The Santeria Priestess

Patricia Benedetto

This is a work of fiction. Names, characters, businesses, places, events and incidents are either the products of the author's imagination or used in a fictitious manner. Any resemblance to actual persons, living or dead, or actual events is purely coincidental.

Copyright @2020 Benedetto Publishing

Paperback ISBN: 978-0-9995791-3-8

eBook ISBN: 978-0-9995791-4-5

Dedicated to Love

PROLOGUE

My name is Hennu.

As a spirit guide, I exist as a light being, an energy force. My heritage many centuries ago, was Egyptian. I was assigned to the Caluda family, to protect them from evil and danger by sending signs that enable them through their lives. Their ancestors arrived as a family of slaves in Cuba, having been kidnapped in Nigeria in the 1700s, though far from the first who arrived 200 years earlier.

By the 1840s, slaves made up forty-five percent of the Cuban population. The wealthy white Cuban elite feared the large numbers. Slave owners were frightened by the religion, by the unknown. No one is sure where the *Santeria* religion originated, but most agree it is a mixture of the Christian and the *Yoruba* Empire's religion which emanated from Egypt. The name itself symbolizes a deviant form of Catholic worship, that of worshiping the saints. The priest and priestess became known as *Santero* and *Santera*.

Originally the *orichas* (oreesha) were their gods, but in an attempt to show acceptance of the Cubans' Catholic religion, the orichas became their saints, each one demonstrating and exhibiting a divine tribute of *Olodumare*, (O-lo-dù-ma-rè) now their one god.

Six generations ago, just after arriving in Cuba, the priestess, Santera Aida, whose name means gift, headed the Caluda family and a Santeria congregation. I was assigned to accompany them to Cuba at the time Spain had begun the imperial reform.

With the loosening of colonial commercial restrictions in Cuba, many slaves were required to perform the additional work. Aida named her daughter Aminah, meaning "putting faith in newborn."

Eshe, meaning 'life' in Egyptian, was the well-respected daughter of Aminah. Born a slave in 1843 Cuba, she was a direct descendant of Carlota, *la rebelde* (the rebel) who, that same year, organized the slave revolt.

During the revolt, Carlotta communicated and organized by drum. The white slave owners perceived the music as a religious practice, but the slaves had already interpreted the kettle drum and sharpened their work machetes.

Gabriela, the daughter of Eshe, gave birth to Martina in 1902. Each generation of first-born females in the Caluda Family was the reigning Santera. As all the women before her, Martina learned her roots, her heritage and her place in the world from her mother. She had difficulty absorbing lifetimes of tragedy and religious-based control. Many atrocities and sins were committed in the name of religion.

Today Santeria is an Afro-Cuban religion.

It is now 1957 Cuba.

❧ I ❧

CUBA 1957

Out of the "Tree of Life" slithers the reigning Santeria priestess, Martina. Her physical movements and mental state are akin to a snake; sneaky and ready to strike at a moment's notice. Today her eldest daughter, Marie, and her two sons, Julio and Juan, accompany the priestess. The boys have been trained to protect Marie. They escort her everywhere, as Martina's brothers do for her.

Marie will shortly begin her one-week initiation; a cleansing and learning of all the Santeria rituals, as she too will become a Santeria priestess.

Santera Martina addresses her daughter. "Marie, pay strict attention, as soon you will be, responsible for overseeing these ceremonies as part of your leadership duties. Today your brothers are christened into the hierarchy of the church and are thus in charge of protecting you and our religion. There are many who would see us dissolved, even if by force. It is fear that drives their hatred."

"Mother, how could I ever have your strength and your knowledge to lead these people?"

"My dear, it is your heritage; born through me, created by Great Grandmother Eshe. Remember your history," Martina continues, "Always remember the trials your great ancestor, Aida, faced and her accomplishments. She brought all of us to this. Shipped here with her Oyo village neighbors as slaves, they were not allowed to practice their religion nor worship their gods.

"Almost three hundred years ago the Papal Synod ordered Cuban priests to adjust African beliefs to the Catholic faith. Aminah incorporated certain ways into our practices, leaving the owners to think we had left our religion for theirs. The slave owners worshipped one god. We adapted by choosing *Olodumare*. We relegated all our other gods to a lesser saint-type level, each overseeing particular needs and blessings. The Cubans now have many saints who they pray to for certain requests. We further adapted by following similar yet different formalities of worship. Certain rituals, such as animal sacrifices, are still done today, though in secret to foster the belief we are peaceful people. As our religion spreads beyond borders, you will be required to implement this deceptive plan of seeming to accept Catholic rituals someday in the United States."

Their arrival at the site brings forth cheers from the crowd of worshipers. Santera Martina takes her seat at the altar. Exercising her regal power, she points the royal scepter, topped with a striking snake head, over the congregation. "We implore Oricha Elegua, to be with us throughout this ceremony and always. Now, let the ceremony begin."

All rituals begin by invoking Elegua. He is known to punish those who do not respect him. The drummers' mesmerizing music fills the cool night air. Wild gyrations of young women dancing quickly produce heat in the now manic crowd. Fires are lit and chants hypnotize the worshippers. Magic of the black vernacular fills the night, producing a malignant insanity. Chants accompany the music. It is a celebration dedicated to Ogoun 'Ogen' the warrior god. The Bata drums, a set of three, are played in his honor.

Through these sacred drums, used only by the men, messages from worshippers reach the Oricha. Dancers face the drums and beseech the god for strength in protecting Marie.

Several young men dance around Marie while she moves seductively to the rhythm of the drums. She drifts with the beat, seemingly unaware of the congregation's attentions to her suggestive body movements. The men dance closer and closer to her. The others gather inward as the young men's intentions become obvious. A wall of worshippers' blocks Julio and Juan from their sister. The congregation is encased in the ensuing madness. The crowd cheers louder and louder for the men to conquer the maiden. Her clothes are being torn from her body. Her brothers draw swords and hack their way through the crowd. Blood spews everywhere, on everyone.

In the chaos, Juan becomes separated. Younger and weaker than his older brother, he hasn't the strength to fight on his own. Someone in the frenzied throng stabs him in the back and he stumbles forward. His gasps for breath and his attempts to stand come to a halt when the sharp blade of a machete strikes his neck. Blood spurts upward like a fountain. Frenzied worshipers trample Juan's lifeless body into the earth without regard. His head rolls down the slight incline, stopped by a row of thorny bushes.

Julio reaches his sister. Wielding his sword, he scoops her up, whisks her out of the inner circle and through the maddened crowd. Marie is hysterical, wearing only a coat of blood, fortunately, not her own. As Julio carries her to the Tree of Life, he steps over Juan's body. Tears come to his eyes when he sees his mother observing the tragedy.

The Santera addresses Julio, "Congratulations my son on protecting the next in line of succession to the throne. Eledumare, ruler of the lower heavens, will protect and console us." Her son knows this to be true as he sees Eledumare standing beside his mother, tears streaming.

"You've now been christened with the blood of the congregation into the hierarchy of the church. Responsibility for protecting our next priestess and her family is in your hands. She will now marry as a virgin and produce her successor. The propagation of our religion is of the utmost importance. We must be ready to sacrifice our lives for it, as Juan has. He is our martyr, and we will honor him as such. Tomorrow we begin preparation for Juan's funeral in three days."

They are gathered in the *casa de santos* 'house of saints' near the Tree of Life. Santera takes her place at the altar. Marie is flanked by her mother and her *padrino* 'godfather.' Behind them stands three distinct thrones draped with royal blue, white, and red satin, representing the seats of the queens, kings, and the deified warriors. A fire blazes in the meadow beside the church.

Martina speaks to the crowd. "Thank you for coming today in celebration of my son Juan's life and his honorable death. Each of you may stand at the altar and address me with a statement or a story of his life and accomplishments."

The congregation begins their ritual today, as always, by invoking Elegua, guardian of the crossroads. He is the messenger between the human and divine worlds. They implore him, as the embodiment of death, to deliver this soul to Olofi. To honor the young man, the altar is draped in black in mourning. It is trimmed in a red outline in Elegua's honor, as black and red are his colors. The candles are lit surrounding the religious icons. The incense is burning; the smoke cleanses the congregation while delivering ancestor veneration. Many people stand and address Juan's life: former teachers, classmates, neighbors, friends, employees, all members of the congregation. Finally, Julio stands to tell his story.

"My brother was like a part of me, a part I'll carry with me always. Our love was a bond. Since we were young children, nothing could come between us. Committed to his position, born to protect our sister, he willingly gave his life to do so. Protecting her is also protecting and preserving our religion. While I have a loss in my heart, I remain committed to our religion and way of life unto death. My mother, our priestess, will now begin the ceremony as we send my brother, Juan, on his voyage to the heavens."

Martina stands, moving ever so slowly to the front of the altar. As candle flames now reflect in her eyes, she surveys the members in front of her. Raising her arms and her head toward the sky, she chants a blessing to her son. Two men approach from the sides carrying an *ebo*, an offering of corn leaves made to the orishas. The members stand and join in the chant. Two women approach the altar and begin to dance, leading a procession outside.

They depart the church and enter the meadow which surrounds the Tree of Life. Here the fire roars, growing higher, becoming more intense. It crackles like lightening. Surprisingly, they can hear the Santeria priestess chanting over the roar of the fire. Cremation is a burial taboo; therefore, the short procession leads all to the cemetery alongside the church. The corn leaves are thrown into the grave, while the worshippers sing and chant throughout the burial.

The congregation now pays homage to their *Egu*, their lineal ancestral spirits. Before leaving the graveyard, the priestess raises her *Egun stick*, a five-foot-high wooden staff, and calls for their blessing. The funeral is intended to pacify and reassure the recently deceased, so their spirit doesn't return to harass the family.

Deafening thunder explodes and lightning flashes, illuminating the skies, right next to the Tree of Life. Rain begins to fall at a tremendous rate, yet it seems to encourage the fire to rage higher and more violently. Martina's chant becomes a harrowing scream.

The crowd is in a manic state; people begin to collapse one person at a time. Thanks to Orisha Chango, ruler of lightning and thunder, the lightning stops. The fire is nearly extinguished. However, he allows the thunder to continue through the day and into the night. Oya, a wife of Chango and master of the winds, is also still present as she rules the dead and the cemetery gates. Their joint presence causes the clouds to change from maroon to red over the next four days. Finally, Juan's body is delivered to the gods.

If the devil were ever going to make an appearance on earth, it would be now. Things begin to return to normal.

2

A wide-open sky of vibrant blue, hosting billowy clouds undulating across her view, fills Marie with emotion. She is excited to begin her initiation, a prelude to becoming a Santera.

She enters their *ile*. These shrines are built by priests and priestesses, often in their homes. The Caluda family shrine is a separate building. She is blessed to be greeted by her Godfather.

"Good morning, my dear. Are you ready?"

Marie is confident in herself and her religion and suffers no trepidation today. "Yes, Godfather, completely. Mother has been guiding me and explaining the process, through which I'll learn the ritual skills and study moral behavior."

Members often come here seeking guidance, but today they are alone. Marie is again in awe of the altar displays; the three distinct thrones reminding her of Juan's memorial service.

"It will be an intensive initiation process," Godfather stresses.

"I'm aware of that, and I'm ready."

"Good. Today, Marie, we prepare you with the ceremony of cleansing. I will apply herbs and water on your head and massage them into your scalp in a distinct pattern."

Following the cleansing, she feels invigorated, anticipating the next day.

"There are four major rituals to undergo this week now that you're cleansed. Tomorrow will be quite intense as you obtain the beaded necklace. The first step is the most difficult, which is to determine the god that will be your guardian angel. The Father-Who-Knows-the-Secret is the Babalawos, the high priest, who will assist you."

Marie walks to the shrine the following day to begin the first major ritual. Her younger sister, Luciana, decides to accompany her on this cool clear morning, Marie is excited to begin her religious journey, and this is her sole focus. Luciana loves the outdoors' natural surroundings and stops abruptly.

"Marie, don't move! Look, over there in that tree!"

"What? What can be so important? Especially today?"

"A tiny pygmy owl! So adorable!"

"I don't see an owl," Marie says in a short-irritated voice.

"Look closely. It's very small, only the size of a robin." At that moment, it flies over Marie's head.

"Why is he out so early in the morning? He's supposed to hunt in the darkness."

"No, not this owl, they hunt in the daytime," Luciana cheerfully informs her.

"Marie is irritated. "Oh, come on Luciana, we're wasting time. I have important things to do today."

Placing the small lace veil on her head, Marie reverently enters the shrine. The high priest speaks to her. "Marie, you will die and be reborn through these rituals. You will no longer be addressed as Marie, but as *Iyawo,* bride of the gods. We begin by determining your own god. The colors and patterns of the beads on the necklace denote the one who serves as your guardian angel. Follow me into the courtyard."

Upon entering the lush garden Marie barely notices the abundant greenery. Her focus is directed to a group of elder members surrounding a lamb, prepared for sacrifice. As the time approaches, Marie is a bit nervous and unsure of her comfort level with this ceremony. The animal blood sacrifice, officiated only by a Santera, is a required part of any initiation, assuring the presence of the gods.

Marie's mother appears and walks to the cement altar within the courtyard. She begins the ceremony, picking up the knife representing the god Ogun. "We petition the gods this day as we begin our purification ritual. We implore you to accept our offering, allowing us sufficient spiritual force to accomplish our beaded necklace today."

Priestess Martina approaches the altar and touches the lamb's head as it hangs off the edge of the concrete slab. She raises her arm far above her head, the blade held tightly in her hand. With great force she brings down the trailing-point knife, the back-edge curving upward, and slits the lamb's throat as she cries out, "*Olodumare*, our almighty god, we deliver this blood in your name."

Marie sees the little lamb go limp; its eyes glaze over. Although dead, the heart will continue to beat for a few minutes longer. They must bleed the animal immediately. With the neck and carotid arteries severed, there are strange sounds from both ends of the animal as they hoist it by the hind legs. The head is decapitated and blood is drained into a large bowl. This sacrifice is made requesting purity for the new priestess, thus the meat is not eaten. It will be placed in a location favorable to the new bride's god.

The high priest and Marie return to the shrine, where he further instructs her. "You will assist me in making this mixture. Sitting on that table is a basket of herbs; bring them here to the sink. We now begin the divination ritual. Bring me your beads. I will place them in the bowl of herbs and lamb's blood. This step must be done by a high priest, to determine a guardian angel."

He then asks the gods to bless the necklace in Yoruba, their native language. His guiding spirit is Orula, the Master Designer. Orula was present when the universe was created and is second only to Olodumare, creator of the universe. Orula is never the guardian angel of the faithful followers. He only guides heterosexual men who have become high priests.

Marie watches intently, observing and learning, as the high priest adds unknown materials and the necklace to the bloody bowl of herbs. This prepared group of ingredients including thyme, parsley, and rosemary have been gathered and blessed by the priest. The cotton string of the necklace will absorb the liquid. The patterns on the multicolored necklace represent the five most powerful gods. They begin asking health, peace, and all things good for the new initiate. Marie prepares herself to receive ritual bathing and new white clothes. She bows over the tub and her head is washed in the Praying Head Ceremony, stripping her of negativity. She feels cleansed and prepared for her new role in life. The necklace is finished and stored for seven days in a special liquid, an elixir of sacred herbs.

Marie knows this necklace provides her with protection from the spiritual world and the physical earthly negative influences and energies.

The following day Marie begins her walk to the shrine early in the morning. Alone today, she takes time to admire the sunrise as it begins to break the horizon. It is so compelling no one can ignore this sight, not even Marie. The colors, red and orange, contrast against the darkness, every shade holding its own brilliance. The meaning is clear to her, red representing love, respect, and power. She feels blessed upon entering the shrine.

If she could pick one of the five most powerful primary gods she would choose Elegua, as he is the messenger, lord of the crossroads. He must be addressed and beseeched before any other. Elegua can form the future; yet he is full of mischief. He controls every road, every door. All other gods require his permission. Marie cherishes this type of power. She craves power, craves control. She would do whatever it took to obtain it. But those five primary gods don't perform as an individual's guardian angels.

Her thoughts are interrupted by the footsteps of the high priest. "Good morning, dear. Today we will begin *medio asiento*, the middle ritual. All your life, the past, present and future, will be reviewed. That information will determine which of the one hundred and one paths of the Elegua you will receive. I chose the materials to be used in constructing the image of his sculpture. It provides protection from evil spirits at your home."

This ritual is only prepared by men, as the gods take some of the santero's manly spirit in the process. Each image is different and made specifically for the individual, taking into account that person's life. Thus, no two are ever the same. The ingredients needed in making the sculpture are now determined. All the ingredients are formed into a small head-shaped object that has eyes, ears, and a mouth made from of cowrie shells. The sculpture Marie receives is not just a representation of the god, it *is* the god himself. The making of the sculpture is one of the most guarded secrets in all of Santeria since the beginning of time. Marie realizes it is always kept in sight of the front doors with the god's usual plate of goodies consisting of candies and cakes, protecting the home at all times.

"Along with the sculpture you will receive miniatures of all seven of Ogun's tools in an iron cauldron symbolizing his ownership of all labor," the high priest tells Marie. "Also, in the cauldron are Ochosi's tools, signifying his rule over the hunt and justice. The last warrior included in the ceremony is Osun, represented as a small silver cup crowned with a circle of bells."

The cup has a lid with a small rooster on it. This god is one of the most mysterious of all. He is generally placed in an obscure location overhead. By falling from his shelf, he alerts the owner that danger is near, allowing time to take the necessary steps to avert it.

The remainder of this ritual is done in secret.

～

Marie walks slowly this morning, anticipating her fourth visit this week to the shrine. She has the feeling she is not alone, sensing a spirit's presence. *Today I will experience my third ritual: Receiving of the Warriors. Yesterday miniature tools were placed in the head sculpture. Today I will receive the actual tools from the high priest, always protecting me from evil. It somehow seems fitting on this cloudy, dark and dismal day.*

The high priest is waiting for Marie as she enters. He begins by telling her, "Today you'll be armed with the protection of the four warrior gods. They walk together and work together to protect you, and strike back at any enemies. Together they oversee your spiritual development. They give these gifts to you: the god of roads and doors opens these for you; the Lord of Iron clears your way and provides you with his seven iron tools. An iron bow and arrow from the Divine Hunter helps you attain your goal as easily as possible, like the straight shot of his arrow. An iron chalice represents the ancestors and is your safe keeper and guardian along the way. This ritual begins a formal and lifelong relationship for you with these gods as they devote their energies to protecting and providing for you on their path."

This was a shorter but exhausting day for Marie. She feels the need to rest before tomorrow, her last ritual in the process of obtaining Santera status.

Early, Marie begins her walk to the shrine for her fifth visit and is preoccupied with her thoughts. She barely notices the drops of water beginning to fall. Finally glancing up, she views a sky black with thunderclouds. She increases her speed, hoping to miss the inevitable downpour. She pauses a moment again to look upward, assessing the situation. An opening appears, streaming golden light on the sidewalk in front of her.

This last ritual of the Santera process is known as Asiento, Ascending the Throne; the most important and secretive ritual in

Santería. She recalls the first day the high priest said, "Marie, you will die and be reborn through these rituals."

This ceremony is a culmination of the previous rituals, where purification and divination take place and Marie becomes "born again" into the faith. She will be as pure as a baby, beginning a new life of deeper growth in the religion. Over the next year, Marie won't perform any church duties. As the new bride of the gods, she will dress in white and avoid those who are not sanctioned in the religion. She will live quietly, avoiding contact with the outside world. Being known in the community by a new name separates her from the old life and wards off negativity."

3

The seven days have passed and it is dawn on Monday when Santera Martina speaks to her daughter. "Marie, the necklace is now ready to be removed from the sacred elixir. I will take it to the river where it can be washed, and will sacrifice a chicken with honey to Osun, asking for a blessing."

Leaving the needed gifts, which include fruits and candies, Martina returns home with the beads. She prepares a holy water bath of herbs and places the necklace in the liquid for an additional seven days.

After a week, Martina removes the beaded necklace from the herb bath. "The colors in the necklace have come forth. Brown and green reveal the god, Ayao, who will be your guardian angel. Ayao, god of the air, a minor god in our religion is a fierce warrior utilizing a crossbow. Appropriately, the angel's numbers are nineteen and thirty-six, the year of your birth. Ayao's favorite home is in the eye of the tornado."

Although this god has substantial powers, which appeal to her, Marie is disappointed to have received a minor god.

The following week, with the full congregation in attendance at the shrine, the necklace is presented to Marie. Every article of clothing she wears is white. The austere neckline brushes against her chin, and the bodice, layered in lace, softens the tailored skirt. It is a beautiful gown previously worn by her mother. She now begins her year of almost total isolation, during which she cannot perform any Santeria duties.

Martina counsels her saying, "As the new bride, the new priestess, you must continue to wear white throughout this year and have no contact with anyone who has not been initiated. You will spend your time meditating, reading, and speaking with the gods."

Marie, of course, speaks with her mother often, discussing her new role and seeking advice. The congregation respects her year of confinement.

~

It is now 1958 and Marie's year is complete, having spent it in isolation and prayer. Her godfather informs her, "Marie, there will be an end of year ceremony, which enables you to consult clients, perform cleansings, provide remedies, host initiations, and conduct religious ceremonies. As a Santeria priestess, you are now regarded as royalty in our religion, and a representative of the gods, vested with the power to work with the forces. The congregation will have a feast to celebrate your consecration."

Marie now views herself as pure and virtuous, passionate and worthy to lead her own congregation. She has the power.

Martina addresses Marie's sister, "Luciana, although the family has no need for your presence at this time, I will allow you to attend the celebration. You will only become important should something happen to Marie; therefore we must make sure you remain chaste and in the graces of the gods."

Departing her home, Marie sees a familiar outline coming into view. As the figure approaches, she recognizes him as her friend and former schoolmate, Hernan, whom she has not seen for a year. She has always liked Hernan. His name fits him perfectly; charismatic, easy going, and caring. She joins him in the walk to her celebration. Hernan would be a good husband. Indeed, he would most likely always give in to her royal supreme wishes and decisions.

Today's Santería *bembe*, the musical ceremony, celebrates Marie's accomplishment, and dedicates prayers to Ayao, Marie's appointed guardian angel. The Bata drums send messages from worshippers to the gods, who respond to their devotees. Through the ceremony, the gods are invited to join in the singing and dancing. Accepting the invite, the gods may "seize the head" or "mount" the worshippers like a *caballo*, causing a person to perform, even to pass messages to the congregation.

Luciana is enjoying herself; eating, dancing, laughing, and drinking, all to excess. The young men are entertained watching her freedom of movement. Her mind is totally relaxed with the drink and the music, her body moves slowly to the rhythm of the drums, her hair flows in the breeze. As the conga drums gradually increase in sound and tempo, her body also increases in movement and intensity.

The worshippers are becoming worked up and excited as they continually invoke the gods to join the festivities. Music is now a driving force; it becomes apparent Luciana is possessed by a fun-loving god that has entered her head.

Marie whispers to her mother, "I know my sister has been possessed by a spirit the community has invited to join the festivities. Maybe Chango."

These possessions are a usual occurrence during drum and dance ceremonies, allowing the entire congregation to witness the religious trance. The night breaks into morning. Few are left standing; most are passed out and incoherent.

4

A Cuban radio announcer sounds excited to report incredible events. "Fidel Castro has divided his forces, sending Cienfuegos and Guevara into the plains with small armies. Castro follows them with the remaining rebels, capturing towns and villages along the way, where they are greeted as liberators."

Martina's family is elated at no longer being suppressed by a Batista fascist regime. With this freedom, they look forward to expressing their religious beliefs fully in the open democracy, a government for the people without fear.

On January 9, 1959, Fidel Castro enters Havana. With him is his closest confident Che Guevara, his brother Raul and supporter Camilo Cienfuegos. The people are celebrating their victory over Batista, dancing and singing in the streets. Change is a concern to Marie. She is deep in thought as she approaches her mother's house.

Entering, she calls out for her brother, "Julio, are you here?"

"Marie, I am just on my way to town for the festivities; there will be dancing, drinking and much celebrating. Would you like to come with me?"

"I am not sure about the celebrating. I feel uncertain what changes will come about to our people, to our religious practices. Most people do not accept change very well and that includes me."

"You worry too much, Marie. Things surely must be better for the people considering how they were treated under a fascist state."

"I will stay here with Mother. You have fun."

～

When Julio arrives in town, he meets Marie's friend. "Hello, Hernan. How are you? Are you enjoying the celebration?"

"I am, Julio, but also concerned as I have been listening to the comrades' idle talk. They plan to bring in all the Batista officials and supporters and put them on trial, but they are already planning their execution: they don't seem to need a trial."

"I for one would love to see them face torture and hanging, or a firing squad."

"That will only instill fear in the people. Innocents could be swept up in the madness."

～

Julio returns home and joins Marie for coffee. He advises her of his encounter with Hernan, "Marie, I do not understand Hernan at all. He seems to think the government should be fair to members of the old Batista regime. Like they were never fair to the people they ruled."

"Yes, under the fascist government the rich got richer, and many people suffered. But, remember change is always difficult, especially when the outcome is unforeseen. The unknown presents its own terror. So many unanswered questions. Which direction will they take? Will they slide right back into a fascist government, or perhaps the pendulum sways to a communist rule?"

Unnoticed, Martina enters the kitchen. She chimes in, "Let us hope for a democratic rule. With the United States so close, it would be to our advantage on many fronts. We have always had a friendly working relationship through open borders, loans, trade agreements, labor forces, training, and advanced educations. It could produce a very comfortable lifestyle. It certainly would benefit us monetarily."

Julio relates some stories he heard throughout the week. "I heard from the soldiers that there have already been several arrests with death sentences mandated in quick quiet hearings. We will see public executions this week, in the stadium, being broadcast island-wide."

Hernan stops at the Caluda home to visit. Upon entering, he hears Julio's last comment and joins the group discussion. He voices the obvious, "They are doing these things to provoke fear in the people. They want us to fear retribution should we dissent. I too have heard the rumors but now I'm assured everything will be handled legally and ethically."

"That certainly is a change from your earlier opinion; 'That will only instill fear in the people. Innocents could be swept up in the madness.' I believe that was your statement."

"I know something of the background of Fidel, Che, and Raul. They are fair men and surely as they remain in charge, the punishments handed down will be fair."

"What evidence do you have to support this theory?"

"The government has approached my father to oversee the trials."

"Why would they ask him? Was he active in the over-throw?" asks Julio.

"Not exactly. He periodically contributed some sensitive information. He knows Fidel and his family for a long time, and being a doctor like Che, they have met in the past. He thinks a communist government would better serve our people."

Marie is astonished by these revelations. "It appears that you are speaking with these people, Hernan. Yes? So, give us some inside information on what changes we can expect. And why would your father oversee the trials?"

"Okay, Marie, it seems I have a lot to answer here. Yes, I am speaking with these people. I know them and my family knows them. I have no great inside information, as you call it. They approached my father because he will not present a challenge to Che, who is in charge of the prison, the trials, and the sentencing. You must realize we need to get along in this new world. That means we need to adapt to change, go along with their plans, and not make problems."

The following day, Martina and Marie are lunching on the veranda, discussing events.

"Mother, my life has changed so much over the past year and our country's changes are monumental. What do you think it will mean for us, for our people, for me?"

"Marie, it is impossible to guess what will become of us and our country. No one can foresee how it will affect our religion. We must set your course for the United States to lead and guide our people there. It is imperative you finish your nurse's training so you have a secure occupational cover when you arrive there."

"Yes, Mother, my studies are going very well. I want to speak to you about Hernan. I know he would be a good consideration for a husband, though I am concerned about his family's involvement with this new government. This could be an advantage or a detriment."

"He has the temperament needed to support your endeavors. With your nursing job and managing a congregation, you will need a caring, objective husband who is not demanding of your time. His family's relationship with the new government could serve us well. Has he mentioned marriage?"

"No, but I'm sure he will, given the right encouragement. I want to keep things as they are until next year when I have my degree."

"Do you care for him, Marie?"

"I do, Mother, and I feel this was meant to be, for my personal life and for the good it will allow me to do for our people."

Julio joins them with his political updates. "They have appointed Che Minister of Industry and in charge of the Bank of Cuba. Castro is already losing some supporters. Wealthy families are fleeing, leaving everything behind. They know under a communist regime they will lose in the end.

"Throughout the past year I've seen many changes taking place in Castro's Cuban government. He appears to lean heavily left. Hopefully, 1960 will go just as smooth"

Marie goes to visit a close friend of the family, so close she calls him Uncle. He is staying at his apartment in town rather than on the farm, unusual for this time of year. From the door she sees his back as he sits at the table with a cup of coffee. "Uncle Ramon, Mother told me you were not feeling well, so I' have come to see how I can help. Perhaps an herbal mixture or a ritual of prayer. What seems to ail you?"

As she rounds the table, she sees her uncle with tears streaming down his cheeks, hands folded on his lap. His complexion is sallow; his eyes appear dead. He does not answer.

Marie kneels at his feet and clasps his hands with hers. She is distraught to find her strong bull-of-an-uncle in such a state. She pleads, "Uncle, look at me, talk to me. What is wrong?" She cannot get him to respond and attempts to call for her aunt. She can hardly speak, trying again and again; finally, she produces a scream.

Her aunt comes running. "Marie, what is it?"

"Aunt Rosario, I don't know what is wrong with Uncle Ramon. Did something happen to one of the children?"

"My dear, something happened to his dearest child, the factory. The government came in and took over the business. It's slowly killing him. No one can reach him. They have implemented agrarian reform; many tobacco growers are being displaced. Of course, we are the largest, most well-known and respected cigar house in Cuba. No, in the world."

"Oh, Uncle, I am so sorry for you. I know of your love for carrying on your family's business. Mother will be terribly disturbed to hear this news. What can we do?"

❧

At home, later that evening, a friend approaches Marie with a newspaper from New York. "Marie, I have brought news from the United States for you and your family. You must know of the news in the free world as it affects the Cuban people. Read this: 'Castro intends to expropriate foreign oil company holdings within Cuba and eventually seize all foreign-owned property.' There is even talk he will issue a government takeover of Cuban-owned businesses. The Soviet Union is offering assistance, making the United States overly concerned with the whole situation."

"My friend, thank you, but it has already begun. My Uncle Ramon has lost his whole factory to the government. He is despondent."

"Marie, the person who brought me this paper is well known for carrying cash from Cuba to the United States at the behest of the casinos. If your family would like to prepare, I will ask him to carry funds for you."

"I cannot answer for the family, but I will inquire."

❧

At the next family Santeria gathering Marie informs her mother and uncle of Manuel's offer.

Ramon quietly responds, "Marie, it would be the saddest day of my life if my family should need to leave Cuba, our home. But, if it became necessary, I know it will be a temporary situation. I see no need to prepare."

Martina is not so sure of things. "I would be interested in exploring all options. It has been over a year since Fidel Castro took power and I only see things getting worse. Would we be able to meet with this person and discuss arrangements?"

"I would think so, as he arrives here in Havana with his empty suitcase, I believe every month. I will advise Manuel that you may have an interest and to arrange a meeting for next month."

A few weeks later, Angela Martinez, a member of the congregation, approaches Martina with a question. "Martina, I'm unsure what to do with my son. You know he's only six years old, such a little one. It seems inhumane to send him to a foreign country all alone."

"Angela, what are you talking about? Why would you send your son away?"

"I'm hearing things that scare me about this government."

"What are you hearing, Angela, that could make you so afraid?"

"It seems anyone who has disagreed with this new government is in danger of having their children taken from them and raised in state schools. Or even worse—having them transported to the Soviet Union and placed in work camps." By now, Angela is broaching hysteria. "What can I do, Martina? What can I do? Please help me. I cannot have the state come to my home and take my child."

"Let me see about this, Angela. I will find out exactly what is going on. And we shall pray on this. I will have my daughter Marie arrange a ceremony to foretell the future. Perhaps an Obi to advise you yes or no. I will contact you in the next few days."

5

"Will I ever see my baby boy again?" Angela cries as she and Martina approach the charming abode of the new priestess. Angela hugs Marie and repeats, "Where or when will I ever see my baby boy again? If the government comes to my home to take him, what can I do? Thank you for performing an Obi. I'm desperately seeking answers for my son."

"I have everything arranged. This will be my first Obi. I'm very excited. I plan to use the coconut shells. Please join me in my prayer room."

Upon entering the room, indeed everything is prepared. The prayer room is sparsely decorated, creating a calming effect. The three women join hands, encircling the artistic hand-made mat on the floor. On a small table beside Marie sits a coconut, severed and displayed in four even pieces with white meat visible.

"Angela, you do realize the question you ask must require only a yes or no answer, nothing complicated. Should you receive an answer, you may ask a second question. And if we don't get an answer the first time and are asked to toss the pieces again, we may not ask a different question. So, make perfectly clear what you want to know."

"I am clear on the knowledge I need to possess. I'd like to ask two questions, but if only the first one is answered, I can make a judgment. Let's ask if the government plans to take the children. If the answer is yes, we will know it is either to raise them in state schools or have them transported to the Soviet Union and placed in work camps."

Marie prays over the dilemma and poses the question. She's terrified of what the answer might be as she gently tosses the quartered coconut onto the mat. There is no movement from the three women who sit as if turned to stone. The pieces are all facing up, the open white side of the coconut appearing to blind them. They have their answer.

"Yes."

Angela is sobbing now, but she has her second question. Should she send her son to Florida? To strangers? "It would break my heart."

Marie slowly gathers the coconut pieces. Her eyes circle the room, pausing on each of the two ladies, bracing herself for the answer. For a second time, she tosses the four pieces to the mat.

The three women gasp as they stare at the floor. No one dares to move or speak; the gods have spoken.

Marie wonders. *Are they teasing us? Why would they do this? This is torture.* Eventually she states the obvious, "The gods are telling us 'maybe.' Maybe is not an answer."

Martina looks at her daughter with sympathy. "Dear, it is disturbing, but we must continue. The good thing about having three white sides up and only one brown, is that we get to ask again. Keep in mind, now we can only ask one more question."

"Let's ask the same question," Angela spurts, "and let's ask it fast."

Marie quickly picks up the coconut, stares at her mother, and turns to Angela. "Do you understand what this outcome could be?

If two, three, or four white pieces are up facing then the answer is yes. If only one is facing us the answer is no."

"Let's ask if the government plans to take the children."

Angela glares at Marie, but does not respond. Marie knows she doesn't want to hear this. Quickly the pieces bounce on the mat, it seems an eternity before they stop and give up their answer. Two of the quarters are facing white side up.

"Yes!" Angela is in shock. "How can I bear to send my child to people I don't know? How can I think it will be better for him?" Terribly distraught and confused she heads for home alone, leaving Martina with Marie.

"Perhaps, Mother, I could go before the children and try to make arrangements for them."

"That might be an option if we had someone for you to work with in Miami. If only you were a bit older and married, you could accompany the children. They would not be alone and frightened. But you are not ready for this type of undertaking."

"Surely you must know someone there, Mother."

"Perhaps Manuel knows someone. He works with all those American people."

"Maybe, but we need a different type of person than one from his casino group."

"I am meeting him and his friend, who transports money, in two weeks. I will broach the subject. His friend did not come last month. Perhaps the profits from the casino are diminishing."

"I want to come with you, Mother."

"Alright, we are meeting at the Copacabana lounge at two o'clock."

"I'll be there."

The radio broadcasts continue relentlessly with rumors concerning the children. The rumors ranged from: "Your children will be shipped to Soviet work camps" to "Your children will be taken from you and placed in communist schools to be indoctrinated." Fear grips every parent.

~

Marie is stunned by the casino's glitz, the opulence, and the bare skin but manages her composure.

Never has she seen such abundance of wealth: crystal chandeliers, sparkling bottles and glasses, draperies of velvet and crepe with gold braided ties, lights of vibrant colors reflecting off the cloth wallpapers. She could barely catch her breath.

Manuel is already seated at an extravagantly covered table. A beautiful black-haired, fair-skinned model is pouring his drink.

He greets Marie and her mother, "Good afternoon, ladies. Please be seated," Manuel motions for menus.

The black-haired beauty arrives with menus and coffee. Marie can barely hear him, over the noise from clanging glasses, music, laughter, and coins bouncing on metal.

"Mr. Carmello will be here shortly, and you can discuss moving funds. I can stay or leave as you like."

"We would like you to stay, please."

Manuel stands. "Here he is now. Mr. Carmello, I would like you to meet my dear friends. This is Santera Martina. She is Priestess at our local Santeria congregation, and her daughter Marie, also now a Santeria priestess. They need to discuss possibly moving some funds to the United States."

"Well, ladies it is my pleasure. And be assured my organization will help wherever possible. "How may we be of service?"?"

Marie turns to Martina, looking for a starting point. She notices her mother is distracted by a dancer teasing a gentleman in the lounge room, almost sitting on his lap. They are both aghast as the scene sexually intensifies.

Mr. Carmello stands and breaks the silence, "Ladies, perhaps we could continue our lunch and discussion at the pool."

"Excellent suggestion," chimes Martina with a little sound of panic in her voice.

Outside, the sun is warm while a gentle breeze cools them. Perfect! Everyone relaxes and their discussion begins with Martina.

"Mr. Carmello, we are interested to hear how we can move money to the United States should we need to flee our homeland. We also must address a new and very sensitive situation, which has caught us completely off guard. Many families are facing a major trauma in their lives. It appears the children need to leave here immediately or be forced into state schools and work camps by the new government. We need to arrange transport and, more importantly, their care. Is there anyone you might know who could help us accomplish this frightening task?"

Martina is visibly shaken; her voice is strained and her hands trembling.

Marie picks up the request. She is much calmer in the face of adversity. "I have made attempts to contact influential people in Miami. We need someone of a high caliber to work with us to assist in this delicate matter. Thus far, my letters and phone calls go unanswered. These are children who will require our help to survive."

"Well this is not an area I'm familiar with, transporting children. My organization strictly handles financial arrangements. Give me time to do some research, and I'll get back to you with an answer. Maybe we can find a way to help."

Manuel joins in the discussion to clarify. "This is an urgent matter requiring immediate attention, Mr. Carmello. Things remain tense on the island. People are frightened of everything and everyone, frightened for their families, children, homes, businesses, and their lives. Their whole world has come crashing down around them."

"I do understand, and I'll have an answer when I return in two months. I'll work hard to have one that is helpful to you."

"Two months? I thought you came every month," questions Marie.

"I did at one time but, as we all know, things are changing. Right now, I'm hoping it is not longer than two months. We do the best we can. And now as we approach the summer, things will be even slower."

~

One-month later, Manuel appears at Martina's front door. "Martina, Mr. Carmello is at the casino and asks to speak with you. Can you come now?"

"Yes, of course. We can stop and get Marie on our way."

They find Marie at home studying; reading the Miami newspapers and practicing English. She is preparing herself for the journey of a lifetime. Everything must be managed perfectly. She could not bear to fail; the results would be catastrophic. This is her chance to make a difference—to be the hero.

~

Arriving at the casino Marie is excited. "Hello Mr. Carmello, we did not expect you so soon! We are grateful for your early return."

"Things have been coming together much quicker than I could have imagined. The response to your needs was without delay. Everyone involved realizes the intense urgency here. Marie, I'm leaving tomorrow night, and you'll join me on my plane. We have arranged an appointment in two days with members of the Catholic Church in Miami. You'll meet first with Father Bryan O. McCarthy, who is influential in the community with politicians and the Church. He's a caring person, especially for the children. And although born in Ireland, he holds a master's degree in Latin American Studies from the University of Miami."

"Mr. Carmello, how did you arrange these things so quickly?"

"My associates have strong ties to the Catholic Church. They provide huge financial support and, often, protection. Contact with the powers-that-be—those who govern any given area, not just the church—are always immediate and addressed accordingly."

"I will be ready," says Marie. "What time do we leave?"

Martina recovers from the shock of how fast things are moving. "You cannot go to Miami, Marie. Perhaps Manuel can go and deliver our plea for help. A young girl unaccompanied in a city such as Miami is trouble waiting to happen."

"Mother, I am not a young girl. I am a woman, a Santeria priestess for god's sake! I can handle myself and any situation that may arise."

Mr. Carmello carefully speaks to the mother, "Martina, everyone I've spoken with is sympathetic to the situation. I've explained Marie's involvement in this movement. They're ready to get behind her and support her. Without her there, I'm not sure what the response will be."

"I do not like this. I fear for her being there alone."

"She'll not be alone. I'll always be with her."

Marie notices that Martina's look of distress doesn't diminish with those words. "Mother, I am willing to do whatever it takes! Our people and our family must come first and their needs, their desires, will be the priority. We want these children to be safe, and if getting them there means taking severe measures, even killing as our soldiers did, that is what I will do. I have no reservations." She sees Martina relax a bit, just a bit. It's apparent that she now realizes her daughter has inherited her strength, the strength to do whatever it takes.

"Marie, perhaps you know that many Cuban families have already arrived in Miami. Although they are the wealthy who could afford to leave here early, the less fortunate and the children need our help. As the Director of the Catholic Welfare Bureau of Miami, Father McCarthy wants to help and has the power to recruit many others. We can build a network of assistance, but we need a force in Cuba to work with us. You must discuss all avenues that are open with Father McCarthy."

6

A sea of stars lights the evening sky. At the airport with Mr. Carmello the following evening, Marie feels invincible, like a superhero ready to fly to a strange land of unfamiliar languages and customs. She is prepared to save her people, her heritage, and most importantly, her religion at all costs. Nothing and no one will stop her, no matter the sacrifice of herself and others. She will conquer all. Her slogan in life is "Whatever It Takes."

The flight is comfortable and short in Gino Carmello's small jet. They land at Miami International Airport just before 8:00 p.m. Mr. Carmello's limo is waiting just steps from the plane.

"Marie, this is Sal, my driver. Get in."

"Sal, take us to my sister's house"

As they enter the small bungalow on the beach, he addresses Marie, "This is my sister, Concetta; you'll stay here tonight. It's safe. Be ready in the morning at ten. I'll pick you up to visit Father McCarthy."

Concetta smiles at her guest. "Hello, Marie. I want you to feel comfortable. Come with me and we'll get you settled in." From her bedroom window Marie can see the moon sparkling on the inter-coastal.

"You can go now, Gino. I will look after her."

"Thank you, Concetta, for taking me in tonight."

Exhausted, Marie falls into a deep sleep and awakens refreshed in time to prepare for her ten o'clock appointment. She's nervous. So much depends on her meeting this morning: the children's welfare, perhaps their lives, and her success as a leader. As they ride to the priest's office, she turns over in her mind exactly what she should say to convince the powers-that-be to help. The responsi-bility she carries is overwhelming, but she is confident.

Walking into the church, Marie's breath is taken away by the beauty. "Mr. Carmello, I have never seen such compelling artwork."

She notices the priest approaching from the side entrance, speaking as he enters. "This church has many generous donors, giving both money and art. Mr. Carmello's group is one of our most appreciated." He extends a hand of welcome. "Hello, Marie, I'm Father McCarthy. Although somewhat familiar with your mission, I'd like to hear everything from you directly."

"Thank you, Father. It is my pleasure to meet you and thank you for your attentions to our request. I am positive you and your church can help us work through our plight."

"Gino, I appreciate your bringing this child-in-need to me. We have much to discuss. Please return for her after lunch."

They take a seat at the back of the church. Marie spends hours informing the priest of all that has taken place since the revolution. She explains how the country had hoped Castro's takeover would benefit the people, hopefully, going from a fascist state to a democ-racy. But the truth was, the people were suffering. They were losing their businesses, their savings and, in some cases, their homes.

"Let's take a little break and have some lunch while we think about this." He leads her through the church toward the altar, out the side door, and to the back of the building. As they enter the garden, Marie gasps.

"My, Father, how beautiful! How do you manage to maintain such a multitude of beautiful flowers?"

"My dear, thank you, but I must give credit to Franz, our heaven-sent gardener, to nature's blessings, and to God Almighty for this beauty. Walk with me through the pathways. It'll help free our minds. The gardens are so lovely in late summer." They walk in silence, soaking in the peacefulness provided by the stillness. Eventually they come upon a gazebo where a woman lays food on the table. Father McCarthy breaks the silence. "Mrs. Simms, I see you have lunch ready for us. Thank you, it looks delightful."

"You're quite welcome, Father. I've prepared a special dish in honor of your guest." She looks at Marie as she continues, "Please enjoy."

Sitting in this fine gazebo, in a lush garden, enjoying impeccable food, Marie relaxes. As she does, she finds herself more confident.

"Are you ready to continue our discussions, Marie?"

"Yes, Father. We beg you to help save our children." She begins explaining her mission for the children of Cuba.

He listens sympathetically. "I'll do what I can, Marie, and I can accomplish a great deal here in Miami for you. There are many factions willing to help. Of course, the Cuban community, most are wealthy beyond your comprehension. Then there is Mr. Carmello's group with holdings worth billions of dollars worldwide. We can collect the children as they arrive, and work out a system of placement as calming as possible. Give us a few months on this. You'll also need the time, as you must provide someone in Cuba for us to coordinate transportation. Someone you can trust above all others."

"I can assure you, Father, I will arrange for a base there to work with you on moving these children. I have someone in mind. One of our local priests. He has already offered to do whatever is necessary. Also, the head of the Ruston Academy has been exploring avenues to move children on his own. He will work with us. We must act quickly, keeping this a secret to avoid repercussions."

She didn't feel the need to tell him that the priest was a Santeria priest, not a Catholic. What did it matter?

At mid-afternoon Carmello returns for Marie. Proceeding to Concetta's house they make a stop at his own to pick up papers he requires for a dinner meeting. His home is like nothing Marie has seen before. The front entrance has a moat. Although she'd never seen one before, she knew of it from books. *Why would one have a moat in Miami?*

"Mr. Carmello, is that a moat?"

"Yes, my dear, it is. There are people who'd like to rob me or even do me harm."

"So, you have water running through it and we cross on that bridge?"

"We do cross on the bridge, but there is no water, dear, that would make the house too easy to penetrate."

As they cross the bridge, shivers run up her entire body. The sounds alone were enough to scare Marie to death. Pit Bulls, gnarling, snarling, growling, barking, and jumping against gated barriers trying to reach them gives her a feeling of "*dinner is served!*"

Mr. Carmello finds this amusing, chuckling as he says. "Don't worry they can't reach you now, but at night I open the gates, and they have free run of the property."

Once inside the house, Marie is mesmerized. She faces one whole wall of glass, two stories high, looking out at the Intracoastal. *What a gorgeous view—in any weather.* She turns around and sees a white marble spiral staircase with a gilded railing. *I can easily imagine one like this leading to heaven.* At the top of the stairs is a wrap-around balcony with an oversized lady looking over the railing and down at them.

"Hello down there! Nice to see you home for a change, Gino. Is this the girl from Cuba?"

"Yes, Camellia, this is Marie. I only stopped a moment to pick up some paperwork for my meeting at Wolfie's tonight."

"That's fine; I'm meeting friends at the Forge Restaurant. Alvin will be there if you want to come by later for coffee and dessert."

"I'll see how my time runs," Carmello says.

Leaving the house Carmello tells Marie, "I'll take you to Concetta's now and return for you in the morning. You'll accompany me to the airport as I'm also leaving—for Las Vegas. You'll be departing for home."

"You will not be on the plane with me?"

"No, not this time. I'll see you in Cuba in a month or two. There's a lot going on between my group and Castro right now. We need to be careful with our exposure on this program. There are many things I need to cover and take care of right now. You and Father McCarthy worked out a safe method to communicate with each other, correct?"

"Yes, he will...."

"Don't tell me. I don't want to know."

The next morning Marie is settled on the plane home. Her head's spinning with so much to take in at one time.

Marie envisions herself as the center of this mission, the heroine, but begins to have serious questions as they pertain to life, her life. She's taking time now to think it all through.

Here I am a new priestess, organizing this exodus from a dangerous country, saving the lives of others, putting the lives of myself and my family in jeopardy. There is the priest supported by a whole-world congregation with nothing at risk, a religion that sees to his every need and comfort, as evidenced by his church and garden. Then there is Mr. Gino Carmello who works for an organization that supports and protects him in his endeavors. Obviously, from his home and cars, he is extremely well compensated.

Now they have both joined their organizations to help us? Why? They don't appear to be people who have ever wanted for anything, nor will they ever. What are they getting out of this? Perhaps notoriety as a "good guy" helping the underprivileged. Is that enough? Something else must also follow.

Without further consideration, upon her return to Cuba, Marie immediately begins to construct an infrastructure and arrange for communication and transport.

Marie is listening to the short-wave radio given to her by Father McCarthy. The broadcast is discussing the fact that Señor Fidel Castro is planning his upcoming trip to New York to address the UN. Things are becoming more tense as the days go by.

~

A phone call goes out from the Hill. "Tom, we need you to work with us for the next month on a very sensitive matter."

"Sure, what is it?"

"That fool from *'way down south'* doesn't want to stay at the most upscale Manhattan hotel we could arranged for him. He wants to stay in Harlem! Of all places, a damn fool!"

"So, what do you want me to do? Force him to stay there?"

"Look, Tom, as a WWII American vet in OSS intelligence, performing clandestine activity, you can come up with something. You're hereby assigned to take control of housing for this *'foreign dignitary.'* Watch over him. Keep him in line and out of trouble. Basically, handle him. Oh, yes, and keep him alive. It wouldn't be good for something to happen to him here."

"You're nuts. You antagonize this guy and then expect me, a nobody in government, to fix things for you? Our relations are in the toilet. Vice President Nixon believes Castro to be a communist, even though Castro hasn't proclaimed this. Our government began months ago to train Cuban exiles to overthrow Castro. What do you expect?"

When the call ends Tom shakes his head in frustration. *Why are we taking this stance with him now, so early in his administration? Why not try to work with him?*

Tom, Castro's US handler places him in the Theresa Hotel in Harlem where he meets with Malcolm X, Langston Hughes, and other non-government, maybe anti-government, leaders.

Another phone call from The Hill comes through. "You're not doing too well at keeping him isolated, Tom. He is meeting with dissidents."

"Do you recall that this is a free country?" Tom asks. "Freedom to meet, to speak with whomever you like."

"You know he addresses the UN today. But he'll be directly attacking the US, which he claims is attempting to destroy his country. Do you know what he is going to say? In his speech, he has certain acts taken by President Eisenhower to cite. Like our continued assistance to Batista, a fascist. And our government's acceptance of that regime into this country, as they brought more than four-hundred million in US funds to our banks. You are well aware that Batista's Communist Repression group tortured and executed thousands of people."

"Tom, listen. He'll talk about the cancellation of exporting all cars and parts to Cuba and requiring oil companies to refuse to refine crude oil from there. And he will close with our international pressures on England to join in embargos, particularly weapons."

"Are you saying he's lying?" Tom shifts the phone from one ear to the other. "Seems he has a few legitimate complaints. Why don't you try to work with him? He could be a valuable ally given his location."

"That cannot happen, and you know it."

Following the address, Tom escorts Castro to the airport without incident. Just before boarding the plane, Castro places his hand on Tom's shoulder, takes off his combat jacket, and gives it to his handler saying, "Thank you, Tom. Thank you."

Tom's next phone call from The Hill is expected, given his new friendship with Fidel.

"Tom, Eisenhower is ordering a ban on exports, including the post office. Everything except medicine and some food, and those require a special license. He's also reducing Cuba's sugar quota to the US, to *zero*, fully canceling our previous commitment. This will cause great financial harm to Cuba. All hell may break loose. We need you to go there and give us some feedback on the temperature. We expect things will be heating up."

"And?" Tom knows there is more to this request. Having spent almost three of his younger years in OSS and a few other acronyms before the CIA, he knows to listen to his gut.

"We want you to start making trips there. We'll provide the cover and alias for you, working with the casinos. Be ready to leave on Saturday."

"What? That's two days from now. Get things organized for me before my arrival."

"Yes, of course. We already have a man on the ground controlling the casinos there. He'll work well with you. His name is Gino Carmello. We want you to use your friendship with Castro to acquire inside information for a possible invasion."

"Invasion? Are you crazy? We have no legal international rights to invade that country."

"Be here in the morning for your briefing."

⚝ 7 ⚝

T om is talking to himself as he lands in Havana on Saturday, September 30th advancing at once to the historic Hotel Nacional. Before entering, he pauses at the breathtaking view of the harbor. Memories flood back, more than he wants. He never thought he would return to a place that held no joy for him. He enters the luxurious hotel, proceeds to the infamous Casino Internacional, and addresses the manager, "I'm here to see Gino Carmello."

Recognizing Tom immediately, he says, "Mr. Carmello is not here. You can catch him at the Tropicana. He had an appointment there. I will call a driver for you, sir."

Tom and the driver travel slowly through lush colorful tropical gardens of the Tropicana, and approach the largest most beautiful club in the world. Tom enters the massive lobby and glances sideways into the immense gaming room. Through the crystal chandeliers, he spots Gino at a table speaking to Santo Trafficante, who owns part of the Tropicana and the Sans Souci, probably part of everything else too.

He enters the hotel casino. Tropical trees of enormous size, occasionally overshadowing a table, reach through the roof to the heavens, lending a calming atmosphere to the ultra-modern building. As he approaches, Gino smiles and gestures. "*Como estas*, Tom. We are pleased you could join us. A great deal has been happening here since Castro took over, even some changes with our group. You know Santo here, right?"

"Yes, very well indeed. It's rare I get to play with someone on both sides of the fence."

Santo growls his disapproval of Tom's innuendo. "You know why you're here, just do your job. We don't want you around any longer than necessary. We've important business to address."

"Like getting rid of a communist dictator?" Tom quips.

"We have managed things on our own in the past." Santo responds.

Tom smiles. "Not always too successfully."

Gino sees that he must put a damper on where this conversation is headed. "Fellas, let's play nice. We all know where we came from, whose interest we represent, and the job we must accomplish. Okay, we're strange bedfellows, but we have been in bed together before, so let's get along and get down to business."

Tom agrees, "Yes, some of us want to go home."

Gino immediately grabs the floor from Tom. "Everyone listen, we are going ahead, straight ahead, with no sideway remarks, Tom. Now let's explore how to accomplish something. The US government does not want Castro in power in Cuba. They had a nice working relationship with Batista, like a good marriage, everyone got what they wanted."

Santo, still sullen, nods in agreement.

Gino continues, "Now, this is the outline we are left to work with: First, the US backed Batista, even when he was unelected and stole the government. Now the US has given Batista protection and welcomed him in with his hundreds of millions. The Cubans hated Batista and his suppressive tactics, selling off major money makers, mainly casinos to mobsters, who gladly shared, fattening Batista's pocket."

Tom quickly rises to his feet, appearing tall and formidable. "The Cuban people are not too thrilled with the new take-over either, as some are losing their businesses, homes, and possibly their children." Tom's briefing is paying off; *always side with the working people*. He is ready to speak for them and the US government.

Gino interrupts Tom midstream and injects a common belief. "So, the US sends people here to make Castro disappear, and they plan and orchestrate an invasion."

Tom jumps in to refute. "The US is not sending people here to get rid of Castro, and an invasion would not be sanctioned by the international community."

Santo growls again. "Are you stupid or blind? Why do you think you are here, Tom? What do you think *my* mission is? You are here to gather information to support our plan for an invasion. I'm here for a more direct and immediate solution. Gino is here to coordinate any event, everything."

Gino is becoming annoyed; his lips are pressed and his shoulder muscles begin to tense. "We all truly know why we're here, to get things back on track. The mob has built an empire here over the past few years under a friendly Batista. They have invested a lot of money and time to accomplish this feat. They aren't willing to walk away and give it up either. The Cubans, especially the wealthy business and land owners, don't want Castro."

As Gino pauses, he remembers the working Cuban people living in fear of arrest and punishment, and who would like to see Castro disappear. He makes a conscious decision not to say this, continuing his argument in a vein that would appeal to his listeners. "So, it's not only the US government, it's also the Mob that sends people here to protect their Casino ownerships."

Tom takes this all in. "You're saying I'm here to represent the government, therefore my mission is to collect data for an invasion. And Santo is here to make Castro disappear, as in permanently?"

"Emphatically, yes," declares Gino.

All three know this is true. Tom isn't sure if Gino knows that Santo, although a mob kingpin and murderer, is also working on this particular problem with Tom and others at the CIA. Their last CIA meeting, included Sam Giancana, and specifically addressed this matter.

"Enough for today. We can continue tomorrow," chimes Gino. "Want to take in a show here tonight? It is fantastic, fifty girls in colorful costumes, under these majestic trees. Great show with voodoo and magic thrown in." He snickers as he adds, "These Santeria girls, the Flesh Goddesses, are very entertaining, if you get my drift."

"I'll see you tomorrow." Santo is ready for some action. He lives here a great deal of the time; he knows where to find what he wants.

"I'll decline tonight. I have things to attend to." Tom has other people to meet.

Gino asks Tom, "Have you been here before? Need any suggestions or assistance?"

"I was right here at the Tropicana on New Year's Eve four years ago when the bomb exploded. Hopefully, means of communicating have changed since then. I have no love for those communist rebels. I'll be staying at the Hotel Nacional, should you need to reach me."

Santo chews on his cigar assuring Tom, "This is a minor setback. It'll end soon."

"Not per your boss. Meyer thinks this is the end of an era. Being the son of Russian exiles, he can spot a communist. And you should be rethinking this scenario after Castro had you and Meyer's brother, Jake, arrested. He knows your group was supporting Batista. Do you want to see the luxurious Tiscornia detention camp again?"

As Santo departs in a huff, Gino leans toward Tom and quietly says, "Later, I'll be introducing you to knowledgeable people who are able to provide you with necessary information."

On a cool October afternoon, Marie and Martina gather at home on the veranda, enjoying the sun and the breeze while listening to the radio. Suddenly a news update. The announcer bellows, "Many Cubans are leaving, though some prefer to stay and fight, forming underground counter-revolutionary organizations. They're requesting help from all around the world, especially the United States, who would like nothing better than to be rid of Castro."

Marie nervously, bites her lip. "Mother, I fear this may call attention to the children's transport. Suppose the government tries to stop us?"

The announcer continues, "The CIA is assisting in the overthrow by training and funding the underground organizations."

Martina hears the announcement but doesn't see that her family and congregation will be affected either way. They're not political and keep to themselves. "Marie, no one will bother us, there is no reason for it. Calm down." But she shares her daughter's fear for the children as they escape the island.

The following day Marie is sitting in the Hotel Nacional lunchroom with Gino working out details on the children's transport. Luciana accompanies Marie but appears uninterested.

"I'm leaving to go back to Miami tomorrow," Gino tells Marie. "Some of my meetings have run over into today and tomorrow."

"That's fine. We have most of our plans worked through by the Miami people and those here in Havana. Father McCarthy has procured funds and most of the required people. Everything here in

Havana is ready. The children of the protesters will be on the first flight."

~

Tom enters the lunchroom and observes Gino with a beautiful, young Cuban lady. He approaches hoping for an introduction.

"Hello, Tom." Gino stands and extends his hand. Tom, this is a friend of mine and a local religious leader, Marie Caluda, and her sister Luciana. Marie, this is Tom, visiting from the states."

"Hello, Tom," says Marie in a voice so cold icicles could be hanging from her lips. She is alluring but cold as ice cubes.

Tom senses Marie's instant dislike, feeling she perceives him as the type of person to take control, be in charge, and do everything to suit his way. He recognizes the same attributes in her. He's too much like her, giving into no one, and wanting no one in her life competing for seniority.

Later that afternoon, Tom is poolside lunching on the house specialty, a fresh savory fish. He analyzes his mission, mulling over ways of acquiring government, military information. *Perhaps through some contacts I worked with years ago. An overt group may already be entrenched in the Cuban hierarchy.*

"Hello, Tom, how nice to run across you again. May I join you?"

Tom looks up at the alluring black beauty. Even fully clothed she is seductive.

"Please, join me, Luciana. Yes, a chance meeting twice in the same day is a pleasure."

Tom smiles. *This woman is enticing. I must find a way into her life.*

~

Luciana has a goal and must now develop a foolproof plan to captivate him. She needs information to develop that plan. Through lunch and light conversation, Tom sizes her up, an area in which he is expert. He decides to attempt a few inroads to see if she responds favorably to him. He hears her speak.

"Tom, you look very much at home here. Do you visit often?"

"Not often. Occasionally I do some work here."

"Oh, what type of work?"

"My line of work is information: gathering it, selling it, buying it, putting it to use." He immediately notices her piqued interest.

I may have just met my information center. Her sister is a Santeria priestess, her mother is also a priestess and heads a large congregation. Then there is the friend whom they address as Uncle Ramon, who produces the finest, most demanded cigars in the world, making him extremely wealthy and well-connected in Cuba and in his homeland Spain. Yes, this is it, I just need to bide a little time and work this woman. Unfortunately, I don't have an abundance of time. Move fast, Tom. You only have two months until the children must leave here.

"Luciana, would you join me for dinner tonight?"

"I would love to, Tom. Perhaps after dinner I can show you some interesting spots in Cuba. Native Places you may not have seen before."

This is perfect. I'm the good guy working to help with the movement of children with Marie, and at the same time, manipulating her sister Luciana to help my government's invasion of their country.

"I would like nothing better this evening, Luciana. Shall I pick you up? How about seven o'clock?"

"Seven is fine, but I will meet you in the hotel lobby."

Tom immediately spots Luciana in the lobby; she stands out anywhere. Her beauty is mesmerizing, her demeanor, compelling. Tom is sure she is a seductive temptress of which he must beware.

"Good evening, Luciana, you look stunning."

"Thank you, Tom, and you are a very handsome escort."

As they enter the hotel restaurant, Tom notices everyone

pausing to stare at the pair. He is feeling very proud, while Luciana takes the attention with a grain of salt, an everyday occurrence.

The waiters and staff treat them like royalty. The dinner is a gourmet delight. Feeling comfortable, and with Luciana leading the way, they venture out into the Havana nightlife.

Luciana leads him to a small doorway with a sign reading "Guarida de Satanas." Tom knows enough Spanish to translate the name, Satan's Lair. They hear melodic jazz as they enter the low-lit establishment, not what Tom had envisioned. They sit at a small table near the musicians. It is obvious that they all know Luciana as a regular. The scent of gourmet food enjoyed at the restaurant is now replaced with a delightful fragrant spice. Tom finds himself relaxing, deeply relaxing.

❧ 8 ❧

Tom rolls over and opens his eyes. His brow furrows. Is he even awake? Perhaps he's still dreaming. Luciana, the beautiful loving sister, stands before an altar next to her sister Marie. Still not sure if he's awake or having a nightmare, he tries to rise. *What's happened to me? I feel like I've been drugged—or—hypnotized. That's it!*

He hears Luciana speak. Is she addressing him? No, she is talking to her sister.

"Marie, he perceives you as the good sister, the priestess, and me as the devilish one, so let's keep that going. He will never realize there is no difference. Only we know that Santeria magic does not differentiate; it all functions on demonic power. We are blessed to know how to use it for good, that is, for our own good."

❧

Tom fully opens his eyes and views the beautiful landscape through his sliding glass doors. Palm trees dance like ballerinas in the gentle breeze with soft pink flowers, resembling tutus surrounding their base. Tom shakes his head clears his foggy memory. *Wow, what a night! What happened? We went to a nice little jazz club, and I don't remember the rest. Did I see Luciana and Marie in a church? Impossible! But what did happen? Maybe I'll have some breakfast to help my memory, I'm starving.*

After dressing, he proceeds to the breakfast room. He smiles at the hostess. "Good morning, Gloria. Are you still serving breakfast this late on a Sunday morning?"

"Oh, good morning, Mr. Tom, you're so funny trying to make me think it is Sunday. Did you just get back this morning?"

"Excuse me, Gloria, I'll be back shortly."

Tom approaches the hotel's registration desk and the clerk addresses him. "Good morning, sir. Nice to see you back so soon. We kept your same room for your return."

Tom glances at the clerk's name tag. "Jorge, could you please tell me today's date? I seem to have lost track."

"Certainly, sir, that is easy to do when traveling and working hard. It is Monday, October thirty-first."

"It's nineteen sixty, right?"

Jorge is laughing as he responds, "Sir, you certainly have a fine sense of humor! Yes, it is nineteen sixty for two more months."

Tom is bewildered, shocked. *How can it be? I went on a date Saturday, October twenty-nineth and came back October thirty first? How can this happen? Am I losing my mind? No wonder I am starving if I haven't eaten for near two days.*

Slowly, Tom returns to the restaurant and orders breakfast. He's replaying his date with Luciana over again in his mind, trying to remember the last two days, or at least more than two hours. His brain is distorting reality.

He feels a tap on his shoulder and hears a familiar voice. "Do you remember me?"

"Of course, I do. You and two hours of your company, Luciana, are about all I remember. What happened?" Tom's voice, though controlled, seethes with anger. "What the hell did you give me to knock me out?"

"May I join you?" Luciana asks and sits before Tom can answer. "I had to be sure who you were and your intentions before I could trust you."

"That's usually what dating's for. You have a strange way of getting to know someone; a relationship where one participant has no memory of it. But it feels as if I had a good time."

"Very funny, Tom. Your name *is* Tom? We do not have time for games nor quote 'getting to know each other.' I had to be sure we were on the same side and you could be trusted. This is deadly business we deal in today, a tug of war that can leave a person dead. The day we met at the pool you said, 'My line of work is information, gathering it, selling it, buying it, putting it to use.' I now know what you meant and what you need to take back with you. I can help you on that. I have knowledgeable friends in many places."

"Most of the information I require comes from governments."

"I know; you do not need to tell me that. I have government friends. I can get the information or introduce you to people. Your need is mostly military procedures, strategies and plans, as I understand it. You need to know where certain secret military stations are located, some military communication codes, and any plans that already exist. You work for the US government, don't you? It's ok, you do not need to admit that. I need a week to get this together."

"I think I'm beginning to see clearly. Did you read my mind using some type of drug? You know my background; I could kill you, and no one would ever know or find your body."

"Of course, you could, and then your mission would be thwarted. What would your government think of that? They need you to get information for their plans and would not be accepting of your failure."

"You think you know everything, don't you, Luciana?"

"I do. We have interrogated you at length."

"That doesn't mean you have secured truthful information nor accurately recorded it. I'm recalling some events now. How does your sister fit into this? A Santeria priestess. I saw you together, talking, in front of an altar. She so different from you."

Luciana leans over the table and speaks in a near whisper, "You do not know that. You only know our outer cover, which we choose to expose. You have no idea whom either of us truly are, nor what we are capable of doing."

"Okay maybe we shouldn't see each other." Tom gives Luciana a hard stare. "Just get me the information."

Straightening in the chair, Luciana is all business. "I will be gathering your information over the next couple of weeks. You should be out of here before your Thanksgiving holiday, twenty-four days from now. We can arrange to meet a few nights each week. We need to make sure you have everything you need when you leave here because the US has now implemented a stop on all travel to Cuba, except for emergencies. You will not be able to return."

Although Luciana has assured him of results, Tom keeps himself busy exploring other avenues of information. He cannot rely on her alone and still has contacts from his previous visits long ago, working with the Batista government and other influential organizations.

Tom remembers after the war when he returned from Europe. Coming to Cuba in December 1946 was a joy. He asked Lucky Luciano how he liked living here. "What's not to like? I have everything I would have in Miami—pasta, wine, and, of course, girls. Do I have girls! Wild, extremely wild, those Santeria girls." Tom wonders if one of those girls was... *no Luciana was only a child, but maybe her mother, head priestess. Hmm.*

For three weeks Tom visits his old haunts only to find things have changed. Nothing is as it was. His old contacts both American and Cuban have abandoned the island. He would look them up later when he returns to the states; perhaps they can be useful there. They have fled to protect their assets, to avoid prison or worse, and to protect their families.

~

Luciana spends the three weeks gathering information for Tom. Of course, she has an ulterior motive; she'll demand help moving the children from Cuba to Miami. She calls Tom at the hotel, carefully choosing her words on the phone connected through the switchboard.

"Tom, we need to meet as soon as possible."

"Let me check my calendar, Luciana."

"Stop fooling. I will be there in half an hour."

Luciana arrives at the hotel, bypassing Jorge at the front desk, proceeding directly to the room and knocks.

"Who is it?"

"Quit fooling, Tom. Maybe you should have been a comedian."

As she enters, Luciana can sense that Tom is immediately aroused by her presence. Her low-cut blouse hugs her strong voluptuous upper body, giving way to the long flowing skirt that dances about her legs, music provided by the breeze from the open glass doors. She sees him blink coming back to his senses when she speaks.

"Today we have serious business to review. In this briefcase are all the files you should need, including the confidential locations of all the planes in Cuba's air force."

"Thank you, Luciana. This is valuable information we can use to bomb these locations first, causing them to be removed from the equation. It will then be impossible for Castro's military to resist the invaders. You're sure these are current and accurate?"

"Of course, Tom. Now, you do not have much time to get out of here. Throw your stuff together and get to the airport."

"Luciana, if there is ever anything, I can do to—"

"Now that you mention it, my sister could use some back up help getting the children out of Cuba and into Miami safely."

"You got it. What can I do?"

Luciana was prepared. She handed Tom a manila envelope. "This contains the contact information, both in Miami with Father McCarthy and here with the Cuban counterpart. If you could, oversee that all is going well and step in if needed."

"I will *and* I'll see you when you get to the states."

~

Castro makes a public announcement to the people declaring, that he will eradicate illiteracy.

This announcement causes Priestess Martina and her daughter Priestess Marie extreme concern regarding the children's plight.

"Mother, we must push everyone to come together immediately on the plans for the children's exit. Whatever we have in place now, we must go with."

"Yes. I will make sure the flight arrangements are in place and ready to go."

Marie contacts Father McCarthy. "We must have the children leave quickly before this new education program is implemented. The parents are becoming more nervous, fearing for their families, and their children possibly being sent to Soviet camps. This could eradicate our culture. I have arranged for you to meet with our priest on your next visit here on December twelfth, expecting movement to begin shortly. He has already begun arranging visa waivers for the two-hundred children of counter-revolutionaries involved in underground activities."

"Marie, I won't be able to meet with him, or you, as all travel from here to Cuba has been denied by the federal government. But you can tell him we're ready to receive the first group. We have prepared housing for them. Placement will be with family members, family friends, or church members. I've contacted Washington DC, and Mr. Tracy Voorhees was sent here by President Eisenhower to assess the needs of these refugees. The president has approved funds at a million dollars to move and care for them. It appears we are ready to finalize this operation."

"Oh, Father, that is marvelous news. Thank you."

"Now we must pick a date, gear up everything, and go. It should be December twenty-fifth. Everyone will be distracted, busy celebrating their winter solstice holidays and New Year's. I'll coordinate with our Cuban connection and establish a time. You prepare the parents. Make sure they have the children there as directed." His voice grows substantially deeper and stronger as he continues, "We can*not* afford any delays."

Marie's concentration has been on moving the children out of Cuba. She phones the Cuban counterpart, James Baker, the headmaster of Ruston Academy, an American school in Havana. He's not surprised Father McCarthy cannot get passage to Havana. "Please tell Father our meeting will still take place. I'll meet him in his church in Miami on the twelfth. We must openly discuss plans before proceeding. Everyone must feel comfortable with the others involved."

≈

Arriving in Miami, Mr. Baker meets with Father McCarthy privately and departs the next day, assured in his mind that all the arrangements are in place.

≈

The holidays are a celebratory time for most religious and ethnic groups. The Santeria celebrations are rarely questioned, as they are similar to the Catholics'. This year is no different in that regard. The Caluda family and their congregation meet at the shrine on Tuesday, December 20th, the Feast of Lazaro. Thousands come to this religious event, some walking many miles to El Rincon this morning, to honor their god, praying to the healer. Of course, Marie's godfather is present as the shrine's high priest. There is no sacrificial animal at this festive celebration. There are other means of honoring this Babalawo healer.

At midnight, Martina calls the faithful followers to the altar to light the fifty-one yellow candles. Each person passes by the three distinct altar thrones, ceremonially draped with royal blue, white, and red satin. The worshiper takes a small amount of grain, wiping it over their body to rid evil spirits. They ask for another year of health and to be here next year to light another candle. The drummer and a guiro player begin their music, invoking the high gods. Martina sprinkles white wine on the floor to sweeten the music and the song of the dark-skinned worshipper, who begins a chant to Elegua, god of communication to the spirit world.

At the morning services for the congregation, Marie issues an invitation to them. "We are thankful for another year of good health and safety, praying this continues for us and the children we are sending away from their homes and loved ones. Tomorrow evening, we will prepare for a Kurova Guva ceremony to be held in two days at the site of my brother's grave. Although we are performing this later than usual, I am sure he will honor our request to return and protect the children as he honorably gave his life to protect me."

Instructions are given by Martina to her son. "Julio, tomorrow you will take Ramon, Manuel, and Godfather, along with our cow, and gather just below the Tree of Life. Outside the shrine, in the field where Juan was killed, Godfather will bestow blessings on the cow, offering it to the gods. Manuel will slaughter the beast and butcher it to feed the throngs of people arriving the following day."

They did as they were instructed and returned home to await the ceremony.

~

Awakening, already feeling tired and depressed, Marie doesn't look forward to today's events but realizes she must perform. Encountering Martina at breakfast, Marie states the obvious, "Mother, it is now December twenty-third, with only two days until departure. I'm beginning to feel the stress of this operation."

Martina assures her. "Everything is in order. Every person has a part to play and is prepared. So, do not worry. We have other responsibilities to take care of today, which means soon your brother's spirit will also be there at the children's departure, protecting everyone, overseeing all goes well."

Marie, Martina, Godfather, and Julio leave the family abode that evening for the short walk to the sacred burial grounds. As they approach the cemetery, Marie is overwhelmed. In an emotionally strained voice she speaks to her three family companions, "Do you see the number of people who are here to join us? I expected many would come, but nothing like this. I see so many dear friends and extended family. We are so very special."

Through the archway, they enter the dark, damp, cold graveyard. Only a few candles light the way to Juan's grave. You can faintly hear the sobbing of those, again, mourning Juan's death. The night can only be described as morose.

Martina, as the mother, is seated and prays; "I await the coming forth of my son, as I did on the day, he first entered this life, at birth." She gathers herself emotionally and waits to again hold and cradle her son in her arms.

Marie addresses the gods beginning, of course, with Elegua. There must be no misunderstanding of their request. She hears the interlocking patterns of the two drums. The dancers come forth with precise movements to the rhythm, their feet mesmerizing.

The family members awaken the night with their clapping, dancing, and music for the ears of the spirit world. Julio begins a chant, singing to Juan, "Your way is clear to return, great-aunts and grandfathers will guide you home."

Manuel brings beer and the beef to the celebration. He places one gourd of beer at the head of Juan's grave. "This is for you, my dear friend."

Marie observes her mother rocking back and forth singing a lullaby to Juan.

Arriving home, Martina assures Marie, "The following two days, Christmas Eve and Christmas will keep everyone busy celebrating and partying. The children have their visas, their movements will generally go unnoticed and, of course, your brother is with you helping you every step of the way."

On Christmas Eve, Father McCarthy receives news that the first children are arriving in Miami the next day. A Catholic Welfare Bureau social worker, Mrs. Louis Cooper, will accompany him to the airport.

"Mrs. Cooper, thank you for assisting me this Christmas Day. I only expected sixty children. I secured housing for that many with the County Welfare Department. When I was told last week that one hundred-twenty-five children will be the first arrivals, I panicked, only able to find nine additional beds at St. Joseph's group home. The one option left was the Assumption Academy, a private school for two hundred girls. Mother Superior agreed to take the children, but they must leave by January sixth, as the students return. She is a gift from God."

It's morning but still dark on December twenty-fifth. Marie can't sleep. She heads to Havana's Jose Marti International Airport early and awaits the priest and the first group of children. She anxiously watches the airline schedules. Pan American flight 422 is ready for departure, but no children arrive to board the plane. She stays and waits, watching the next flight to Miami, National 452, leave again with no children on board. Depressed and confused, Marie leaves the airport for home.

∾

Christmas morning in Miami finds Father McCarthy and Mrs. Cooper anxiously awaiting the first arrival of Cuban children.

"Father, the children are so lucky to have such a warm day on their arrival here. At eighty degrees and a light wind, they will feel so much at home. There are two flights from Cuba this afternoon, Pan American's 422 and National's 452. I assume, since we are here, they are arriving on the earlier flight. Is that right?"

"I'm not sure, Mrs. Cooper. We just wait and pray they arrive safely."

Pan Am arrives. No children are on the flight. Filled with trepidation, they await the second flight. After what seems like an eternity, National finally arrives, with no children. Their anxiety peaks.

"Father, what's gone wrong? What's happened to the children? I pray to God they're safe. Do you think Castro has stopped them from boarding?"

"Mrs. Cooper, we'll return tomorrow to again await their arrival and the next day, and every day until they are here. God will provide us with a solution to this dilemma. I'll contact Marie on the radio when I arrive home and call you with an update."

∾

"Marie, Mrs. Cooper and I were at the airport awaiting the children. What happened?"

"Father, I was also frightened when no one showed up at Jose Marti airport, no children and no word from the organizers. When I arrived home, Mother informed me that Priest Backer had a warning from Hernan. You know his father is close to the new heads of government. Evidently, large numbers of guards were being positioned at the airport, and Hernan feared they might stop the children. You know that anyone, even students, caught plotting or working against Castro's rule is immediately executed, no trial necessary. Neighbors are watching neighbors. The paralyzing face of fear is everywhere."

The priest could not put the children at risk. "We are going to try again tomorrow. Pray for us."

"I will, Marie, and we'll be there every day necessary to meet the children."

"Thank you, Father."

On December twenty-sixth Marie awakens to a beautiful clear day for a flight, but depressing clouds of doubt and fear linger. She again makes her way to the airport observing only a small number of guards. Strained with tension, Marie notices how utterly dismal the waiting room has become.

Her friend Manuel approaches her in the departure terminal. "I'm here to wait with you, Marie. Hernan has told me that today should not raise any problems, but I want to help if I can."

"Thank you, Manuel. It could be a long day of waiting."

Marie sees two children enter the terminal with their mother. She wonders. *Are they traveling with their mother, awaiting an arrival, or are they a few of the departing children?*

The police pool all the outbound passengers together like a school of fish. As they begin interrogating each passenger individually, tensions rise. Every suitcase is opened and inspected. Marie notices valuable items are removed, supposedly confiscated for the good of the regime. All cameras are seized along with jewelry, wallets, and some photos. As the Pan Am flight readies for departure the police remove several people and allow the remainder to board. Marie's eyes meet the eyes of the children's mother who is now alone and silently crying, tears streaming down her cheeks.

"Manuel, do you notice the police have not allowed the children on the plane? They have placed them in that room with the big glass windows, without their mother."

"That is the 'fish tank,' the holding room for children traveling alone."

"Do you think they are part of our group? There are only two of them."

"There, over on the side is a man looking through the glass and crying. I would guess he is their father, so most likely they are part of our group."

"Manuel, stay here, and only come forward if I need help."

"What are you up to?"

Marie ignores the question and approaches the room. Nodding at the police officer, she enters the fish tank.

"Hello children, are you here alone? Where are you going today?"

They cower back, reluctant to speak to her.

"Do you know who I am? I'm Priestess Marie, a friend of your priest and am here to help you. Where are you going?"

The eldest child, a little girl, speaks, "Our parents and our priest brought us here today to fly to Miami."

Marie flashes a smile to Manuel as she opens the door allowing their mother to enter. He understands these are the children, but only two? That can't be.

National's flight 452 arrives at the gate. After many torturous hours of waiting and intimidation, the two children board the plane at dusk, viewing the last light of day and the last sight of their parents and their country.

❧ 10 ❧

The Flight, the first flight carrying child refugees arrives in Miami in the dark of night. Nothing is darker than the two little faces departing the plane with no one to look for, no one to care. As they meander down the walkway a bright smiling face, a glowing sunlight of welcome appears before them.

Mrs. Cooper's normally soft voice bellows, "Good God, it is our children! Father McCarthy, our children are here!"

Father McCarthy, also smiling, is busy thanking God. Upon his return to the church, he radios Marie. He assures her someone will be at the airport to meet new arrivals each day. "You have accomplished a miracle for these children. A job well done, Marie."

"Father, I do not look at this as the end of a long journey, but rather the beginning of one; a journey that will carry me to all my desires, all of my wants." Marie envisions at the end of that journey she will be in total control. Family members and associated people will abide by and do her will.

~

Tonight, is the celebration of New Year's Eve, a joyous celebration when all the church members gather at the shrine. Martina fills a large bucket with water, placing it in the center of the altar. As the clock strikes midnight, Julio helps her carry the bucket outside and empty it beside the Tree of Life, discarding the previous year's problems. Now, godparents come forth carrying their white pigeons. They release the pigeons leaving the children purified.

Martina has brought the grapes with her. "Each member will remove twelve grapes from this large bowl as it passes. Place a grape into your mouth and make a wish. All twelve will surely come to pass sometime during the year."

Everyone is jovial, popping grapes, making wishes, and devouring large gulps of wine. Uncle Ramon provides his beautiful cigars and more wine.

New Year's Day morning, a Sunday, Marie awakens to balmy breezes and a sunny world. A bright beginning for 1961. Children are moving to Miami. Given their efforts, the church is prospering. Marie and Hernan are making wedding plans. The family members each pack a suitcase and walk around the block, a traditional rite, to guarantee travel and love in the upcoming year.

At noon, the family gathers at the shrine, the godfather does readings for the congregation and helps everyone offer food to their god. The priestess offers prophesies to the congregation. There is an ebo ritual, the offering of a sheep to ask for a good year.

Martina informs the congregation, "A blood sacrifice will be made to guarantee the presence of the gods. There is no consecration without the gods. We will all gather in the forest, in full view of mother nature."

Upon arrival in the woods, everyone chants and forms a circle to observe the offering. Godfather approaches the animal encircling its head with his left arm. His right arm quickly swoops down with great force and slices through the animal's arteries. He holds the animal at an angle to capture the blood in a ceremonial bowl. The head is placed on a silver tray. "We will feast on the meat and provide the food of blood to the gods. May the Orishas and all spiritual entities fill you with love, success and great things during this holiday season and may the new year bring you all that you wish to have."

~

Two days later, Manuel delivers a message from Tom to Luciana. "Meet me at the Hotel Nacional at three this afternoon."

Tom enters the hotel at noon. Things are uncertain, and he doesn't like this additional trip added to his agenda. He pauses at the entrance, marveling at its grandeur and tosses a silver dollar into the wishing well. "Perhaps I have gone mad, giving some credence to this Santeria mumbo jumbo, but I have nothing to lose."

He says to the well, "I just want to go home and live quietly in peace. May the Orishas and all spiritual entities fill me with love, success and great things during this new year."

He turns to approach the desk and bumps into Luciana. "My, it appears you are here early, aren't you?"

"I am, and it appears you've seen the errors of your ways. Taking a new direction?" she asks, referring to his wish.

"No, not really, just fooling around."

"Okay, why are you here, and how did you get here?"

"How is not important, why is. I need to reconfirm these military locations and strategies. We can't afford a mistake. We have one chance to get this right. Locations where we will drop bombs need to be precise. Exact locations are imperative."

"Yes, I am sure there are no changes."

As they approach the desk, they overhear the news on the radio, "Today President Eisenhower has severed all relations with Cuba."

Tom's in shock. In just over two weeks John F. Kennedy will be sworn in as President of the United States. *It seems Eisenhower could have left that decision to the new president. Kennedy must be saying, "This is a fine mess you've got me into, Dwight!"*

~

On January 20, 1961, Kennedy is sworn in as President and begins to orchestrate the demise of the Castro regime. He is relying on many avenues of information, including Tom's.

Luciana and Tom visit her Uncle Ramon. He has been working for meager wages while his factory continues to reap and enjoy rising profits.

"Ramon, why do you stay here in these conditions? Come back with me. I can get you out of here with your money."

"I cannot leave. My life and my heart are here. Do you understand this is my home?"

"You can't stay and continue to work and live like this, Ramon."

"It will not last long. I can wait."

"Very well, but please let me help when you change your mind."

Upon his return to the United States, Tom submits his reports and hopes this is the end of his involvement. He knows many Cuban-born men, now living in Miami, are standing by to take back their homeland. Victor has been instrumental in supplying information to the CIA and is one of Tom's closest friends. He fears for this determined warrior.

Tom sits in his living room in a trance. His thoughts are in turmoil. The day is April 17th 1961. *Right this moment a group of Cuban exiles, including my friend Victor, are preparing to leave Nicaragua in American B-26 bombers painted to look like Cuban planes. I fear for his safety. In two days, it will all be over.*

Kennedy is relying on the CIA for accurate information and plans. As the day goes on, he acknowledges their air strike has been fraught with problems from the beginning. It is apparent Castro and his advisers knew about the raid and relocated out of harm's way. The president begins to suspect the clandestine plan is "too large to be clandestine and too small to be successful."

Two days later, Marie is listening to her radio, as she does every evening, waiting for Father McCarthy's call with an update on the children. A radio outpost on the beach immediately reports the invasion. The station is broadcasting every detail to listeners across Cuba. Marie calls to Luciana. They sit and listen to all the reports. *"The Cuban exile brigade invades an isolated spot named the Bay of Pigs."*

Luciana knows the problem; the CIA advance team has failed to spot the outpost. She will be called to answer for that.

The radio broadcaster is still reporting. *"Some of the invading ships are hitting coral reefs, and paratroopers are landing in obscure places. The invaders are pinned down on the beach and forced to surrender. All this in less than a day. One hundred fourteen invaders are reported killed and eleven hundred taken to prison."*

Uncle Ramon now acknowledges his folly; Castro would reign, at least for a while. He decides to leave Cuba with his family, knowing in his mind that he will return shortly. He contacts Tom by radio. "Tom, we need to leave immediately. Can you still help us?"

"Ramon, I have a boat docked on the west end of Malecon. Go with your family now. I will radio the captain."

Suffering great inner pain, they leave hurriedly, taking only a few possessions. Ramon will find only poor manual labor in an industry he loves, separating leaves in a Connecticut tobacco house. Like so many others, his life is changed forever.

In December, following his heroic win, Castro makes his announcement. "Cuba is now a socialist republic. Che is appointed Ambassador and thus structures the bond with the Soviet Union. I am a Marxist-Leninist and shall be one until the end of my life.... Marxism or scientific socialism has become the revolutionary movement of the working class. Communism will be the dominant force in Cuba."

~

The new year is passing quickly. Marie keeps busy with her religion and the children. Visas are not a problem, as they are no longer mandated. Logistics and transportation continue to require constant vigilance and attention.

Father McCarthy confides in her. "I am hearing rumors that our situation may change. Travel *to* Cuba has not been allowed for two years, and now travel *from* there is becoming more difficult. I do have some good news, though. An announcement will be made tonight. If you listen to your radio, you will hear that, 'Father McCarthy is bestowed the honor of Very Reverend Monsignor this day October fifth, nineteen sixty-two.'"

"Congratulations, Father, err, rather Monsignor. You deserve it and will make a fine leader, always caring and helpful. I'm happy for you." Marie is hopeful his new position would create easier passage for her and Hernan next June. She always considers her own advancements. Surely the priest's advancement will facilitate Marie's entrance to the US.

It seems the world is falling apart, but Marie is planning her future. *This will be my life. Everything is planned, everything. At twenty-seven, I will marry Hernan and move to the United States to begin my own congregation. In three years, I will have a daughter to train as a priestess. Everything will be perfect, my way. The wedding is the start of my new life, my own life, on June twenty third nineteen sixty-three, six months from now.*

On this cool evening, Marie listens to the radio and hears the President of the United States delivering a nation-wide address. He is making demands on Cuba, placing a naval blockade there, and demands the Soviet Union remove their missiles from Cuba. She listens intently and fearfully as she hears: *"It shall be the policy of this nation to regard any nuclear missile launched from Cuba against any nation in the Western Hemisphere as an attack by the Soviet Union on the United States, requiring a full retaliatory response upon the Soviet Union."*

For the next thirteen days, Marie is not sure the world has a future. All commercial flights are cancelled, impacting the moving plan for her and Hernan. No one is leaving Cuba.

Marie is depressed by the turn of events, withdrawing to her thoughts. *Any remaining children are trapped. No available exit. But I find solace in the fact that as a major contributor to the movement, I have been largely responsible for the relocation of over fourteen thousand Cuban children to safety in the United States. Because of my successful efforts, I should be allowed to travel.*

❧ II ❧

The year 1963 arrives without further incident. The Soviets had removed the last of their missiles two months ago, and life is more relaxed. On June eleventh, more is heard from young President Kennedy. It has been a full century since President Abraham Lincoln signed the Emancipation Proclamation. The president addresses the nation with a civil rights proposal, being the first president to call on all Americans to denounce racism as morally wrong.

Marie and Hernan listen intently. *"I hope that every American, regardless of where he lives, will stop and examine his conscience about this and other related incidents. Our nation was founded by men of many nations and backgrounds. It was founded on the principle that all men are created equal, and that the rights of every man are diminished when the rights of one man are threatened."*

Martina enters, curious to hear what is so interesting. Marie motions her to be quiet; she points for Martina to sit. They hear the U.S. President continue, *"Today, we are committed to a worldwide struggle to promote and protect the rights of all who wish to be free."*

"Shush, sit, be quiet," Marie orders.

"It ought to be possible, in short, for every American to enjoy the privileges of being American without regard to his race or his color."

As the speech concludes, Martina addresses her daughter. "This is why I am so excited to see you go to the United States. You will be free to do whatever you please, including conducting your religion. We may never enjoy that freedom here."

June 23rd is a hot 87 degrees with a balmy wind. It's a good thing the wedding is in the evening, when it will be a bit cooler. Marie has chosen Playas del Este for the ceremony, a most beautiful, enchanting beach just east of Havana. It will be conducted in their native tongue from their homeland of Yoruba, Nigeria. Hernan and the congregation await her arrival. In their ceremonial dress, they appear as a rainbow on the sunny beach. The pounding surf provides a sparkling white backdrop.

The drummers have been washed and purified. Now the Bata drums can begin. Dating back five-hundred years, these instruments accompanied the Nigerian people to Cuba. They are soon joined by the chékere, a shaken gourd-rattle, keeping time with the beat. An acoustic guitar and a soft flute can be heard in the background. The bride and her mother arrive in the wedding carriage. Although Marie is an average looking woman, Hernan is breathless when he sees her appear. She is glowing; her dress movement is hypnotic. The congregation begins dancing around the couple. The late afternoon sun produces long, dark, dramatic shadows moving rhythmically across the sand.

Forming a circle creates a liturgy that follows a sacred formula for communication with the gods. They summon the Orichas, first invoking Elluga, and glorifying Chango, the Great Spirit. The Babalawo joins the couple to perform a water blessing and draw an image of a circle in the sand. The chanting increases as he sprinkles and tosses fruit with water, proceeding to rub each of their bodies with the fruit. The couple experiences the spirits' angelic possession, clasping hands and calling upon the gods, shaking, shrinking to the earth.

The sudden silence is deafening as the priest digs a small hole in the soft beige sand and begins a quiet chant. He slowly tosses sand back into the hole. His chants grow in intensity. Sand and fruit funnel into the ceremonial glasses. The groom kisses the ground while the bride sings a chant. Holding the glasses, they wade into the roaring surf and toss the fruit into the sea. Everyone kneels except the priest. He leads a prayer evoking the gods and massages his hands in circles over the sand image.

The bride stands and says, "We offer this bridal bouquet of brown and green, the colors of my guardian angel, as an ebo spiritual gift to Ayao, who lives in the tornados. I see by the thunderous waves she is with us today, blessing our union."

Hernan then declares, "I join my wife in this offering of flowers, prayers, and blessings as an ebo to my guardian, Aggayu, god of the deserts and guardian of river crossings. We ask your assurance of a blessed life."

This appears a confusing contradiction, yet fitting for this couple; deserts, rivers, and tornados, not to mention fusing a religious priestess' family and a political family. Perhaps that is why Hernan was given Aggayu as his guide; this god who is not sure if he is the father or the brother of the god Chango.

The sun begins to set on the tumultuous ocean. A light rain begins, the drizzle increases and the moon disappears, leaving only total darkness.

Marie is questioning her carefully constructed life plan. *Six months ago, we had a complete darkening of the night sky with a total lunar eclipse. I pray this is not an omen, darkness at the beginning of our married life. How can we move to the United States and establish my congregation now that we are married? How can that happen when transportation is frozen?*

~

A month later Marie becomes more hopeful that moving time is near. The radio reporter announces the news. *"President Kennedy is calling for peace, establishing a hotline between himself and Khrushchev. They are signing a limited nuclear test ban. The current United States president is quoted as saying, 'For, in the final analysis, our most basic common link is that we all inhabit this small planet. We all breathe the same air, we all cherish our children's future, and we are all mortal.'"*

Months pass by and Marie becomes more stressed. She is working at her mother's shrine, but is becoming increasingly impatient to have her own.

Nearing the end of the year, she has word from Monsignor McCarthy. "President Kennedy is coming to Miami next week. I'll be meeting with his people, possibly with him. Hopefully, there will be some inroads on our programs. I'll keep you up to date. Also, there's a safety concern. A letter mailed from Miami Beach, addressed to the Chief of Police of Miami was received today. It's from a group called the Cuban Commandos and threatened both President Kennedy's life and Miami Mayor Robert High. Have you ever heard of them, Marie?"

"No, of course not. How do you know this?"

"I was told by a member of the police department who was formally instructed to keep it quiet. He told me because it is rumored that a 'Padre' is involved. He thought I might have heard something through my Cuban involvement. He'll be here Monday, November eighteenth. Special precautions will be taken. None of the usual motorcades, he'll move about by helicopter."

~

Four days later, Marie is resting on the veranda. It's almost noon, and she's enjoying a cool drink before lunch. The salad looks fresh and delightful. Engulfed in the delicate fragrance of flowers from the garden, her relaxed state is interrupted by the radio's annoying beep, announcing a special report is coming.

The announcer is choking, trying to catch a breath. He's hardly able to speak. Marie can barely understand him. *"The world has suffered an overwhelming shock. President John Kennedy and Governor John Connally were shot today as they rode in an open car motorcade proceeding through Dealey Plaza in Dallas Texas."* Later that day, she learns the president has died.

Another two days pass when Monsignor McCarthy calls Marie on the short-wave radio. "Marie, I'm not sure how much you are hearing there; Kennedy's killer, a man named Lee Harvey Oswald was captured today. As he was being moved from the police station to a jail cell, he was shot by a man named Jack Ruby. Ruby will go to trial even though everyone saw him do it live on TV. I also want you to know I'll not be available tomorrow, as I'll be attending the president's funeral.

"On a good note, inroads are being made on travel. You should be able to come here in the near future. We're succeeding in our efforts to convince government officials to reunite families. The first allowed to enter will be the parents of the children we worked so hard to bring here and who came alone. I'm establishing a committee to assist the Spanish side of the operation, and I think you should head it. We would need to have you here as soon as possible. I'll keep you posted as the plans progress."

Marie's ego grows, envisioning her future in the United States; her congregation of souls, her power and control.

The Christian holidays are approaching as Martina addresses the congregation at their next gathering. "We know at Christmas and

New Year's everyone will be immersed in their own holiday preparations and ceremonies. The Santeria holy service will, as usual, go unnoticed. I will officiate at the ceremony, assuring the gods are duly impressed with our prayers and offerings. We meet at the Tree of Life on Sunday, December twenty-second, which is the Winter Solstice. Be there at dawn. We will ask for a solution in the new year, allowing Marie to receive her transport papers.

The morning of the ceremony springs to life. An abundance of pink light streaked with yellow, accents the blue sky that is brushed with billowy clouds. The only sound is from the tree palms, fondled by the cool breeze. The gods have sent an inspirational sunrise.

Priestess Martina addresses the gathering, "We begin our worship here at our tree, by offering thanks for this inspiring day. Later we will proceed to the shrine for prayers."

The congregation focuses on the colors of the sky as they petition the gods with their requests, and acknowledge their received blessings. By noontime, they march in procession to their shrine. The priestess leads the believers in formal prayer in observance of African traditional religion. Spoken in the Yoruba language, they offer solemn respect and honor.

Four days later, as the family lunches on the veranda, Marie answers a knock at the door. The visitor, Manuel, hands Marie an envelope.

"This was sent to the casino from Father McCarthy. I thought it would be important."

"You mean Monsignor. Thank you, Manuel," replies Marie as she tears it open. "Wow! Marvelous!"

"What is it, Marie?" Manuel is very curious.

"It is all the final paperwork for me to enter and live in the United States."

"How is that possible considering today's travel freeze?" Manuel is confused.

"It appears Monsignor McCarthy has been contacted by a church in a place called Georgia, and a family there has agreed to sponsor me on a Christian housing program providing a place to live, food, and work in the community."

"Does that include Hernan?"

"Yes, of course."

"Well, I wondered when you said, 'It is all the final paperwork for *me* to enter and live in the United States.' So, I wasn't sure."

"I must go tell my family and make arrangements to leave as soon as possible."

Proceeding to the veranda she calls out, "Mother, Luciana, Hernan. You will not believe what just came in the mail."

"What is it, Marie?" All three ask as she enters.

"My dream has come to pass. My prayers have been answered by the gods. I am leaving for the United States!"

"Is Hernan going also?" Luciana asks.

"Of course, why does everyone ask that?"

Martina becomes excited. "Oh, Marie, you will love Miami."

"I'm going to someplace called Georgia."

"Where is that?" her mother asks.

"I'm not sure. It must be very close to Miami since Monsignor needs me to head a committee to assist the Spanish side of his program to reunite families."

Martina is jubilant. "The congregation will be notified and we shall meet to celebrate a new beginning on Tuesday, December thirty-first. Praise the gods! Praise Obatala, father of all the gods. Praise Egun, our ancestral spirit! This new year we pray for our religion, the congregation, all our families, and ourselves. Mostly we pray for success through the efforts of Marie and Hernan as they begin this new life in a new country.

"Late evening on New Year's Eve, we will gather at the Tree of Life, and spend the night, welcoming members to the most formal ritual, the blood ritual, Eyebale. The gods require the sacrifice of the black she-goat. Manuel, you will bring one from the field. We will petition the gods to bless Marie with the birth of a daughter"

❧ 1 2 ❧

On this cold New Year's Eve, the Santeria followers gather at the Tree of Life, intent to spend the night. Martina leads the worship and Hernan accompanies Marie today as an equal.

"Welcome to the most formal ritual, the blood ritual, Eyebale," says Martina. "This communion with the gods requires the sacrifice of the black she-goat. As we call on Oya, our powerful warrior, and serve up her favorite food, we petition her to guide Marie on her crusade in the United States. Oya is a force of change and we ask her to use this force, wielding her machete as needed, for Marie's success. We also ask the gods for Marie to give birth to a daughter who will later lead our members in the foreign country."

They approach the central altar, the *boveda* table, which is covered with a white cloth. "Marie, place six stemmed glasses of water on the altar." Martina brings a seventh glass, slightly larger than the others, and places it on the table; saying, "This glass, containing the cross represents Marie's spiritual consciousness and connection to her Spirit Guardian."

The congregation members place images of the deities, a white candle, and flowers on the cloth. Hernan lights the candle, places a crystal ball at one end, and fans for the gypsy spirits at the other.

Marie rubs perfume through her fingers and flicks it at the altar, petitioning the spirits to cleanse her and carry away all negative influences. She utters her intentions to Ayao, her spirit guide. "Accept this fragrance as an offering and may the alcohol feed and nourish your dead spirits, enabling them to manifest their energies around you and cleanse my aura." She turns to address the congregation "Please join me now in reciting the Our Father as I light the frankincense and myrrh."

As the sun quickly sets, Marie knocks on the altar three times, a greeting to the spirits. She begins speaking quietly with them and listens to their advice. She becomes excited. "They are sending me an image, a baby! Repeatedly she exclaims, "Let us offer a prayer of thanks!"

In the silvery light of the full moon, shimmering blades of high grass dance to the rhythmic sounds of the drums. Sacred drinks are passed to all, and feverish body movements begin. Martina approaches the goat, grabbing its head, and slits its carotid artery as she prays, "We invoke the Orisha, Oya, and ask her to possess Marie. Lead her to her destination."

Marie begins to speak and act as the Orisha. Madness embodies the priestess. Fear is etched on the faces of the crowd watching Marie wield her machete and scream in a language no one recognizes. She finds herself at the altar, again reciting the Lord's Prayer, knocking on the altar three times while blowing cigar smoke on it, honoring the gods. She turns to her mother and sister but their faces are not familiar. Her eyes search the crowd for anyone she may recognize. She is very confused. Martina takes her arm and steers her in the direction of home.

Marie joins Hernan on the veranda for breakfast. "Good morning, dear, did you sleep well? Oh, and Happy New Year."

She recites the blessing to him, "May the Orishas, the Lwas, and all spiritual entities fill you with love, success and great things during this holiday season, and may the new year bring you all that you wish to have." She bends to kiss his head.

"You're a bit late, Marie, two days late."

"Impossible! Absolutely ridiculous! Yesterday was New Year's Eve."

"Do you remember the elixir of the gods you asked Luciana to administer to her friend Tom?"

"Yes. Why?"

"Well it appears you had a taste of the same medicine."

"Luciana did that to me? I don't believe it."

"Apparently, she cared for Tom and decided you should share his experience. And as you know, Santeria practices are most often used as a strategy to resolve conflicts between people. So, how was it, Marie? Do you feel less conflicted with your sister? The sister you have taken advantage of all these years? You have always treated her as a lesser person, almost as a servant just because you are the first-born daughter and thus entitled to be the priestess."

Martina walks into the veranda saying, "Good morning. How is everyone today?"

"How would I know? I thought this was January first. What did I do for four days?"

Marie hears loud laughter from indoors. She turns to see Luciana laughing so hard tears roll down her face as she says, "I'll never tell."

Marie growls, spurts obscenities and flees from the veranda. She enters the shrine and approaches the altar to address the gods, "How can you have allowed this to happen? Have I not been a faithful follower and worshipper? Do I not bring people to worship you? Perhaps I should change sides and begin working for Olosi, the bearer of evil. Lucifer may appreciate my devotion and energy given to success."

❧ 13 ❧

Four months later, Marie nods to the pilot as she boards a private plane to Georgia. "Hernan, I am so excited at our prospects. I can hardly wait to get to work."

"You know, Marie, you need to proceed slowly and feel your way. Let's take our time and let them make the first moves. We will soon learn when it is safe to venture into our own dealings. First, I need a job."

Landing in Atlanta full of hope and plans, Marie has her own ideas of what is to come. "The church in Atlanta sent instructions saying the family we are staying with will meet us at the airport. Mr. and Mrs. Johnson do not have any children and spend a great deal of time on church projects. We should be arriving soon."

The flight and the landing are smooth and easy. The host family is at the airport to welcome them. Marie and Hernan are experiencing a bit of anxiety, anticipating the differences in culture and language. The Christian church, which is spearheading this endeavor, has organized everything and, thus far, all has gone perfectly.

"Hello, Marie and Hernan, it's so good to have you here."

Marie extends her hand. "Thank you, Mrs. Johnson, your generosity is overwhelming. We appreciate your kindness."

"We are happy to help your people who seek freedom within a Christian life. And please call me Peggy Sue. This is my husband, Charlie."

Greetings and pleasantries are exchanged as they walk to the car and load the suitcases. The conversation is met with great difficulty and repetitiveness. Hernan and Marie's strong Cuban accent is as difficult to understand as the extreme southern drawl of Charlie and his wife. During the drive home, Charlie points out interesting sights to the newcomers.

Marie and Hernan are impressed with the accommodations. They stand in front of the Johnson's home, absorbing the feeling of the neighborhood and its large two-story brick homes with columns in front, most supporting a balcony. Tall thin evergreens form a line of separation between neighbors.

Hernan is the first to speak. "What a lovely area, Charlie. An enchanting street lined with many oak trees, beautiful flowers, and grass that looks like a carpet."

"Yes, we are all very proud of our grass."

Peggy Sue interrupts their botanical discussion. "Let's get you settled and unpacked. We can sit and talk over dinner." She walks them to their bedroom suite.

Marie is taken back by the beauty of the room and its furnishings. A dark mahogany four-poster bed sits against the wall to her right, with a matching rocking chair on her left alongside an antique dresser. A large bay window faces her from the opposite side of the room providing a scene of a golden sunset veil over Atlanta. The room overlooks the new spring buds coming to life in the garden. She is spellbound. *This budding garden is just like me, finally coming into my own life.*

Hernan stands speechless for a moment, drinking in all the opulent decorations.

"Marie," Peggy Sue says, breaking the spell, "when you and

Hernan are unpacked and rested come into the dining room. There is no set time, so don't rush. It will all keep warm. If there is anything you need that I may have overlooked, just ask. We hope you are comfortable and feel at home."

Marie thanks Peggy Sue. She whispers to herself; "this is nothing like home!"

Hernan heads for the shower, hoping it will reduce some of his stress. "Marie, get in here quick! You are not going to believe what you see."

Marie rushes in asking, "Is there a problem?" only to be stunned speechless. The appearance of her surroundings has left her frozen in place. Finally, her eyes travel in a semi-circle, pausing to take in every inch of the stately riches. Mirrors everywhere cause the small candelabra-shaped chandeliers to illuminate the scene. "Never have I seen anything of this magnitude! I am heading for that glass enclosed shower. You'll have to wait your turn, Hernan." As she adjusts the water flow, a full waterfall descends on her body engulfing her in bliss.

Having showered and feeling refreshed the guests enter the dining room. Tastefully decorated in soft blue tones sprinkled with dark green accessories, the room's immense chandelier sends bits of sparkling light flittering across the green satin drapes. The china and silver come to life on the tablecloth. Dinner begins with a blessing, of course. Peggy asks, "Marie, would you or Hernan like to say the blessing?"

"Thank you, Peggy Sue, but this is your home and beautifully prepared dinner. Please, you should set the tone for the evening."

Peggy Sue and Charlie reach forth their arms offering their hands to the young couple. They pray together, a prayer of thanks for the food, the move, and new friends.

"Marie, I've made arrangements for you at the nursing school. Although you cannot simply transfer your license here, you can take a course to qualify and then receive your Georgia license. I'll take

83

you tomorrow. Now, tell us about your trip here. Was it a pleasant one, and what life do you dream of here in the US?"

"Our trip was uneventful, which is good—and as it should be on such a grand day."

"Is today a holiday or religious day in your country?" Peggy Sue asks.

"Yes, May fifth is Cinco de Mayo."

"What's the meaning of Cinco de Mayo?"

"It is very important, and well known in the Spanish communities, even in the United States. It celebrates a victory of the Mexican Army over the French Army in the Battle of Puebla."

"But that's Mexican and you're Cuban, so why the celebration?"

"Yes, true, but we are all Spanish descendants."

"I see, so all the Spanish cultures celebrate Mexico winning that war?"

"They all celebrate winning the battle. It was like David conquering Goliath, but unfortunately, Mexico lost the war."

"I never knew the French ruled Mexico. What war was that?

"It was the Mexican Civil War, known as The Reform War."

"At some time, the French left or were overthrown. How did it become Spanish again?"

"It was one hundred years ago, eighteen sixty-four. The Americans came in to help the Mexican Government after the United States Civil War ended."

"What an interesting story, Marie. It was also one hundred years ago, that General Sherman captured Atlanta."

Marie is misrepresenting herself as Spanish when her true heritage is Nigerian.

Charlie jumps in during a short lull in the ladies' conversation, "Hernan, I've made inquiries in the surrounding neighborhoods to find you some work. This area is active with commercial businesses nearby. You could get to work by walking or taking a bus. I've written up a few places for you to visit. Places I know are hiring."

"Thank you, Charlie." As Hernan looks over the list, he

becomes a bit perplexed and questions Charlie. "I see here that most of these jobs are menial. Do you know I am qualified to operate a business? I have worked in upper management with governments, religious groups, and businesses like import / export companies. Surely there must be a professional job that I can fill?"

"Hernan, please recognize things will take time to develop for you. Bigger offerings will come your way eventually. But right now, people here will need time to adjust. Initially they'll see a foreigner. One who speaks with an accent and has dark skin. You are in the *Southern* United States and things in the South don't change quickly. Be patient, take a job, and prove yourself. This is Tuesday; take a few days to look things over and adjust, after which you can go on these interviews."

Hernan is feeling angry and hurt. *How can these Southern people judge me by my speech and my color? I will watch the news each night to keep informed, enabling me to make educated decisions.*

Over the next week, Hernan visits local businesses and interviews for jobs. On Tuesday, the twelfth, as he is watching the news, students begin burning their draft cards and protesting the Vietnam War.

While continuing to look for a job, he meets others from his homeland that are also here thanks to the church sponsorship. It is reassuring and comforting to meet others like himself. Ten days later, the TV is showing President Lyndon Johnson deliver a speech at a college calling for an end to racial injustice and poverty. He outlines an agenda for his four years. Hernan is excited. *This is great! No more racial problems. Maybe now I can get a professional job.*

The following week, Hernan approaches professional businesses with his resume. He's given a cold reception at each location. Perplexed, he asks Charlie for some guidance. "What am I doing wrong here, Charlie? I am dressing in a nice suit, my resume is professional, and I am always polite to the first person in the company through to the personnel department. With the end of racial injustice, what do you think could be the problem?"

"Hernan, the problem isn't with you. Just because the President calls for no more racial problems doesn't mean it's going to happen quickly. That's why he implemented a four-year program. I know your government makes things happen immediately. You have Batista and a certain fascist way of life one day and in the snap of a finger the next day it's completely changed to a Castro Communist dictatorship. Not so here, my man, not here."

Marie is disturbed today, Sunday June 21st, the Summer Solstice. She is not hosting a ritual; she has no followers, no congregation, and no altar. She's suffering a major depression. To make things worse, the heat is breaking records. Hernan assures her that she'll succeed in time. At 97 degrees, with a straight seventeen days of abnormally extreme highs, the summer grows warmer and so do the friends and potential members of a future congregation Marie gathers. Amazing, the number of potential members in the medical field. She finds them at the library, noting their reading material. Those, in turn, introduce her to others as everyone is anxious to have their home religion available to them here in this new country.

Hernan listens to the news. "Three activists fighting for civil rights in Mississippi are presumed murdered." *How long does it take here to enact a law after a president issues a mandate?*

In July, the news reports on television tell Hernan, "President Johnson is signing the Civil Rights Act, prohibiting discrimination on the basis of race, color, religion, sex or national origin in employment. It also ends segregation in public places, and outlaw's segregation practices common among many southern businesses."

"Marie, come and listen to this. Hurry." As she listens, Hernan tells her, "This is directly said to the *Southern* people and businesses. That means I can get a decent job now, finally."

"That is good news, Hernan, because I have ten more months to get my work permit."

Over the next month, Hernan is mesmerized by the news media. A white police officer kills a black teenager, and over the next six days, violence explodes in Harlem. The North Vietnamese torpedo a US destroyer. The bodies of three freedom fighters are found in the south. Congress allows the President to declare war. Lee Harvey Oswald alone killed Kennedy, no conspiracy.

"Hernan, I finally have enough Santeria worshippers to hold a ceremony. We are going to meet in a park on the little Kennesaw Mountain. We arrived here near the hundredth anniversary of the Battle of Puebla, and now we hold our first ceremony here at the location of the Battle of Kennesaw Mountain. We will meet on October fifth, a perfect night. One with no moon."

❧ 14 ❧

It is early evening when the couple sets out for Kennesaw Mountain, traveling with new friends. Marie addresses the small group standing before them in a white mask adorned with shells. It seems to glow in the pitch-black night. The sky is an endless pool of darkness. No sun, no moon nor stars.

She begins, "The ceremony this night is calm and uplifting. We need to be careful as we progress in our gatherings to avoid any confrontations or complaints. Tonight, we meet for the first time as a congregation, appropriately on Satan's Night. The Darkness encompasses us on every level. Last night I blessed and slaughtered a chicken for our offering, which we now share with the Orisha. As we feast on the meat, I offer this blood to the gods. By this offering we know they are with us."

Marie recites a prayer, "I beseech you to be with us and share our food. Bless us, guide us. Help us to grow and succeed in our quest. Help us to gather more followers for your worship."

She turns her attentions to the small congregation. "Often new members are lost souls looking for a meaning in life. They are prostitutes, sex addicts, thieves, even murderers. These souls often look to religion when things go terribly wrong. Let us help them. We will close this evening with songs bidding the gods to oversee our growing congregation and our safety in this new country."

As they arrive home Marie remarks, "Hernan, I am in love with this Georgia autumn. The falling leaves are forming a kaleidoscope of color, covering Charlie's grass. What kind of tree is that?"

"Charlie says it is a Sugar Maple, and in the fall no other native tree matches the brilliant yellow, orange, and red coloration of the leaves."

Hernan listens to his favorite news station. He can hardly believe what he's hearing. A black man, Dr. Martin Luther King, is receiving the Nobel Peace Prize. *My, what a contrast to Nelson Mandela, a peace activist who is sitting in prison.*

~

"Wow, Marie, I enjoy this Thanksgiving holiday," says Hernan. "Great food! But you realize now, Christmas is almost here. What do you suggest we do about the Christian ceremony, which will surely confront us again? It may not be so easy to make believe in such close quarters with the Johnsons."

"Yes, Peggy Sue has already given me the schedule of church ceremonies, prayer vigils, and dinners. We will make do, Hernan. We will find a way to satisfy them and still have our spiritual needs met. This year, their church days are not the same as our ritual days, so we will do both."

A couple weeks before Christmas, Hernan's favorite news show is reporting, "The US Government is charging those men in Mississippi with depriving the freedom workers of civil rights. Why, because murder is not a federal crime? Where is the peace and justice?"

Ten days later, he hears China has tested a nuclear bomb. *Where is the peace?*

~

"Marie, Hernan, we're ready to leave for Midnight Mass. Hurry, Charlie's waiting for us in the car."

"We will be right down, Peggy Sue." Marie's not happy about attending the mass, but realizes this is something they must do to reach their desired end. "I really dread this, Hernan. It disturbs me immensely, pretending to be a Catholic. It angers me to be perceived as a devoted follower. Mostly I hate being in a situation where I have no control, no control at all."

"I understand, Marie, as a Santeria priestess it is hard for you to act out something you do not support. Perhaps you could find some comfort in the similarities."

"No, Hernan, this is much like our religion worships, only because we have adapted. Their saints are almost identical to our gods, each one helping with different needs. They named the slaves' religion Santeria, meaning 'the way of the saints,' I consider a derogatory term. The worshipers themselves did not use this term. They referred to themselves as *La Regla Lukumi* meaning the 'Way of the Lukumi.'"

"Oh, I did not know that, Marie. It has been called Santeria for as long as I can remember."

"Yes, Hernan, it is not something often discussed. When our ancestors left Nigeria, they were transported as slaves to many areas of the Caribbean, not just Cuba. Our religion became known by many different names in those areas, all of us hoping to hide our true beliefs."

"Your mother told you this history?"

"Yes, it is handed down through the priests and priestesses."

"So," says Hernan, "sit back during this ceremony and see how many similarities you can find."

The Christian holidays pass without incident. The new year arrives in Atlanta, warm and comfortable. Marie and Hernan celebrate, looking forward to the blessings they know await them.

Today is special-order perfect, warm with a cool breeze. Spring arrives. The sun is shining, and cherry blossoms fill the scenery and the senses. "Marie, you must be so excited about your graduation. I know I am. My wife is a nurse in the United States. I never thought I would say that," Hernan says.

"Yes, it has been a long-fought battle. I hoped it would only take a year, but the language barrier was extremely difficult to overcome. Now, I can get a job, and we can afford a place of our own."

"I am sad that I cannot support you by myself. I am a failure as a husband."

"No, Hernan, you do what you can, working at the restaurant. If we grow the congregation, perhaps, we could make up some income with donations. Considering the apartment lease dates and the amount we need to pay to move in, I would like to move by the end of summer."

"I will look at apartments this week on my days off."

Within three days, he finds just what they need.

"What a perfect quaint apartment, Hernan. I noticed a little park and playground across the street. Maybe we will have a daughter playing there next year."

That evening at dinner, they talk to the Johnsons. "Peggy Sue and Charlie, Marie and I want you to know how much we appreciate everything you have done for us. Without your help, we would not be at this point. You have been as kind as family to us."

Marie agrees, "Yes, your help with school and language enabled me to graduate. I won't forget."

Peggy Sue is choking up as she looks at the two of them and says, "We'll miss you being here, but are so happy you've been able to get your own place. You must stay in touch and visit often. And maybe within a year you can visit with a little one; I know that means a lot to you."

"You and Charlie are part of our family, and always will be. You have been like parents to us, and we hope you will be grandparents to our children."

"Oh, bless you both, we are thrilled to be grandparents. When?"

"Not yet." Hernan chuckles. "Give us some time to get settled."

～

Following the move, Marie schedules a "Full Moon" celebration.

Peggy Sue calls Marie, "Please come for dinner next Friday and let us know how you are doing."

"Sorry, Peggy Sue, next Friday is September tenth, and we have plans for the evening."

Peggy is wondering just where the young couple goes on these evenings out. They are always so mysterious and never disclose their plans.

～

"Hernan, as the members come into the restaurant for café con leche, let them all know, we will meet at the Little Kennesaw Mountain Park on the evening of September tenth at six thirty. We now have a small but substantial congregation so we will begin to ask for church donations. And today at work you should approach the restaurant owner and ask Mr. Barzaga if he would like to join our congregation."

"I'm not sure if that would be good for my job. Suppose he objects?"

"Give it a try; there is not much to lose. We can manage on my salary for a while, and you can always get a restaurant job."

At this point, Hernan feels depressed, not very needed. As always, he'll do as Marie asks, even if it costs him his job.

≈

Hernan comes in from work with his boss alongside him. "Marie, Mr. Barzaga would like to talk to you."

"Yes sir, what can I do for you?"

"I would like to hear about your religion. I remember my parents talking about this when I was young. Like all youngsters, you hear things, but I don't understand the whole concept."

Marie sat with him for hours explaining the religion. He had so many questions. Marie was good at convincing people of anything. He would be joining them on the tenth.

≈

"Charlie, let's follow Marie and Hernan and see where they spend their evenings."

"Why would you want to do that?"

"Just curious, very curious. Only because they are so secretive."

"Okay, I'll get the car out or I know I'll never hear the end of this." They pull up near the front of the apartment and wait in the darkness. A car stops in front and the young couple gets in. As the car pulls away from the curb and heads forward, the Johnsons follow at a discreet distance.

≈

Marie and Hernan arrive at the park. After a short hike, they make their way to the open field where there is always a pleasant breeze giving voice to the leaves. No one could approach from the west, as that edge of the field slopes severely downhill into a valley. They have come to feel comfortable and safe here, having never seen another person in the area. Marie addresses the congregation.

"There is no tree even slightly resembling the *Tree of Life* we have at home. But the view from this mountain top is spellbinding and can provide us with inspiration. The treetops below us, in every imaginable color, appear as massive assorted bouquets gently gliding over the dance floor."

Marie has everything prepared for the sacrifice. The drummers begin their soulful music, motivating people to move their bodies with the rhythm. Ceremonial drinks are served. Everyone is singing praises to the gods.

The congregation builds a fire and becomes quiet as Marie approaches the park's makeshift altar. "It is seven o'clock and the full moon is now peeking over the tree tops, while the sun, still visible, is fading into the pink horizon on the opposite side of the sky."

She begins her prayers and requests. She bows to the heavens and summons the gods, expressing gratitude for their blessings on her wishes. Her ceremonial dance becomes fierce, as she flings her body from one end of the altar to the other. Even the glistening stars appear to be dancing, in-between the sun and the moon.

Peggy Sue watches in shock. She cannot believe what she sees.

Marie sings out, "We have the gift of this spiritual sky tonight as we praise the Orishas."

The sacred drums intensify, inviting the gods to come and walk among them. Marie is dancing wildly toward the ceremonial ground and begins to tear off her clothes.

The people are building to a frenzy. Marie steps up to the altar carrying a chicken in one hand and a knife in the other. She dances wildly reciting familiar prayers, shedding the last of her clothing. The chicken is exsanguinated. Blood flies in all directions as she dances with the sacrifice. Covered in blood, she continues to repeatedly throw herself over the altar, calling the gods to possess her.

Peggy Sue lets out a low moan, which no one hears.

Hernan approaches the altar and does possess her, taking her bloody naked body right there on the altar. The music continues for hours carrying everyone into exhaustion.

Peggy Sue faints dead away. Charlie is more scared than ever before in his life.

As the moon wanes, the congregation gathers at the west side of the field. Peering down the slope affords a vantage sight to view the full moon as it slowly disappears into the lower level horizon.

The fire has cooked the chicken. They share the bounty with the gods. The Orichas consume the blood. Without the blood sacrifice, there would be no gods present.

Charlie helps Peggy Sue stumble back to the car. They leave just moments before the congregation arrives in the parking lot.

Last night the moon kissed the sun while the stars danced. This morning is a mental reflection in total darkness lasting nearly an hour. The sun has not kissed the moon.

As daylight creeps over the mountain, everyone departs, declaring the full moon worship a successful religious experience.

"Our own place together for the first time, Hernan! We will continue to have so many firsts here. This will be our first autumn, our first holiday season alone together, and our first new year. We have been so blessed, coming here to freedom, friends, the beginning of a congregation, and our little girl on her way to us."

The phone ringing interrupts Marie. Hernan answers, *"Buenos días. Un momento, por favor.* Excuse me, I mean one moment, please. Marie, the Monsignor from Miami is calling for you."

"Good day, Monsignor. How are you doing?"

"I'm fine, thank you, Marie. I need you to come to Miami and help out here. The government's allowing entrance to the families of our Pedro Pan lift. The children will finally be reunited with their parents. We need help organizing, and with translations. These people know you and will trust what you tell them."

"This is marvelous, Monsignor! Exciting that they'll be reunited. How will these parents support the children and provide for their families?"

"They'll have a great deal of help from the government paying for everything: transportation, getting established with housing, food, jobs, things like that. President Lyndon Johnson is their savior. The churches will oversee and help if anything is needed. Or I should say *when* things are needed, and that time will come."

"When is this happening?"

"We begin December first. There'll be two flights a day, called The Freedom Flights."

"The children must be so excited, and, of course also the parents. When do you need me there?"

"Yesterday would have been good, Marie." He sighs. "There's so much planning to do before the parents start to arrive. We need to secure things like clothes, medical, moral support, and others we haven't even thought of yet."

Marie is on the next available flight to Miami. Mrs. Simms greets her at the airport and takes her to the rectory where the Monsignor is already at work.

"Please wait in the garden, Marie. I'll bring tea and let the Monsignor know you're here."

Marie doesn't mind at all. She has always loved this garden. Unlike Atlanta, Miami is always green and blooming beautifully in the winter months. *Will I be asked to contribute to the cause again this time, and what will I get out of it? Last time I got early consideration to enter the country. This time, what?*

"Hello, Marie, my dear. Nice to see you again, and looking so well. Tell me how things have been for you in Atlanta."

"If you do not mind, I will, but first I am anxious to hear about The Freedom Flights and what I can do to help."

"Yes, I'm sure you are. President Johnson has established this program, noting our government is sponsoring the refugees' flights. Cuba isn't stopping anyone from leaving there. They depart from Varadero Beach twice a day. When they arrive in Miami, they're escorted to the Freedom Tower where our government has established an office for the U.S. Cuban Refugee Resettlement Program."

"I am happy to help, as always, Monsignor. I would like to be given a consideration, if I may ask. I wish to relocate to Miami, to be near my people, those whom I have helped."

"That won't be a problem, Marie. You just let me know when you're ready."

"I would like to consider July or August, giving me time to have my daughter and recuperate."

"Congratulations Marie! A baby girl; how precious and exciting for you."

"I will stay now for a couple months to establish a presence and get things started. That way I will be home before the holidays. After the baby is born, I will come to Miami as soon as we can work it out."

Marie sets up shop attempting to organize for the unforeseen problems and inevitable confusion. By performing well and establishing a workable format, she has been sure to create a need for herself. They will most definitely bring her back to Miami.

Marie is in labor expecting a child of the gods. This will be the girl to maintain their family's hierarchy in the religion. The next Santeria priestess, born on the half-moon night, June 23, 1966, *plus* having been conceived at the Full Moon ritual, surrounded by the dancing stars will surely be blessed by the gods.

The doctor enters the waiting room and addresses Hernan, "Congratulations, sir, you have a healthy son."

Marie is despondent. She won't talk to anyone. *A boy! A boy!*

"Don't worry, Marie." Hernan tries to console her. "We can have more children; we are young and healthy. Besides, it will be good for our daughter to have an older brother to protect her, the way both your brothers did for you."

"Healthy, yes. But I am thirty, with few producing years left."

"What shall we call him, Marie? We have not even thought of boys' names."

"I don't care. Name your son whatever you like."

"I would like him to have my name, Hernan."

"That is terrible, but if you insist, we must have a nickname. We will call him Chico."

Charlie asks Peggy Sue if they should visit Marie and Hernan's baby. Peggy's a bit unnerved but agrees to go. "We saw it conceived; we may as well see it born." Of course, when they get to the hospital they coo and giggle over the little one.

Charlie corners Hernan. "I want you to know that Peggy Sue and I followed you both one night. We were worried about you. Being new here, we were concerned you might get into a situation you couldn't handle. That being said, is there anything you want to talk about? Something you need help with? A problem bothering you?"

"No, Charlie. Why would you think that?"

"I want you to feel comfortable and know you can tell me anything. I'm here to help you in every way possible. Like today, Marie doesn't look happy."

"Thanks, Charlie. We are doing fine. It's just that,"—Hernan pauses and takes a deep breath before continuing—. "You know Marie had her heart and mind set, totally convinced it would be a girl baby. So, she is a little disturbed. By the way, when was it that you followed us?"

I can't tell him which night I followed them. If I did, they would know what we saw. I don't think we could ever get past that if we said it out loud. "Oh, it's not important."

"Fine, but I want to know. When was it?"

Charlie is stuck now. He doesn't know any other night to refer ence. He didn't keep track of their numerous nights out. "It was some night in September, not sure which one."

"Really, Charlie? There was only one night we were out in September, only one night. So, I know where you followed us and what you saw."

"Hernan, we didn't mean to spy or intrude on your life. We were only trying to protect you, to keep you safe."

"Well now, Charlie, the way I see it, you owe us a consideration."

"What can I do?"

"When Marie gets home from the hospital you both will come to our home and Marie will explain everything about our religion to you."

Shocked and surprised Charlie blurts out, "That was a religious ceremony?"

"Yes, a ritual, you will understand later."

He doesn't mention this to Peggy Sue. He would have no idea how to even begin that conversation. *It can wait and, as Hernan said, Marie can explain everything when she is released and feeling well.*

Upon arriving home, a message is received from Mrs. Simms. "Almost every child has been reunited with their family. The flights end this month, so we're winding down. Not too many problems to work out. With the federal employees working here, we're doing fine. You just stay home and rest, recuperate and gain your strength. You should not be flying so soon after giving birth. We'll get together later, I'm sure. Congratulations on that baby boy!"

That last sentence is grinding on Marie. *"Congratulations on that baby boy."* She knows she will hear that for months to come.

Hernan notices Marie seems to be coming out of her depression. "I am so happy to see you cheerful again."

"I have come to realize the boy will be very useful to us as time passes."

"How do you mean?"

"In my last meditation, I had a sign. Hernan, I would like you to invite Peggy Sue and Charlie over to see the baby, and I will talk to them about our religion. I want them to understand and accept. It is good for us to have friends like them."

"Okay, I will call Charlie. What kind of a sign did you receive?"

"In my trance appeared a cloud, drifting slowly. As it passed by the light, dark shades seemed to rearrange themselves. Slowly the darkness moved to the center and separated into three sections. They rolled and reformed into Chico's birthdate."

"Really? I don't understand the meaning of that."

"His birth date Hernan. His date is June 1966. That is 6/66. Do you understand now?

"We must have a ceremony welcoming the child, asking the Orishas to embrace and protect him. I would have chosen Sunday July third, at the first full moon of his life, but that first weekend in July is a big outdoor holiday for the Americans. The parks will be crowded. Therefore, we will hold our welcome ceremony on Sunday July seventeenth, the first new moon after his birth. Let everyone know we will meet at sunset."

Over the next three weeks, Marie begins aggressively tutoring Peggy Sue and Charlie. She starts with the similarities so they will be receptive. She interweaves stories of Cuba and family life. The Johnsons are becoming quite relaxed with the religion. They are anxious to attend little Chico's Santo, his baptism.

Hernan wonders how receptive they will be to blood sacrifices. Marie has purposely avoided this area in her discussions.

Marie approaches the altar with her tall wooden staff to ceremoniously call for the blessing of the ancestors.

"Welcome everyone on this day to celebrate our little Chico's entry into the Santeria religion. As the act of birth has blood associated with it, so will our ritual tonight. Our ancestors fought and survived in the face of slavery to preserve our ritual observances. Symbolically, Chico will observe the sacrifice so he can appreciate the lives of the animals that are dying to save him, and help him spiritually evolve."

Peggy Sue watches as Hernan steps forward holding a beautiful pigeon captive within a small cage. She notices the silver-gray feathers shimmering in the setting sun. The drums and dancing facilitate a group trance, which allows the Orisha to descend upon the head of the new member controlling the child's frenzied movements.

Aghast, Peggy Sue lets out a blood-curdling scream as Marie lays the bird on the rock altar, raises her arm over her head, and quickly lowers it. The cleaver neatly removes the head from the body. The blood flows into a bowl on the side of the rock. The sky becomes invisible in the darkness.

"We are not sharing the meat with the community today, as the sacrifice is used for purification. This blood we share with the Orisha and with our new Santero, allows this child to be born into a new life as a child of the Orisha." Marie pours the blood over the sacred stone and feeds a small amount to the baby. Peggy Sue is off to the side near a tree, vomiting.

❧ 16 ❧

All day Hernan is enjoying a new commercial with the lyrics "the wheels on the bus," and again tonight as he's enjoying his evening news show as usual. It is April third, and tomorrow is the grand opening of the big new buses. The trolley cars have been converted.

"Marie, I think I will try taking that new bus tomorrow and see how it goes."

The next day he arrives home excited. "Marie, I can't wait to tell you how nice the new buses are. A big improvement!"

"I can't stop now, tell me at dinner."

"Alright, I'm going to check the news now."

Hernan likes to keep informed, especially on the issues of immigrants and discrimination in the job markets. The announcer is saying, "It's April fourth, nineteen sixty-eight, and I am being handed a breaking news announcement. Dr. Martin Luther King Jr., in Memphis today to address the Southern Christian leadership conference, was shot in the head at six o'clock this evening. We will keep you posted on his condition."

Shortly after seven, they announce his death.

"How can this happen in these United States, Marie? A man should be able to speak; it is one of the freedoms we came here to enjoy."

~

The weather has been quite rainy but now the heat and humidity are setting in.

Hernan, having become interested in the political scene, is watching his favorite news show. ABC is just signing off the air when the announcement comes. "The assassination of Massachusetts senator Robert Francis 'Bobby' Kennedy, brother of assassinated President John Kennedy, took place shortly after midnight today during a presidential election campaign event in Los Angeles, California.

"Oh, how terrible! Marie, come see the news. Robert Kennedy has been shot. Just two months ago was the shooting of Dr. Martin Luther King, and now this. What are we coming to? How can this be happening in a free country?"

"I feel sorry for his family," she mutters.

"Marie, how can you be so unfeeling? I don't understand you sometimes." He is striving to understand his wife's uncaring attitude.

Hernan listens to the news all the next day. He plays audio tapes done by radio reporter, Andrew West, who had just recorded the speech and turned off his recorder. Following Robert Kennedy to the exit and hearing the gunshots, West had immediately turned the recorder on.

Hernan is tormented with the thought, *what a sad day for that family*.

~

Over the next two years the Johnsons periodically get together with the Caludas, Marie explaining the Santeria religion beliefs and rituals. Marie now performs her worship with many believers attending. For now she must remain in Atlanta to service the growing number of worshippers. No one could take her place. By Christmas of the second year, all four are attending the Santeria ceremonies on a regular basis, although the Johnsons also attend the Catholic Church.

New Year's celebration brings an abundance of members including both families. The congregation gathers in the park just before midnight. All are wrapped in heavy coats, as it's forty-five degrees and the wind on the hill brings a chill to the bones. Hernan is carrying a bucket of water to the altar.

A bit later in the evening, as the clock strikes midnight, he and Marie approach the altar with their son, Chico, now two and a half years old. He seems right at home there. Hernan picks up the bucket and walks to the cliff. Facing the strong wind, he tosses the water. The members watch the water cascade down the steep hillside, releasing the old year. They welcome the new. They can only follow the water with their eyes for a short distance. Although the moon is almost full, the fog is dense and creates the impression of swallowing the water. Every worshipper has a bag of twelve grapes, and with each one, they make a wish for the new year.

Peggy gives Charlie a quizzical look. He surmises her question concerns the water toss. Pulling her close he whispers, "Their version of our New Year expression, 'out with the old and in with the new' I suppose."

Priestess Marie greets her congregation with the standard greeting. "May the Orishas, the Lwas and all spiritual entities fill you with love, success and great things during this holiday season, and may the new year bring you all that you wish to have. In Cuba, we would now walk around the block with our suitcase hoping to travel. Our wish has already been granted, as we are here in Georgia. We offer thanks to the gods. We will now have this year's readings and feast on our roast pork. May we all share in good health this year." Marie inwardly petitions the gods for another child, a girl.

The newscaster on television is lamenting the weather. "This is the longest cold spell in our recorded history. From February ninth, until today, March eighteenth, we have endured the longest bout of frigid weather. Ladies and gentlemen, that is thirty-eight consecutive days! Stay indoors, cook a pot of soup, and cuddle up!"

Hernan is thinking this is a grand idea. A perfect way to spend this Tuesday afternoon. "Marie, the soup needs to simmer a bit, so let it sit. Come here and simmer with me for a while."

"Hernan, it is time to leave. The ceremony begins at nine this morning. We need to finish before the heat of the day."

It is Saturday, June 21, 1969 the Summer Solstice. The ceremony includes a blessing for Chico.

"It's hard to believe that in two days he will be three years old. When he was conceived on that altar, I used the 'way of power' to approach the spirit with an ebo offering of the chicken, whose blood I poured on the sacred stone, feeding the god, petitioning for a daughter. Following his birth, at his baptism, I offered the pigeon to Elluga utilizing the 'way of values,' requesting the dead ancestor spirits to provide *ashe*. Whether Chico is right or wrong, good or bad, the ancestors will always protect him."

"What are you trying to tell me, Marie? Is there a message for me in all this?"

"Yes, Hernan, because of these offerings, I am telling you that

Chico has been blessed with my great-aunt, Carlota, la rebelde. She is reincarnated in our son."

"How can that be, she has been dead over two hundred years?"

"Yes, that is why it is possible. If she were only a generation away, we could not invoke her."

"Why have you done this, Marie? What possible reasoning could be behind this?"

"My age for one thing. I never thought I would have another child. I feared my son might be forced to become a Santeria priest and lead the congregation. It should have been a girl. The religion belongs to women. I realized with his birth date numbers, 666, he will be able to do this. So, I gave him every protection."

A couple months later, Marie rushes in the door calling, "Hernan, come. I must talk to you now."

"What is it? What is so urgent?"

"Sit down."

Hernan is nervous. *What is wrong? But she is smiling so nothing can be wrong? What is so important?* He can't stand the tension. "What is it, Marie?"

"Hernan, we are expecting another child. I did not think this would happen. We waited so long for our first child. Now I am thirty-three years old, but here we have a second chance to have a daughter!"

"Oh, Marie, this is wonderful news. I am so excited. Is everything alright? You went to the doctor? What did he say? When is it due?"

"Wow, slow down, Hernan. Everything is fine, so far. According to the doctor, everything appears normal. We can expect her in December. The next ceremony will include a petition to the gods for a girl baby. They really owe this to me."

"How do you see that, Marie?"

"I worked hard and sacrificed to become a priestess; learning and studying for over a year, giving service to the gods."

Hernan retorts, "This was not a sacrifice. It was a position in the community, and in the church you wanted in order to feel fulfilled."

"Look at what I have done, left my homeland, my family and my friends to establish our religion in this new land, again giving service to the gods."

"Marie, you craved this. You did not sacrifice anything."

"I worked and led over fourteen thousand children to freedom, saving them from communism and camps. Now they have the freedom to choose and to worship the gods."

Hernan is becoming agitated. "For which you received the right to come here when others did not. And do you really think they now have the freedom to choose? Like us, when we first arrived, they are living with Christian families."

"I host our ceremonies honoring the gods, offer sacrifices, hold special ceremonies like the Obi for Angela Martinez, and help people wherever I can."

"Well, Marie, I guess you deserve a girl. What about Chico?"

"What about him?"

"Well you have been grooming him to become a Santeria priest. Do you still plan for him to be the priest and lead the congregation?"

"Of course not!"

"How can you justify that? You have requested the gods to bless him with *ashe*, the power to make things happen, so he will be seen as an invincible leader. Unbelievably, you have your great-aunt Carlota reincarnated in our son! Now he is to stand aside?"

Marie informs him, "It cannot be undone. But he can be controlled and remain submissive to his sister. I will see to it."

"You may damage him."

"It would not matter; my daughter will be the head of the hierarchy."

Hernan needs to make decisions and he struggles with his thoughts. *I have very few choices at this point. I can walk out, which would mean leaving my son behind. I could never do that. No matter how I feel about Marie, I could never abandon my son. My other choice is to stay. And how can I bear that? I will be completely submissive to Marie. As Priestess, she controls our life, making all the decisions in church and at home. I will look weak in the eyes of my son. What would that teach him? How will he mature being under the thumb of his mother and his sister? How did I find myself in this position? How did this happen to me? I am ruined and I have ruined any chances my son may have had in this life.*

God help us all.

17

By September the heat is calming, outdoors and indoors. The phone rings and Hernan answers. He can be heard saying, "That is great! What a nice surprise. You must come here and stay with us. No, you could never be any trouble. Lucky for you the daytime is a cooler eighty degrees, nice to be walking outdoors. We will see you shortly."

"Who was that on the phone," Marie asks. "What person will be staying with us?"

"It is your sister, Luciana. She has just arrived in Atlanta and is coming to visit."

"Visit? For how long?"

"She didn't say. We'll find out everything when she arrives."

Shortly the doorbell sounds and Hernan opens the door to Luciana. He is happy to see her and hopes she can reason with Marie. He welcomes her warmly.

"Luciana, we are overjoyed to see you. Welcome to our home. I am going to take a walk and let you two sisters catch up on the last five years."

Marie appears from the kitchen, hugs her sister, and asks, "How is Mother?"

"She is doing fairly well. A few age problems. At sixty-seven things start to wear out, you know. But the big discussion here is you. I didn't know you were expecting another child. Congratulations. When is it due? Are you feeling alright?"

Marie informs her, "Our daughter is due in December, and I am doing fine. And how are you doing? What brings you here? How long are you planning to stay?"

"Wow, lots of questions. Perhaps you are not happy I am here."

"Not at all, just eager to hear your plans."

"Oh, nice. I won't be in Atlanta long, maybe a couple of weeks, if that is okay with you. Just here for a short sister visit. First thing I want to do is see my nephew, then back to my home in Miami."

Marie is in shock. She is the one trying to get to Miami for years and now learns her sister is there. "How did that happen, and what are you doing there?"

"My, you really do ask a lot of questions, Marie. There was not a pressing need for me in Havana. I never felt truly welcome, having no religious position there. You were the next priestess, our brother the protector. The fact is I barely have a family position, especially after you left. I really missed working with you on our many accomplishments. Remember Tom?" They chuckle at the thought. "So, let's see that little Chico, and tell me what is new with you and Hernan."

Just then, they hear Chico waking from his nap. "Look at this big boy. How beautiful you are, my little *bebe*. Marie, he is beautiful. Let's sit here and watch him play while you tell me about your life here in Atlanta. You have done well for yourself, judging by your home."

"We have done fine and have worked hard to achieve it. New followers have joined our congregation here. I am myself waiting to move to Miami, sponsored by the Catholic Diocese."

"The family is going with you, right?"

"Yes, of course. Why would you ask such a question?"

"I just wondered. You always do what you must to achieve your goals."

Luciana had realized by now; it has always been all about Marie. She only considers herself, first and foremost.

As the afternoon progresses and Marie prepares dinner, Luciana plays with Chico. She watches him closely, observing his moves, his thought process, and his overall interaction with toys and with her; truly analyzing Chico.

He seems older than his age. Not necessarily more intelligent, but more aware and more, I guess, manipulative. The way he plays with the little wooden toy people. Must take after his mother. Luciana laughs to herself.

Joining Marie in the kitchen Luciana says, "I would like to spend time with you. Maybe I can help you in some way again. I also want to get to know my nephew, but I must leave before the end of this month to prepare for my classes."

"Oh, you are continuing your education?"

"No, oh no, I am teaching at the university. When you move, you must stay with me until you find a place."

"Oh! We would make you too crowded."

"Not at all. I am by myself in a big house. Plenty of room for the three, err, four of you."

"I'm not sure when we will be arriving. I helped organize the entrance of the Freedom Flight parents, who joined their children after living apart for up to six years. They would like me to be back already, assisting with many parents who are just now arriving here. You can image how nervous and concerned they are. It's been too difficult to get things organized to leave Atlanta. Now I must wait until this baby girl is born."

"How exciting, Marie! I am sure Chico will love a little sister. Speaking of Chico have you noticed anything unusual about his playtime, especially with his wooden people? More like he is controlling them rather than playing."

"He is very bright."

Under the waning crescent moon on Sunday, December 7th, the night is freezing as they make their way to the hospital. Marie is hopeful this moon is not a depressing signal from the gods. A few hours later, one could hear her wailing throughout the entire hospital. The doctor did not need to tell Hernan he had a son. It was evident upon hearing the anguished cries of his wife.

Marie is terribly distraught. The doctors have her heavily sedated. She cannot be released in this state of mind. She is sent to a rehabilitation center. Hernan visits when he can get away from the restaurant and get extra help with the children.

Two weeks later Dr. Brimmar tells Hernan, "Marie has somewhat improved, that is she has passed the hysteria. She's ready to go home now. I've written her a prescription for valium; it'll bring her back to her old self again."

Hernan is not sure about that. "Maybe we should wait and see how she progresses on her own before starting the valium."

"That's not a good idea. Right now, she needs help."

"Okay doctor, we will give it a try. Mother's little helper, right?"

"Right, Hernan, she'll be fine in a few weeks."

The doctor was right. In a few weeks Marie is up and about, appearing to be like herself again.

Hernan had not heard anything about the holiday plans yet. He is concerned about Marie's attitude, wondering if she is up to doing this. She was so angry with the gods. "Marie, do you have the outline done for the New Year's ceremony, or do you need some help?"

"No, Hernan, I am planning to do something different this year."

"Really, what exactly are you doing?"

"Palo Mayombe."

"Marie, you cannot be serious, that is a powerful black magic. Why would you, a Santeria priestess even think of such a horrible thing? It is the religion of darkness. And you would not even be recognized as a priestess."

"It is a part of Santeria, you know. They do have Palero priests and gods, maybe they will favor me more than the ones I address now. I want my son to be an important leader, and he will be as the Palero have that power. It is an honor to become a part of them."

"Do you realize that chapter of Santeria demands a lifelong commitment? And you cannot just join; you must be accepted by them."

"Of course, I do. I am a Santeria priestess. I know the governing rules."

"Marie, what are you be thinking? Your ancestors were all Santeria. Then, of course, there was the little problem with your great aunt Carlota. She did dabble in the art of black magic."

Marie is able to get an introduction to a Palero priest. He meets with her and listens to her request. After contacting the spirit world, including Marie's ancestors, he tells Marie, "I'm not sure this is the place for you. First, it is highly unusual for a Santeria priestess to request membership here. You would be required to accept all our rules. It is a full commitment. That being said, I was able to learn of your aunt Carlota. It seems she did practice some black magic, but was not a one hundred percent Palo Mayombe member.

We would not accept that today. I suggest you meditate on this matter and return at a later time."

The next morning at breakfast Marie opens the discussion.

"You know, Hernan, I was a bit too upset yesterday when I was planning my changes. I took some more Valium before bed, and I feel calm and more clear-headed this morning. I could never leave my church, or my congregation. I have worked too hard to get where I am to just walk away from it. We will have our new year's celebration as we always do." Hernan feels relief as he leaves for work.

Things are back to normal. Hernan is again relaxed in his home with the family. Everything is going smoothly. Before dinner, he retreats to his television news show. "Marie, good news, today, January fifteenth, is a day of celebration. It is the end of the war in our homeland."

"There has been no war in Cuba, Hernan."

"No, not Cuba, our real homeland, it is the end of Nigerian Civil War. Those poor people have been dying of starvation for years."

From the floor a voice says, "Papa, what does that mean, do we have a home some other place?"

"No, Chico, this is our home now. Our ancestors lived some-where else and came here."

"Who are ancestors?"

"Everyone in our family who was born before us. Like grandparents and their parents."

"Can we see them?"

"You just saw your Aunt Luciana."

"How about grandmas? Most of my friends get to go visit their grandma."

"You do see your Grandma Peggy Sue."

"Yes, but I mean our real grandmas, mothers to you and Mom."

Hernan is not sure how to respond as he looks to Marie, who addresses Chico. "Yours are far away. Maybe someday."

She knows this is not going to happen. Marie is not about to share control of her family with anyone.

Marie continues her position and duties as Priestess of the rapidly growing congregation. Secretly she begins in-depth study of Palo Mayombe.

They have not accepted her as a member, yet she seeks the security and control she perceives this religion offers. It is always about control.

❧ 18 ❧

Spring arrives. Tiny drops of rain sprinkle their magic crystals. Tulips are blooming in every imaginable color. Delicate bright daffodils sparkle in the sunlight after the mid-day shower, their trumpets announcing that spring is here. A mesmerizing rainbow engulfs the Atlanta neighborhoods.

On this cool May evening Hernan is checking his favorite newscaster before dinner. He cannot believe what has happened. The announcer is showing a photo of a young girl, visibly shaken to the core, partially kneeling over a body. Her arms outstretched begging and crying. At the same time, he reports, "Earlier today there was a protest at Kent State University, similar to the one they held there on Friday, just three days ago, and like so many taking place in colleges across our country today. It is a time of unrest. The governor calls the protesters un-American, revolutionaries, and requests the National Guard to keep peace."

∾

Marie foresees the next few years pass without incident. She is thrilled with the growth of her congregation. Although she would like to be in Miami, she can't give up her status in Atlanta. With summer approaching she decides the family should make a trip there. They could stay with Luciana, who would be thrilled they are coming. She has not seen Chico since he was three and has never seen Juan. Marie will never leave her congregation; the power she wields is keeping her here. A move would mean starting again.

They arrive at Luciana's beautiful house in Coral Gables. Marie is struck by the architecture and the beautiful surroundings. The home and gardens are bordered by an artfully constructed concrete fence, which has an oversized archway and gateway to enter. Luciana greets them here.

"Marie, Hernan, how nice that you could come, and this cannot be the same boy I remember; he is too big. How old are you now, Chico?"

"I'm twelve, thirteen in a couple of weeks."

"My, where did the time go? You certainly are a handsome young man. And Juan, how old are you?"

"I'm ten, and I play soccer."

"How nice. We will find activities for you."

Once inside, their breath stops in awe of the gardens. Luciana takes them on a guided tour.

The pathway to the house is graced with light purple fluff, formed by miniature flowers Luciana calls Creeping Thyme. It is framed by floating pink feathers of muhly grass. A winding path reveals stately bamboo palms shading orange and deep pink bird of paradise. They make their way down the path, guided by white snowflakes called White Delight Carpet, even their name sounds comforting. They are backed by long, deep red Dwarf Chenille surrounded by Liriope's white and green leaves. It feels like Christmas. This opens to a large entertaining area housing a gurgling waterfall and clear-as-glass pool. The boys are ready to jump in. Hernan stays to watch them.

As they enter the lanai, Marie pauses, a questioning look on her face. "Luciana, the whole side of the house is open to the entertainment area. There are no walls or doors. Why is that? You must have windows."

Luciana chuckles, "Marie, there are sliding glass doors. You just can't see them because they slide into the walls on the two sides. It has the appearance of no walls, with no braces showing. Nice, huh? I really enjoy it. Now, tell me why you are really here. I don't want to hear, 'vacation.' We haven't seen each other for over ten years, so something brought you here. What is it?"

"Okay, I never could keep secrets from you. I have been doing some studies on Palo Mayombe. I have decided to stay with the Santeria, given my position and stature in the Cuban community there, and, of course, the large congregation I have built here."

"With large contributions, I'm sure."

"Yes, of course, but it is more than that. It is my home, my efforts created it."

"Which makes you a god of creation?"

"Stop teasing, Luciana. I deserve everything I've built."

"Okay, Sis. So why are you here?"

"I have found a Palero here in Miami who is willing to give me instructions without my full commitment to the membership. He knows I want to learn how to work the black magic to my advantage when needed."

"Is it the Church of the Lukumi Babalu?" Luciana asks.

"No, why would you ask about that church in particular?"

"Because they are the first Santeria Church in the States to become incorporated. I am really surprised you found a Palero priest to do instructions without a commitment. Does Hernan know about this? Is he alright with what you are doing?"

"He knows nothing about this. And you will not tell him."

"Marie, maybe we could do a 'Tom' on him and that will give you four days of unknown activity. Let's go indoors for a drink and discuss this priest you are going to visit."

Luciana leads Marie inside to an area of large overstuffed white sofas, as inviting as soft clouds, with a handsome view of the pool through the lanai. Turning left, they enter the kitchen, ultra-modern copper everything. Luciana crosses the room and pushes the espresso button, giving Marie time to compose herself. Her eyes move around the room, first landing on the hand painted tiled breakfast bar, leading to the convection oven, progressing to the copper stove with glass top, next to a serving window that opens to the entertainment area.

"Marie, would you grab us some cookies from the butler's pantry?"

"Sure." She walks into what she considers a small grocery store. *Hmm, cookies, where would they be?*

They relax at the breakfast bar sipping their drinks, watching the boys at the pool. "Marie, tell me your schedule. When are you going to visit the Palero?"

"I have an appointment at eleven o'clock on the morning of June thirtieth, this coming Monday."

"I would like to go with you, Marie. Would that be alright?"

"It would be fine with me, but we should ask permission. Although he has agreed to help me, I am not sure if he would like an audience."

Luciana surprises her by saying, "Or he may not like a witness. After all, most likely the church would not approve of him sharing."

"Good point, very possible. Would you please keep Hernan and the kids occupied while I am gone?"

"Sure, I will. We have some outings planned."

Monday morning Hernan is sleeping in; it's his vacation. The boys are enjoying the pool. Marie is up and sharing coffee with Luciana, who brings breakfast to the lanai table and calls the boys.

"Wow pancakes! Thanks, Aunt Luciana."

"I am leaving shortly for my meeting," Marie says. "Would you tell Hernan I went to meet some religious friends for lunch? Please."

"Yes, of course. Why not? That's the truth."

Marie arrives at the shrine on time, more than a little nervous. She approaches the door with caution. It is dark wood, beautifully carved with symbols of the gods. She knocks and hears footsteps. Slowly the door opens. Standing before her is an average looking man wrapped in a white robe garment. He has a friendly welcoming face, a big smile between his light brown mustache and beard. He has unusually light skin color, much lighter than hers.

"Welcome, Marie. Please come in. Join me for some lunch."

"Thank you, Reverend D."

This entrance places them behind the altar and heading towards the living area. As they approach the kitchen door, a woman brings tea and sandwiches to the table. "Marie, this is Fatima, my helpful servant."

"Nice to meet you, Fatima."

She gives a short curtsey and leaves.

"I am interested to learn why you are seeking instructions in Palo Mayombe, especially as a Santeria priestess."

"Reverend, I will be completely honest with you. Originally, my interest was to explore the possibilities of your religion, but I have since decided to examine and learn certain aspects. I already mentioned to you, I want to stay right where I am as Priestess to my congregation."

"Alright. I would need to know what it is you desire to learn and why. I hope you do not have the preconceived idea that all of us are evil black magic worshippers. We are not Voodoo sticking pins in dolls." He laughs. "Some do, but not us. Much, if not most, of our religion is identical to yours. You know we are part of the Santeria group of worshippers. We differ in spells and potions."

"Yes, sir. That is exactly what I want to learn, the spells and potions."

"Give me an example of what you might like to accomplish."

"Well, Reverend, I have two children. I have always petitioned the gods for a girl to take my place, as I took my mother's and hers before that, but the gods have not blessed me. They have given me two boys."

"Are they strong healthy boys?"

Marie nods. She knows where he is going with that. "Yes, I know that is a blessing, but not what I asked for. In the future I will most likely face other needs, wants, and challenges. The spells and potions would help me in those matters."

"I see. You are quite accustomed to getting what you ask for, yes? What else? I know there is more."

"Yes, I want to make sure my family is always protected and treated fairly."

He already understands her. "You mean, as you see it, or as you want it, correct?"

"Is that so bad?"

"No, Marie, it is not. I am going to agree to coach you. How long are you in Miami?"

"For one month. I can return from time to time if needed."

"That is not very long, but it will provide a good start. Come every other day at noon."

M arie pulls in the driveway and walks to the back pool through the lush gardens, the fragrances enveloping her. Hernan approaches. "How was your day? Did you enjoy time with your religious friends?"

"Yes, immensely. They asked me to work with them while I am here. Teach some classes, I may even take a few myself. Is that okay with you and the boys?"

"Marie, it is your vacation too. We are here to relax. If that is what you find relaxing, definitely do it."

Wednesday morning Marie returns to her first class. The boys are planning an outing.

"Dad, let's go to the zoo today. Can we? Huh, can we?"

"That sounds like fun. Let's go."

Friday Hernan is prepared for their requests. "Dad, let's go to see the Flamingos. Can we?"

"Sure, let's go."

On Monday, the kids are ready to pounce on Hernan with another request.

"Surprise." Hernan walks into the kitchen. "Well, boys, it is my turn now. Let's go see the Monkey Jungle. Can we? Please, can we?"

The boys are laughing and rolling on the floor with glee. The children enjoy this extra time with their dad. Every other day they would tell their mother about the special place they went. The days Marie was home were study and pool days. Departure time came quicker than anyone imagined.

They returned home to Atlanta, to work and school. On the first day back, Hernan is checking his favorite local newscaster, who reports that two young boys, fourteen years old, have disappeared and foul play is expected.

"Marie, you must tell the boys to be on guard and always tell us where they are going. Two boys Chico's exact age are missing and probably murdered."

They keep extra vigilant watching the boys.

"Okay boys, up for school. Let's go," says Hernan. "Hurry."

Chico is now in eighth grade and Juan is in fourth, a bit older than the other kids, having started late due to his December birthday.

"Good-bye, Marie, I am off to work. I will try the new MARTA transit, and see how it is."

The moment they were gone Marie begins her studies.

Over the next few months, she has visions. Some are quite troubling, but she is not yet sure what they mean. She studies harder and decides to visit Miami to consult with the Palero priest. She would prefer to stay in Atlanta. She loves the autumn, which they never had in Cuba. From the airplane window, the town's brilliant colors mimic a painter's palette.

~

"Marie," the Palero priest says. "I told you this was a difficult religion to grasp unless one is completely committed to it. Near impossible to pick and choose parts of and still remain in control. It is like doing half of anything. You need to put in your all to realize a full return."

"Still, I would appreciate a few explanations and answers to my questions."

"Tell me your concerns, and I will see what I can advise."

"I am having visions in my sleep that don't make sense to me. Two are repeated often, others are frequent, while there are always a few new ones appearing. One often-repeated vision involves a young girl with long dark blonde hair. I see her crawling through my front door. She turns into a yellow-haired dog, padding into the kitchen, but I cannot get past the kitchen entryway as it requires a key. The other one is a young skinny black bird attempting to fly in through a bedroom window. I slam the window down across the neck. It shrivels, shrinks, and dies. What does this mean?"

"I cannot be positive regarding the meaning. It could be a premonition. They never come exact; you need to decipher based on your life, considering the people and things in it. Then again, it could just be a reoccurring nightmare."

"It is not a dream. It is too real and disturbing. There must be something I can do to understand."

"Our minds are open to different levels. Perhaps yours is searching for a solution to a problem. These dogs and birds are probably symbols, maybe from a past memory, perhaps something in your subconscious that you need to resolve. Go back through your childhood and see if anything fits these scenarios."

Marie flies home with a great deal of thinking to do.

~

Chico prepares for high school, keeping his grades up and already thinking of college. He wants Tulane. Marie would make sure he got it. Over the next four years each member of the family works toward their own goals.

~

Four years pass, and Marie continues to conduct ceremonies for her congregation and, of course, remains diligent in her studies. Her night visions are more frequent and more terrifying, mainly because she cannot control them. She must ignore this problem and concentrate on Chico getting into college. He has already made his applications.

"Hernan, I am planning an elaborate ceremony petitioning the gods for Chico. Now that he is a senior, we need to have this university secured. Since his god is Osain, we will have it on his holy celebration day, Sunday, December thirty-first. We will begin at seven, his ritual number, and end in the early morning. He will be honored. We will make a selected offering and request his blessing on Chico's education."

~

At seven o'clock on New Year's Eve, the congregation gathers in the park. The trees appear to be ghostly silhouettes floating across the almost full moon.

"Marie, we will not be able to stay here all night. It is ten degrees, and with this wind on the hilltop we will freeze."

"We will do what we can, Hernan," Marie says scanning the crowd. "We have a good attendance; then again it is New Year's Eve."

She turns to address the congregation with the usual new years' blessing. "May the Orishas and all spiritual entities fill you with love, success, and great things during this next year."

"Blessings to all. Tonight, we will have a divination. We will ask the gods' help, using the Diloggun method, cowrie shells, to make requests and tell the future. We address Osain, god of magic, petitioning blessings for Chico as he ventures into college, and ask any bad luck be removed from his path."

The people look uncertain.

"Most of you have probably not seen this ritual before. It must be done only by a fully initiated santero or santera. I have eighteen cowrie shells. We will use sixteen. I throw the shells on the floor of the altar twice, to provide us with a pattern. We can address any god. The throws may be preceded by a question and have a number as well as a name associated to it. As I continue to throw the shells, a story will form to answer our request. This communication with the universe relies on respect, and proper interpretation of the responses received. We now pray in the traditional language."

"We will begin with the Oti. This cane alcohol is used in many Santeria ceremonies. We now offer to Osain the flowers, candles, and rum. Let the Congo drums begin."

The rhythm is hypnotic; the faithful sway and silently offer prayers to the gods.

Marie pauses, before she begins to speak in slow melodic and rhythmic patterns. "We call upon our ancestors, who have gone before us to be here with us tonight. Great Aunt Carlota, we call upon you to be our spiritual guide tonight."

Up the hillside, across the wraith like trees to the altar, the wind arrives whispering a message, *"I am here with you."*

Marie casts the shells across the altar floor, and then again, a second time. She now asks her questions.

"Will Chico go to Tulane, the school he most desires?"

Again, she throws the shells, eight from each hand. She reads the pattern, *yes, he will.*

Another question, another throw. "Will he marry a nice girl to become the new Santeria priestess?"

She reads the pattern. It is a bit confusing. The eight thrown with her right hand say, *yes*. The eight thrown with her left hand say *no*.

"I don't understand." Irritated she asks, "How can the answer be both yes and no?"

Aunt Carlota whispers, *"Maybe you need to ask one question at a time. Or maybe you got both of your answers, 'Will he marry a nice girl—' yes '—to become the new Santeria priestess' no."*

"That cannot be my answer. I will try again." As she throws the shells, she asks simply, "Will he marry a nice girl?"

No answer comes forth, and no pattern supports her needs. She tries again and again. Repeatedly, there is no answer.

As the clock strikes midnight Hernan carries the bucket outside and tosses the contents over the hillside, discarding the previous year's problems. Now, godparents come forth and cleanse the children with their white pigeons. They release the pigeons leaving the children purified.

Marie is troubled at the outcome, but feels sure the gods will bless her request, especially coming through Aunt Carlota. Santeria is nature based. Ceremonies that channel *ashe* from plants and animals toward one's goal is vital. Osain is the most powerful Orisha utilizing magic of plants.

Upon arriving home, young Juan asks his mother, "Please tell me how Aunt Carlotta can talk to you when she has been gone since eighteen forty-four?"

"Our ancestors, the egun of our religion, can visit us, instruct us, and provide guidance with knowledge. And often they may ask us, especially a priestess, to help them spiritually. It is part of nature. Spirits can communicate and even interfere with our lives."

"Maybe they are causing your bad dreams?"

"Maybe."

"You could ask her, right?"

"Yes, I might just do that, Juan. Thank you."

"And maybe she can help with Chico's school."

"I'm working on that."

Marie will consider any means to get what she wants. It is about eight months until he needs to report to the college. Confirmation of Acceptance will be mailed in April or May. She may need to resort to other matters for him to attend the school of his choice.

Chico enters the room calling out, "Mother, it is already April and almost everyone I know has gotten their college responses. It is less than eight weeks until registration. I don't understand."

"I am working on it, Chico, so don't worry."

❧ 20 ❧

Chico graduates from high school, concerned he has not heard from the college of his choice. Tuition will also be a consideration for his parents, at almost twenty thousand dollars a year plus books and living expenses. As a nurse his mother does not even make that much, and neither does his father managing a restaurant. Together they make only slightly more than the cost of tuition. Chico has good grades, but not enough to qualify for a scholarship. He does not live in state to get a reduced rate. And he is not athletic material as he is considerably overweight.

Marie has been studying and practicing everything that Reverend D has been teaching her. Armed with the black magic knowledge of potions and spells, she needs to put her practices to work. She feels confident. Having worked all the Santeria gods with offerings of their favorite foods and ceremonies to no avail, she must resort to stronger methods. She has repeatedly addressed her Orisha, Ayao god of air, to intercede on her behalf. Nothing has produced the outcome she seeks. In black magic, most times the spirit will only reject an individual because Palo Mayombe is not for that individual's spiritual path, or because the person may not yet be ready to handle or understand the responsibility of being a Palero. Normally success depends on expertise gained through experience. Marie has no experience.

Marie decides to use the Palo Mayombe Crossroads Method of addressing these gods, in particular, Lucero, god of crossroads. Chico is at a crossroad in his life and, apparently, so is Marie. She has found a location, in a site known as the Dead Angle. The cemetery is near the park on the little Kennesaw Mountain, very quiet with little to no activity. It must be secure, as she needs to return every morning at sunrise to meet with the spirit Lucero. He continues to instruct her as she seeks success, mastery, and personal power.

Her visit is planned with an offering of The Candles, purple in color, designating royalty. After all, she is a priestess. She makes a sachet sprinkled with glitter. She gathers hair from Chico's brush and a copy of his college application. She returns each day burning the candle for an hour at sunrise.

Lucero counsels her to do a spiritual bathing. Upon arriving home, she calls her eldest son to her. "Chico, I have been petitioning the gods for you that you may be accepted into that school. We must conduct a spiritual cleansing. I have done many. It is most powerful when administered directly by a holy person, so I will conduct the cleansing, producing strong positive effects towards success. Your body will be motivated, your mind will be open, and your soul will be purified. Following this ritual, you will accompany me to the crossroads with the candles, oils, and a few curios. We will address the gods together. Come with me I have already run a nice warm bath for you."

They enter the bathroom; she sprinkles a potion on the bathwater as she calls upon the gods. Slowly undressing, Chico enters the tub. She chants as he washes, cleansing his spirit. "Chico, step out so I may bless you with the oils of success." She holds the bottle of oils, as he steps out of the tub. She begins at his head.

~

The next morning, before sunrise, the two depart for the cross-roads. Marie brings the candles for the final day of lighting, the oils to be used in the cleansing ceremony, and honey to sweeten the request. The additional sachet powders are sprinkled with the oil.

Marie lights the candle and addresses the gods with gifts and prayer. In a whisper, Lucero responds; *"The gods have looked kindly to your request, especially the king of magic, Siete Rayos. He loves anything sensual."*

As they arrive home, they find Juan waiting for them all excited. "Mother, Chico, a letter has come from Tulane University. Hurry, hurry and open it."

Chico's hands are trembling as he slowly and carefully opens the letter. A bit of trepidation encompasses his whole being. Will the gods bless him and answer his mother favorably? He does not want to consider anything else.

Juan is now jumping up and down, "Hurry, Chico, hurry. I can't stand this."

Finally, the envelope falls to the floor, and Chico unfolds the letter. He is reading to himself and then slumps into his father's worn overstuffed recliner.

"What is it, Chico?" Marie and Juan are both yelling at the same time.

"They accepted me. They actually accepted me! By all the gods, they have accepted me!"

Marie laments, "Now all we need to do is find a way to pay for this. We may need some additional ceremonies and rituals for twenty thousand dollars."

"No mother, it's not necessary. It says here that I have been given a minority scholarship."

New Orleans. How appropriate for their beliefs, a mix of Santeria and Voodoo. Chico will be comfortable there, and Marie, of course, will visit often. Juan is going into high school. He is not as strong as Chico, but he has his own way of making things work. He'll be fine.

❧ 21 ❧

Chico leaves for Tulane in the Fall, while six hundred miles away a pretty, young girl is beginning her senior year in private high school.

Intelligent and studying hard, she is already excelling in a special program offering Harvard college courses. The girl is strong willed and determined, falling right into a good definition of the Irish. Aside from her beauty, she's a formidable athlete, excelling in track, taking numerous awards. She knows her goal in life, marine science. Her parents have been encouraging her, sending her to summer classes in the Florida Keys.

She has her eye set on University of Miami, one of three colleges currently offering that course. Nothing else is acceptable. Cost may be a barrier, but she will receive lower in-state resident tuition and a set amount of scholastic scholarships. There will be no athletic scholarship, as girls' track is not an eligible sport. She has been offered full scholarships elsewhere, scholastic and athletic combined, but nothing will do except UM. She continues working for Publix, now in the office and making enough to pay her tuition considering her scholarships,

Pell grant and small loans. Her parents help where they can. Her name certainly fits her determination and her strong will, Erin.

~

Erin graduates high school with honors and prepares to enter UM. She requests exemption from certain classes as she has already excelled in them in the special Harvard program. She doesn't want to waste time and money redoing a class. She is denied. She asks to see the school's president.

"Miss Erin, I understand your argument against retaking these classes, especially given your high grades, unfortunately, your credits are not transferable. I like your spunk and confidence. I'll make you a deal. We can't give you dispensation on the classes, but I will say, if you take the courses and pass on the high end of the grading scale, I'll personally pay for the classes."

~

Chico is in his sophomore year at Tulane and excelling, on his way to achieving his business degree. His mother, Marie, continues to lead her congregation.

Her personal study and practice of Palo Mayombe is gradually taking her down a new path. She is prepared to help her son and herself on every level.

~

Marie plans a visit to Chico, and to see a few sites in New Orleans. Having researched hotels and tourist areas, she has her trip mapped out.

"How long will you be gone, Marie?" Hernan asks.

"Just one week."

"I know Chico will be glad to see you. He was home for such a short time over the year-end holidays."

"Can I go too?" Juan pleads.

"Of course not, you have school," his mother states, coarsely.

Juan hears Marie on the phone. "Yes, I want to leave Atlanta on Saturday the thirteenth and return the following Saturday. Yes, of course this month. Yes, I realize it is a busy time of year, just three days before Mardi Gras." Finally, he hears her say, "I will pick up the ticket at the airport. Thank you."

She turns quickly bumping right into Juan.

"Are you eavesdropping on me?"

"You're going during Mardi Gras. Now I really want to go." He says using his most demanding voice.

"When you're older, maybe."

"I'm in high school, a junior already."

"Exactly, a baby, way too young for Mardi Gras."

Marie is careful to book her hotel and sightseeing activities when Juan is at school.

Two days later, Marie sets out to Atlanta Hartsfield Airport. With the temperature at forty-seven degrees, she has a large wrap to keep her warm. From her vantage point at take-off, the landscape below has turned to brown.

Arriving in New Orleans, the city's vibrancy warms her, and brown has become every neon color. Every pore of her body absorbs the excitement in the air.

She walks up Bourbon Street and approaches the Lafitte Guest House. The desk manager appears to be one of the ghosts, as she is parchment white. But she asks, "May I help you?"

"Yes, I have a reservation for this upcoming week. I specifically reserved room number twenty-one."

"I see that, very unusual. You must be Marie. Most people don't want that room. Do you know the history there?"

"I researched it before I came. A young girl, suffering with yellow-fever died there."

That's right. It was originally her mother's room. The girl reclaimed it. She was too upset to leave here."

"I understand her name was also Marie, correct? I'm hoping we have things in common."

"Well you may see the light go on. Marie likes to walk at night. But she never goes far. She only walks here at the hotel; only at 1003 Bourbon Street."

"Marvelous, just what I am looking for. Thank you."

The first night goes without incident, or else Marie has slept through it. It's thirty-degrees; maybe young Marie decided not to take a walk this night.

The next morning Marie calls her son. "Chico, come explore with me today. Let's venture into the dark side. It's Sunday; maybe we can find a few religious ceremonies to attend. Let's see what's available in New Orleans, starting with the French Quarter."

She is shocked at his appearance. It seems he has lost half of his body weight. "My, Chico, you look so lean and healthy."

"Yes, Mother, I'm working out. I'm in Triathlon training now. I feel great."

"That is fantastic. I am so happy for you."

They go looking for the Haitian Vodou. "Some of these believers also came from Yoruba, as well as the Congo and Taino. They were influenced by the Haitian French Catholics, unlike the Yoruba in Cuba who were influenced by the Spanish Catholics."

Walking through the French Quarter, they near a worship center, evidenced by the plastic dolls on the altar representing the spirits, very common in this type of worship. They also use images of saints to honor the spirits of Vodou.

"Chico, this congregation is composed of five different groups; the Yoruba people, the fiery spirits of the Congo, the Taino, modern-Haitian people, and the spirits of the dead, by way of the French Catholic."

Heading out the side door Marie feels a chill down her back. Immediately she realizes this is the cemetery. She observes the puppet stuffed in a shoe and nailed to the big live oak tree, which acts as a messenger to the other side. The spirits are not welcoming her. She can hear their whispers as they float to her on the breeze. She walks through the area with Chico reading the tombstones.

Marie has worked up an appetite. "Chico, want to stop for lunch?"

"Yes, I know a place. They have sandwiches called po-boys, similar to our Cuban sandwiches."

Finishing her sandwich, Marie agrees they are marvelous. "Let's find a Louisiana Vodoun Church. How about it, Chico?"

"We just went to a church."

"That was a Haitian Vodou. They would not have permission to conduct a Santeria ceremony. The Louisiana Vodoun is quite different. It's really a mixture of religious and magical practices found in the southern United States. They include a little Haitian Vodou, a great deal of Catholic saints, and select sections of Hoodoo."

"Hoodoo?"

"Hoodoo is not a religion. It is folk magic. It uses magic and black magic to conjure things up. Often it appears like European folk lore and other times like American Indian beliefs."

Marie stands up saying, "Maybe we should get moving. Let's just explore."

They walk for a few hours, playing tourist and occasionally asking directions. Chico has had enough religion for one day.

"Let's stop and rest with a cool drink. We can do more research and play tourist again during the week. I suggest we head toward the hotel and see what we find."

They walk a few more blocks when Marie spots an old building. "Look, Chico, right there," she says, pointing to a crumbling building, "We are only a block from the hotel. Let's stop here."

"Are you joking Mother? It could collapse on us."

"No, it won't. Come on, we are having an adventure, something different."

"Dying would be different."

She gives him a don't-give-me-a-hard-time look, and he follows her into the bar.

"I can hardly see. There are no lights, just candles." He notices there are few people in this drab colorless room. The bar itself appears to be hundreds of years old; the silver back of the mirror is flaking off. The smell confirms he would prefer not to be in here.

"Oh, I love candles. Listen to that music. It's an omen. Cole Porter's song, 'You do that voodoo that you do so well!' It sounds like Frank Sinatra's nineteen fifty recording."

❧ 22 ❧

The barmaid approaches. "Hello, would you like to sit near the fireplace or in the courtyard?"

Marie asks, "Which is more comfortable?"

"It's almost seventy degrees; outdoors is most pleasant."

"Why is the fireplace ablaze in warm weather?" Chico is perplexed.

"It always has a fire burning, never allowed to extinguish."

The courtyard is more dilapidated than the building; broken statues, overturned birdbaths, brown leaves cover the patio and dying vines hang overhead. Chico orders a beer, and Marie orders a fancy umbrella drink.

When the barmaid returns, Chico inquires, "What is your name, honey?"

"No, it's Betsy," she replies coyly.

"I see."

Marie asks, "Well, Betsy, can you tell us the history of this ancient building?"

"Sure, most tourists come here because they are already familiar with the stories, and there are many. It was originally owned by Jean

Lafitte. You know, the buccaneer. It was The Lafitte Blacksmith Shop, built in seventeen seventy-two, but, really, this is where the pirate ran his smuggling business. We keep up the beautiful French architecture. It's important, because we're in the French Quarter."

"Yes, I can see that," responds Chico as he eyes the crumbling mortar next to their table.

"He was a real hero, you know?" Betsy says.

"No, I didn't know that. Tell me about that part of his life?"

"The Battle of New Orleans. He helped Andrew Jackson defend New Orleans against the British and got a presidential pardon. That's one reason I sat you here. He guards the fireplace. I often see his red eyes staring at me through the grate. You might see him from here. He is really guarding a treasure between the bricks in the fireplace, which is why it is never extinguished."

Marie excuses herself for the ladies' room. She climbs the steep staircase. The door is difficult to open. She pulls with both hands until the creaking stops. She steps up to the mirror,

where, while applying her lipstick, she notices an old ragged woman standing behind her. She turns to address her, but there is no one there. Turning back to the mirror she sees the woman laughing at her, and the pitch of her voice is ear piercing. She quickly turns to confront her, but again no one is there. Marie grabs her purse and runs. The door is stuck as she jiggles and pushes; it won't budge. Finally, at Marie's point of exhaustion the door quickly and easily swings open. She stumbles and rolls down the stairs.

Betsy comes running over, "Marie. Lay still. I'll get help."

She looks up to Betsy, fear in her eyes she mumbles, "She was there. I know she was there. I saw her, but then she was gone."

"Don't be frightened, it was just the mirror ghost, Marie Laveau or maybe Madame Lalaurie."

Chico sees the commotion and comes running from the court-yard. "Mother, don't move. We'll get you to the hotel to rest."

As Marie regains her composure, she is upset with herself for allowing a ghost to get the better of her. *Wait until next time.*

They take a taxi the short distance to the hotel. Chico helps her to the room, with number 21 printed on the door. He makes sure she is comfortable, getting aspirin and an ice bag for her swollen foot.

"I'll be back in the morning to check on you."

The clock chimes three and wakes Marie. She reaches for the water and aspirin on the nightstand when, something grabs her wrist. Unable to move, she speaks softly, "Mother Marie, is that you?" Marie waits. No answer. Her wrist is still immobile. "I would like to talk to you. My name is also Marie. Like you, I dreamed of raising a daughter. That never happened. I can sympathize with you."

She hears a moan. It grows gradually louder.

"Appear before me, Mother Marie. I frequently have visions. Maybe I can help you."

Another moan and throaty guttural sound forms words. "I am not a vision. I am here. How can you help me? Can you bring my daughter back?"

"Perhaps I could bring her voice to you. You could speak with her." Marie responds in a soothing voice.

"I don't need you for that. I want you out of my room."

"I won't do that. I'm booked in this room for a week."

Marie's wrist is jolted, and she is catapulted to the floor. She feels paralyzed.

"You Santeria priestess women always think you can out do us Vodou. You think yourself superior, because we cannot conduct a Santeria ceremony. Be aware, New Orleans' Yoruba population is Haitian; your Yoruba Cuban magic has no power here."

Marie is in excruciating pain now. Her wrist throbs, her foot is pounding, and her head is unclear. Now, lying on the floor, her back is absorbing an inordinate amount of pressure. She can't stand. She can't move. She vows to get even with this woman, just as she passes out.

~

The following morning Marie is stiff and sore. Walking slowly, she ventures out to find a store with the supplies she needs. After shopping, she stops at the Lafitte Blacksmith Shop and sits near the fireplace, ordering an iced tea. Marie glances at the courtyard where they sat yesterday. She sees a murder of crows upon the overturned bird bath. The fireplace flames dance before her eyes, as she explores every brick and the mortar that separates them, searching the hot walls for the treasure. Suddenly she sees the two red eyes. Starring at them she hopes they'll direct her to the treasure. She realizes it's in the overhead bricks forming into the chimney. If the fire never goes out the treasure will remain in the possession of Jean Lafitte.

Marie leaves her table to visit the ladies' room. The door opens easier today. She approaches the dressing table without looking in the mirror. Opening her bag, she places a black candle, a spray bottle, and a bowl holding netting wrap on the table. She lights the candle and proceeds to spray the room as she chants in Spanish. She picks up the netted ball from the bowl and begins waving it around the room. She continues to alternate between shaking the netted ball and spraying, while reciting a Spanish spell.

Suddenly the mirror emits a blinding sunlight, burning throughout the room. It is Marie Laveau attempting to enter. The light is circling in a vortex with a deafening sound.

Marie continues to swing the netted ball, chanting louder, she turns abruptly and sprays the mirror. An explosion occurs followed by dead silence. Marie now looks deep into the mirror. No one is standing behind her. Silence and calm fill the room. The door swings open easily. She proceeds down the steep staircase. Betsy is standing there having just arrived at work.

"Oh, Madame, are you alright? You went up to the ladies' room alone? How brave you are."

"Betsy, there is no longer anyone living in the mirror. And if that fire ever goes out, please call me. Here's my number."

Marie returns to her hotel room and opens a small shopping bag. She places a new shiny red candle on the nightstand. As the candle flares up, she recites Spanish phrases gradually increasing in volume. She opens a new bottle. It looks like perfume. She sprinkles it over the nightstand, continuing her chant. "Descanse en paz a ti mismo, para los justos no desamparado." *Rest yourself in peace, for the righteous are not forsaken.*

She leaves the room and approaches the clerk at the front desk. "Checking out, please."

"Yes ma'am. Did you enjoy your stay? Did you get to meet our Marie?"

"I thoroughly enjoyed my stay, and yes I did meet Marie. I think you will find her much friendlier in the future."

Erin finishes her first year and arrives home for the summer. She is pleased with her progress. "Mom, I have aced my first-year classes at UM with a 3.7 average. Therefore, the president will pay for the classes I was required to take a second time."

Her parents are extremely proud of Erin and encourage her at every crossroad.

Chico arrives home for the summer having completed his junior year. "Mother, I have decided that I will do my masters study at University of Miami. I have applied and have already been accepted. I need to be there before August of next year for the sports program, with funding in hand."

"That is fantastic news, son, I know you really wanted that. What about the cost? It is an expensive private college."

"Yes, Mother. It is expensive because it is a private school, but also because it is one of the best. A degree from there really means something. I need to have that."

"So, tell me about the expenses."

"Probably about forty thousand for the two years."

"We will make do somehow. Based on your Tulane degree, can you get any scholarships and surely a business job while you attend classes?"

"I don't think so, but I can apply for that and there are grants available. We can also inquire for student loans. Given all that I will still need financial support from you."

"And you can work during this summer break. Surely, you can manage a job."

"I can look into both of those, Mother. And perhaps you can do some of your magic worships. Maybe perform another cleansing ritual?"

"Hernan, could you come to the living room please. I would like to discuss something with you."

Marie hears Hernan shuffle the newspaper as he enters the room. "Yes, Marie what is it?"

"We need to start planning and preparing for a move. It is time to leave Atlanta. We are moving to Miami, at long last. See if you can find a realtor to list the house for sale."

"That is very sudden, Marie. What has brought this about?"

"Our eldest son is taking graduate courses in Miami next year. And Juan will be graduating from high school. He can begin his first year of college in Miami. We need to be there."

The following winter, Marie calls her sister. "Luciana, could you recommend a realtor to help us find a place in Miami?"

"You are moving here? I am so excited. This will be great. Yes, I know someone, my friend, Carlos Garcia. I will e-mail all his contact information. I can't wait for you to arrive, to see the kids again."

"They aren't little kids anymore, Luciana. Chico is twenty-one and Juan is eighteen now. They will both be going to school there. Chico for his masters and Juan is starting college. He is graduating high school this month."

"So, Juan will start college here in the fall?"

"Yes, at Florida Atlantic University. We will all be together in Miami."

Early the next morning Marie phones Carlos and advises him exactly what she is looking for and when she would like to move after her sons' graduation. He forwards many selections to her over the next few months, giving her an idea of what is available.

Erin is overcome with excitement starting her senior year at University of Miami. A few of her friends from high school are also entering their last year at UM. They're all thrilled, looking to the future with wide eyes, anticipating their rosy future.

23

Finally, after a few trips to Miami, Marie finds the house size and price acceptable to her. Upon arriving home in Atlanta, she begins to tell her husband all about it. "Hernan, this house is in a neighborhood known as Krome. It's only about a hundred blocks straight east to the University of Miami and buses run all the time. The town also houses the immigration processing center. It is referred to as the Krome Detention Center; some call a holding facility for immigrants entering the US. They are processed to stay or to send back. The surrounding areas house many Cubans granted asylum; most Haitians are denied. We will feel right at home." Three months later the Caluda family moves into the new place, just before summer ends.

~

Chico has graduated from Tulane and heads straight to Miami for sports and graduate studies. He is making friends quickly. One new friend, Ron, is also there for the triathlon. "Hey man." The friend waves him down. "Come with us for a few drinks tonight. We'll introduce you around."

"Great, where are we going? I don't have a car here."

"No worry, we're staying right on campus at the Rathskeller."

"There's a bar right on campus?" Chico asks a bit surprised. "We had our share of partying in New Orleans, a big party town, but none on campus."

"So, now you can walk home, if you can walk," he laughs. "See you there about eight."

Chico arrives on time. Strutting in like a German officer, the new man on campus is looking good; tall, dark, and muscular. It's a typical busy Friday night and his new friend introduces him to people. Through the night, he meets many who share his interest in business and sports.

By the time the school year starts, Chico is comfortable with the school, the area, and of course, the beaches. He's walking through the sport field when he stops short to stare at a young lady running laps around the track. He admires her form, all of it. He's thinking of a way to meet her when he sees his friend Ron on the outside of the fence.

"Hey, Ron. Got a minute?"

"Sure, Chico, what's up?"

"Do you happen to know that girl over there? I would love an introduction."

"No, but let me see if I can find someone who does. You know the old rule, six degrees of separation." Ron heads up to the main gate to find a track member he might know.

"Hi, David," says Ron, "let me ask you something. Do you know that girl who is just coming up from the track?"

"Not really. Why?"

"My friend Chico would like to meet her."

"I know him. I've seen him at the pool. Triathlon, right? You know she spends many hours at the pool, too. She's a diver. He's just got to be there at the right time. I've seen her diving mainly in the evenings. She's been helping one of the football players because players are not supposed to be diving, according to coach."

"Thanks, I'll let Chico know."

Chico now swims daily for his triathlon training, but he has changed his routine from morning to evening. He's appearing at the pool, hoping to spot Erin there. On Thursday, she's taking a structured diving course, being very helpful to that football player. Chico wonders how involved they are.

He makes sure he's standing where she needs to pass at the end of class. He smiles and says hello. She smiles, nods, and quickly walks on by. He's not happy, but not giving up. He hurries through the locker room and waits in front for her to exit. She never appears. He must have missed her.

He continues to work out in the pool every night, hoping. On Sunday, he is there mid-afternoon and sees her enter the pool alone. He waves and smiles. She smiles back. He swims over. He needs to start a conversation and ask a question to engage her.

"Hi, I'm Chico, practicing for triathlon. I saw you here the other night. Are you on the swim team?"

She gives a little laugh saying, "No, I like to swim and it helps with my diving classes."

"You must enjoy diving. It's a great recreational sport."

"Yes, but for me it contributes to my degree in marine science."

"Didn't I see you running track the other day?"

"Running is just something I love to do. I have been on the school track team all through high school, with a few medals in the

PATRICIA BENEDETTO

mile. Unfortunately, there is no scholarship for girls track team. What are you studying other than triathlon?"

"Very funny, I'm here doing my master's in business. How about having a bite with me after our swim?'

They walk to the Rathskeller, talking all the way. It's amazing how much they have to share, with almost nothing in common. He's all business; she's saving the planet. As they are seated and order they find one common ground, athletics, mainly swimming and running. He knows enough to be attentive to her stories and she appears to appreciate the attention, an excellent combination. They attend each other's events and date frequently over the school year.

~

Spring is approaching and the two young people are getting closer and more involved. Chico invites Erin to his parents' home for dinner and she accepts.

"Mom, I'm here with Erin. Dinner smells fantastic."

Marie enters the room and inhales deeply, placing her flat open hand on her chest. She is speechless. Luckily, Hernan enters the room to break the silence. He smiles at the girl and invites her to sit in the living room as Marie retreats to the kitchen.

Following a short conversation with Erin and his Dad, Chico says, "Please excuse me I want to check on the dinner."

"Mother, what was all that about? If not for Dad appearing on cue, I'd have been embarrassed by you."

"How can you say that? I would have embarrassed you? You are the embarrassment to your family! You nonchalantly show up here for dinner with a gringo! How could you? How could you do this to me? You can't find a nice Cuban girl in Miami?"

"Mother, I like her. She's beautiful, athletic, in good shape. She comes from a good, respected family in the community. She is

150

smart and can hold her own intellectually with anyone. She'll make a perfect executive's wife."

"Wife? Are you trying to kill me? If so, you are right on track. This will do it. You are thinking executive wife? You need to be thinking Santeria wife. Have you forgotten your station in life? In the church? Are you prepared to walk away from your obligations?"

"We're going to leave, Mother. We can't sit through a dinner with your attitude."

"You'll leave when I tell you to leave," Marie pauses, her face flush with anger. "Now I will tell you—leave!"

Chico enters the living room looking drained.

"Erin, I'm sorry but Mother is upset that she has burnt the dinner. I think it best we leave."

"Why don't all of us go out to dinner, Chico?"

"No, she says she's too upset. One of her headaches has sent in, so she has gone to lie down. Bye, Dad, sorry it did not turn out differently."

"Bye, Son. We'll do it another time."

As they close the door, Marie confronts Hernan. "How could he bring that girl here? How could he hurt us like that? He's the chosen one to replace me. How can he do this with her? He needs a Cuban Santeria wife. We must work on him constantly, never letting up for a minute until he's convinced."

Erin is home on spring break. Her parents are thrilled to have her back, even if just for a week. It's Friday night and the doorbell rings. They know who it is; Erin has told them Chico is coming to pick her up.

Erin's mother, Catherine, greets her daughter's new friend at the door. "Come in, Chico, and have a seat. It's so nice to finally meet you. Erin has told us so much about you that we feel as though we know you." She finishes just as her husband enters the room. Chico stands and shakes hands with him. They chat about school, sports, goals in life, and family.

~

On December tenth; Erin leaves UM with an environmental degree, ready to save the planet. As a crusader and hard worker, she just might do it. Everyone is so proud of her. Erin is excited to enter her new ecology position with the state. The whole family attends and applauds her success. They are dressed and ready to celebrate Erin's college graduation and accomplishments.

"Let's go to that dinner we've been planning." Catherine is so excited she feels they all deserve to celebrate the long four years.

"I'm not going with you, Mother; I'm going with Chico."

"But, dear, we have been planning this forever!" Catherine is heartbroken. Doesn't her daughter understand this is a family celebration? They *all* worked towards this day.

~

As summer arrives, Chico is living at home and working for a local firm. Marie is continuing to work on him mentally regarding an interracial marriage. She has great arguments against him marrying outside of their nationality and their culture, which also involves their religion.

Chico is gradually beginning to realize the hurdles he would face. How could he be true to his religion and keep Erin in the dark? Right now, it is relatively easy. He attends the Catholic Church with her, which is not uncommon among the Santeria. He knows he could not sustain this cover-up forever. He cannot become a Santeria priest fulfilling duties to his people if they are married. She would eventually put it together. He's confused and knows he must make a decision, a plan that includes his mother.

~

Juan appeals to his brother, "Chico, I need some advice. I'm madly in love with this girl I'm dating. I must bring her home to meet the family and tell them we are getting married. Any advice for me?"

"Yes, just elope and then tell them."

"You know I can't do that. Stop joking and help me."

"Okay, first question, is she an American?"

"No."

"Good. Good beginning. Now, is she an islander?"

"Yes."

"Great! Don't worry, you've got it made. Mother will approve."

"Not so sure about that, Chico. The island she is from is not Cuba. It is Jamaica."

"Oh no, Juan. She will never approve."

"Come with me, Chico, when I tell her. Please."

Dinner that evening is overshadowed by an ominous cloud. Juan is suffering with his dreaded thoughts. Chico suffers the anticipation of the forthcoming war of words.

"Mother, I have been dating a lovely lady. I would like you and Dad to meet her before I ask her to marry me."

"My sons are growing up. Tell me about her."

"She is caring, helpful to those less fortunate. An only child, she is educated and her family is very nice to me."

"You have met her parents, but she has not met us? Why?"

"Mother you know the girl's parents always want to meet before you even date."

"Well, yes, those are careful parents. Tell me more about her. Where in Cuba is her family from?"

He hesitates. "They are not from Cuba. They are from Jamaica."

Marie lets out a bloodcurdling scream. "I have two sons, and neither can find a nice Cuban girl in all of Miami? My God, this is Miami! There are as many or maybe more Cuban girls here than in Cuba. What is wrong with you? Must you deny your heritage? We need to carry on our cultural traditions and our religion. Chico will tell you about differences, as he accompanied me to the Haitian Vodou in New Orleans."

"Mother, please just meet her," begs Juan.

"Yes, I will meet her. Bring her here."

Marie thinks she will be smarter this time and rationally bring out why Juan should not marry this girl.

❦ 24 ❦

Juan is struggling with his plan to take his girlfriend, Adriana, to meet his mother. He can't do it, he can't face his mother, nor submit the lady he loves, to the scrutiny. He knows his mother would be merciless, sparing no words. He's shaking at the thought. He continually makes excuses and postpones a meeting.

He decides to call Chico. "Please come for lunch with me and meet Adriana. I can't introduce her to mother. She'd never give her approval to my beautiful lady. She is too different."

"How different? You know she's not going to be as judgmental of you as she is of me."

"First, you know Adrianna is Jamaican; so, she's English, not Spanish. Second, her religion, Obeah, is also very different, which is a major factor. It originated in Africa's Gold Coast, today's Ghana, not far from the Yoruba in Nigeria, but a whole other world. Third strike, she's very dark."

"What does that matter?" Laughing he adds, "Do you know you, yourself, are very dark?"

"Of course, but you know how mother feels about marrying dark. Chico, please just come."

"Yes, okay, I'll be there for lunch tomorrow with Erin. The two of us may need to break away to talk. Erin can keep Adriana company."

"Thanks, brother."

Juan opens the door to Chico and Erin. He looks relieved. "Hi, and thanks for coming." They follow him to the kitchen. "Adriana, I want you to meet my brother, Chico, and his friend Erin."

They exchange pleasantries and sit down to lunch.

"This is delicious," says Erin in between bites. "It is really fabulous."

"Marvelous, truly marvelous," Chico chuckles while still chewing.

After lunch Juan asks Chico to join him for coffee in the living room, while the girls talk during cleanup duty in the kitchen.

"What do you think Chico? What should I do?"

"You know only you can decide that Juan. I like her. I think she is a lovely person and a great cook," he chuckles. "But you're your own man and must decide your own life. I can't tell you what to do. Listen, hear the girls talking and laughing in the kitchen? They seem to get along nicely."

Chico dreads answering this call, it's his mother. "Have you seen your brother lately?"

"Depends on what you mean by lately."

"Don't get funny. When did you last see him?"

"About a month ago; we had lunch."

"Good, that's nice. Now tell him to come to dinner with you on Sunday. He has not returned my calls all week."

"I'm not sure I can make it. I'm supposed to . . ."

"You'll be here with your brother."

Chico sighs. "Sure. I'll let him know." He phones his brother. No answer.

Chico goes to the campus pool for a swim. Afterward he calls again, still no answer. He calls Erin. "Can you drive me to Juan's house to see if he's okay? It's Friday and he hasn't answered his phone all week."

Erin picks him up in her classy Chevy, a gift from her parents when she entered UM. They arrive at Juan's but no one answers the door. Chico goes to the adjoining apartment and knocks. A young man answers.

"Hello. My brother Juan lives next door to you, there," Chico says as he points. "No one has heard from him in days. Have you seen him? Do you know where he might be? We are all concerned. This isn't like him."

"Hey, nice to meet you. Want to come in?" He opens the door, and Chico enters. "Juan speaks of his big brother often. Two days ago, he asked me to drop them at the airport."

"The airport?" Chico asks, surprised.

"Yes. They flew to Jamaica for their wedding. Adriana's mother is so excited. She has everything planned. Nice family. I met them last month when they came to meet Juan. I think they plan to be gone two weeks. Didn't he tell you? I think the wedding is Sunday."

"No, he didn't tell me. Besides, I have classes at school. I'll see him when he gets back. Thanks for letting me know."

On the way to the car Erin asks, "What are you going to tell your mother? She will be furious she didn't know and won't get to attend the wedding."

"Oh yes, she'll be furious, but for other reasons."

Chico's in a precarious position. His mother will be furious, alright, that Juan married against her knowledge and approval. Sunday will be a busy day in two countries. In one there will be a wedding, the other a murder. His mother will kill *him,* blaming him as he is the older brother. He must make a decision. Does he show up alone for dinner? Does he call and try to cancel? *Fat chance.* Surely, she won't take this well. He has two days to make a decision.

Chico's enduring torture as he talks to himself looking for a solution. "I'll call, that way I can just hang up. No, I should go and look really sad maybe get some sympathy. No, that won't work. I've got it – a telegram."

Chico outlines a telegram. *Mother, I can't make it to dinner tonight as I am getting married today in Jamaica. Your son, Juan.* Yes, that's it. Juan needs to take responsibility.

On Sunday, Chico sends the telegram. A couple hours later his phone is ringing nonstop. He doesn't answer. What can he say? He calls his dad. Luckily, his father doesn't answer. Chico leaves a message. "Sorry I can't come to dinner. I have a workout scheduled."

～

Ten days later Juan calls Chico. "Hey brother, I'm really sorry to leave you with that, but I couldn't face the challenge. Forgive me?"

"Sure, brother. Believe me, I wanted to strangle you, but I completely understand. You know Mother's still going to make you pay one way or another."

"I know. I'm going there tonight about eight to get it over with."

"I'll meet you there."

"Thanks, Chico."

～

Marie is ice cold to her two sons, angrier than she has ever been. Betrayed by her own family. Juan is one thing, and she'll work on him, but Chico is her replacement. She must take control of what's going on with this girl who has him entrapped. Whenever they're together Marie drops comments like drips of water. "Chico how's that fragile white girl you are seeing?" Or, "Is that Christian girl able to keep up with your religion?" And sometimes, "Are you letting that little girl lead you around by the nose?" Always something to make him think less of Erin and make him think being with her is also making him less. Marie knows as a strong Cuban man he would never stand for that, no matter what.

~

Erin is working at the same job she has had all through school. For the past year, she and Chico managed to see each other on weekends. She always enjoys his company and sees him as an intelligent, patient, and giving person. A person she could share her life with, a good caring husband, a good caring father. A father who, with his education and intelligence, would be a good provider, who makes sure she and the children have the best of everything. Her station in life is extremely important to Erin.

~

November comes around, the beginning of the jolly season. Marie thinks, *the Christian sentimental season of love—time to take advantage of that*. She knows just how to manipulate this scenario.

"Chico, Thanksgiving's coming up soon. Maybe we should try to plan something with Erin's parents. What do you think?"

He's taken by surprise at the offer. How nice and caring of his mother. "Erin was telling me her father loves to cook, especially for a holiday. I'll speak with her and see how we can get together."

Marie's mind is speeding a hundred miles a minute as she sits smugly in her living room chair. Just let me at them and I'll destroy them, the unsuspecting saps.

~

Chico asks Erin if they can plan a family get-together for Thanksgiving.

"That would be great," she says. "I'll call my parents."

Her mom answers, "Sure, honey, I think that's a good time to get together, but as you know we're in a temporary hotel apartment waiting for movers. I doubt if Dad can cook a holiday dinner. There's not much here to work with, and there's not much room. Let me know how many, and we'll see. If it's too large to handle here, we'll take them all out to dinner. Your grandmother will be here also. She arrives Monday before Thanksgiving."

"Great, Mom. I'll let you know."

She immediately calls Chico with the good news and asks him to find out how many will come. After checking with Marie, he gives Erin the count. She then calls her mother.

"Hi, Mom. Chico says we'll be eight, five of us and three of them."

"What about his brother? We've included your brother in our count, we should include his."

"I thought of that and asked. Juan got married and is spending the holiday with his wife. I asked to include her, but they declined the invitation."

"Okay, your dad would still prefer to take everyone out to dinner as we just don't have the facilities here. It's tough just making breakfast."

"That's fine. When and where do you want to meet?"

"You know your dad's friend Sal who owns the Italian Restaurant? They have great turkey dinners on Thanksgiving, heavily booked every year. Of course, we have a table for eight, even more if we need it but must confirm in advance. So, are you positive the invitation was extended to all?"

"Yes. I made double sure but will ask again. Thanks, Mom,"

"Erin, you know we want this young man's family to feel comfortable."

Erin calls back and confirms the get together is for eight. Juan and his wife won't be attending.

Thanksgiving Day arrives and Erin's parents are watching football before getting ready to meet Chico's family. The phone rings, it's Erin. She sounds unsure of herself, which is not normal. "We have a little problem and I need to ask you a favor."

Her mother steals herself. What could cause her daughter such concern? "What is it, Erin?"

"Chico's mother called to say that Juan and his wife are coming, if that's okay. I told her I wasn't sure. I know the restaurant is busy and we're able to get a reservation because the owner is a friend of Dad's. So, what do you think?"

"I don't need to think; we asked three times, and each time they said no. We couldn't do more than that. We can't call now and ask to extend our reservation. It is unacceptable for them to request this. They can't rationally expect this to happen on the busiest restaurant day of the year."

Erin relays the message to Chico who calls his mother informing her of the response.

Chico, asks Erin to try again noting two more can't matter that much.

Erin understands the situation, but shortly phones back to her dad. "Chico said to ask you to at least *request* they make room for two additional people. He says if they're overcrowded two more won't matter."

Dad says, "Obviously, he never ran an upscale restaurant. You don't just squeeze in a few more. I won't ask my friend to do that."

"Hold on a minute." Her father can hear them conversing, but not exactly what is being said. She returns shortly. "It seems reasonable that you could at least ask the restaurant."

"No. We invited all of them, they said no three times. So now it is no."

They all meet at the restaurant. Chico introduces his parents; Hernan and Marie. Erin introduces her parents; Frank and Catherine. The air is a little tense as everyone makes small talk. Erin's parents apologize for not being able to *squeeze in* two more. They could have accommodated if they had known initially. His family offers no apology for putting Frank in an uncomfortable position. Erin's brother is being picked up by his girlfriend after her family's dinner. She arrives and approaches the table. The maître d' observes her and brings a chair asking her to sit. Catherine reacts quickly, "No thank you. She is not staying, just here to pick up my son."

With a superior air about her, Erin speaks out. "Well, it appears your friends could have accommodated one or two more."

Surprised at her attitude, her father kindly replies, "That is not the issue. We asked, the invitation was declined repeatedly, and it's not acceptable to then ask for additional invitations."

Marie is pleased she is able to create tension and stress in the girl's family. Enough stress and they will fold.

Driving home Erin's parents discuss the situation. They are concerned over the way the evening unfolded. Catherine reviews it out loud to her husband. "First Erin calls me to ask us to add two people at the last minute after they repeatedly refused. Then she calls again speaking to you and asks again, noting Chico asked her to call. She asks you to wait a minute, while Chico gives her further instructions on how to speak to us. This does not appear to be the strong independent girl we raised. I have seen her stand up to teachers, employers, us—her parents, gosh, even a college president. What is happening to our little girl?"

❦ 25 ❦

T he following week Frank and Catherine call Erin. "We are taking your Grandmother to see Vizcaya; would you like to join us?" They enjoy a lovely day exploring the gardens, admiring the fountains, and viewing the house. At the end of the day they are thinking of dinner.

Grandma looks at Erin saying, "Thank you for joining us, Erin. I'm glad to get a chance to see you again before I leave. It was such a nice Thanksgiving."

Erin becomes hysterical, screaming insulting accusations. Catherine freezes in shock "What the hell just happened?"

Through her hysteria Erin counters, "What do you mean what happened? You know very well what happened. You ruined Thanksgiving. You insulted Chico's parents. You offered a holiday meal and then ruined it. They must think I have the most awful family. It was so embarrassing."

Stunned, Catherine finally regains enough composure to reply. "How can you say that? We offered the whole family to come and they refused. You can't blame us for that."

"I can, and I do," Erin screams. "Even Chico said how insulting and embarrassing you were."

"Oh, even Chico? Is he now thinking for you? What's happened to you? Have you lost the strength and conviction of your own mind?"

Erin heads for her car and leaves them stunned, bewildered, insulted and upset.

~

They don't hear from her again for two weeks, when she calls and says, "Chico would like to stop over tomorrow night and visit for a bit. Is that alright?"

Her mother is a bit confused about this request. "Are you coming with him?"

"No, he says he wants to speak to you."

This seems strange, but she agrees, hoping not to rehash Thanksgiving.

Catherine is brewing a fresh pot of coffee when she hears the doorbell. "Come in, Chico. You can join Frank in the living room, and I will bring coffee." She gathers the cups and heads to the living room.

"Well this is a surprise. Is there something I can do for you?" Frank says, offering Chico a chair.

Catherine enters with a tray. As she pours, she hears Chico say, "I have come to ask for your daughter's hand in marriage."

Slosh, slosh, coffee puddles all over the table. Catherine runs for a towel, pausing to catch her breath. She isn't sure what she expected the night to bring, but that had never entered her mind. She returns to the living room having forgotten the towel. Her husband is speaking, but she isn't sure what he's saying. She stands, "Excuse me." She returns sipping a glass of wine, wondering, *does his mother know what he's doing?*

Chico is addressing Frank. "Considering all the girls I have dated; your daughter is the best."

Catherine takes a sip of wine, peering over the glass at Chico. *He didn't just say that, did he?* She is numb through the remainder of the visit. She can hear voices but no words.

~

The next day Erin comes by to speak with her parents. She's all bubbly and anxious to begin making plans. "Did Chico speak to you last night? He said he wanted to do things the old-fashioned way and ask you for my hand in marriage. Isn't that romantic? How did it go? Nice, I bet, right?"

Catherine couldn't bring herself to tell her daughter how he compared her to "all the girls" he dated."

Frank volunteered, "I think it went well considering we were totally unprepared for the discussion. Have you talked about dates or arrangements at all?"

"Well, Chico will complete his masters within six months, and he's very secure in his position with the company. Hopefully, I'll finish my masters within the next year. It isn't easy while I'm working, but I love my job improving the environment and enforcing the regulations. We're planning to get married in one year."

Catherine pops in with, "First of all, Erin, I want you to know, without a doubt, the happiest days of a mother's life are when she can plan her daughter's wedding. We should start to form our plans early, choose bridesmaids, colors, the church, invitations; there's so much to decide. I'll get some wedding planner books and next time you are home, we'll start making arrangements. Churches and reception halls book up way in advance at the holidays so that should be our first consideration. You both should start on your list of guests which may affect some of our decisions."

"Will you make the list for our family?"

"Of course, dear. I'll do as much as I can. You should be relaxed."

~

Catherine has been so preoccupied; Christmas arrives before she's prepared. Chico and Erin are here for a small part of the day. His gift to her is a beautiful engagement ring. Erin's on cloud nine, as they leave for dinner at his parents' home.

Catherine starts the family and friends list. First is her mother, Grandmother of the Bride, what a nice title. Her father had passed away a long time ago.

The following month, when Erin is home for a visit, Catherine goes over the list with her. "My sister will come with her extended family, your brother with a date, and your sister with her son. That's sixteen people including your dad, grandmother and me. Closest friends are on the list amounting to fourteen, only four will attend. The others can't make the long trip. That's twenty people. If his mother has twenty and you kids have twenty, we can expect sixty people."

"That sounds reasonable," Erin says. "You know all my closest friends through high school and college. They'll come. I'm sure Chico has the same, although some may not come from Atlanta."

"This year will go fast. Ask Chico if their list is done so we know how many invitations to order. We need to do it six months in advance, so before June. Let's go to the stationary store tomorrow and look at samples. We can do lunch while we're out."

"Great, Mom, sounds like a fun day. I'll let Chico know to tell his mother."

~

"Erin needs a guest list from us so they can order the invitations."

Hernan asks Marie, "Do you need my help putting the list together tonight?"

"No, Hernan, I am not going to do it tonight, or this week, or this month. Let her sit there wondering what to do next. I will enjoy this little game of torture. Chico, don't give her any inkling of this."

"Don't worry, Mother. I'm with you on this. It's a good way to start to drive a wedge between Erin and her mother. We must make Erin see her mother as unreasonable and non-supportive, allowing us to slowly introduce her to Santeria. Thanksgiving was a good start."

It's March. Chico plans to take Erin to the best Cuban restaurant in Miami, with great food and music. "Just the two of us lovebirds," he tells her.

Erin's mother calls. "We're hoping you will come by for a visit so we can celebrate your birthday."

"Sorry, Mom, I just have too much going on, and Chico is taking me to dinner."

"Well, of course he is automatically included. We always celebrate your birthday together. Ask him to come. I still don't have an invitation count for Chico's family. Can you check with him about their list of guests? We need a total for the invitations. What is taking them so long to do this? We only have two months to order them."

That evening Erin cautiously broaches the subject. "Chico, my mother would like us to come there for my birthday dinner. She always does something outstanding for my birthday."

"So, you don't want to have a romantic dinner with me? Fine, I get it. You would rather be with your mother. How are you going to leave her and be my wife? Maybe we need to wait until you grow up."

"No, I didn't mean that. I meant for us all to be together, that's all."

"Well, I would prefer just you and me. I thought I made that clear."

"Yes, I'm sorry, just not thinking clearly with everything going on. We'll go to the restaurant, just us. Oh, my mother asked if Marie has the invitation list done yet. It's been three months now."

"Wow. Your mother never gives up, never stops, does she? Constant nagging. She's done with her list so what? Is she trying to prove she's better than us? I can't help it if my family is larger and my parents have more friends than yours. Is this a bad thing? It sounds like she is trying to cause trouble."

Erin visits her mother, dreading the conversation. "We spoke to Chico's mother about it. She said she's working on it, and a few other things."

"What other things could she be working on? Oh, do you mean the tuxedos and rehearsal dinner?"

"I'm not sure, I guess so. I know they are having a hard time narrowing down to thirty people. They have many relatives and an abundance of friends."

April brings Catherine excitement. "Erin, I have some thrilling news for you. Your Dad's friend Sal has offered to close the big room at his gourmet restaurant for the night, the one with the full-wall fireplace, to host your wedding reception. Isn't that marvelous; food for the connoisseur, beautiful room, great musicians, romantic atmosphere. You couldn't ask for better. Remind Chico's mother that I need the names and addresses for invitations. They must be ordered by June."

"That's great, Mother. It's beautiful and the food is the best. I'll remind Marie."

"Chico, I know you don't like to be reminded, but it has been another month since my mother asked for the guest list. She really needs to order the invitations. She has gotten us a beautiful place for a reception. Sal's brother runs the other restaurant they own, and it is beautiful, all delightful gourmet food."

"So, she's at me, again, right? I don't think she likes me, or she nags me because I'm special."

"She just needs the list to continue with the arrangements."

"How could she book a reception when she does not have attendees counted yet? And she didn't even bother to consult us. She really is choking us, isn't she? Dictating numbers and, now, where we celebrate. Always constant nagging. Whose wedding is this, hers or ours? When are you going to stand up to her for us? We deserve a big beautiful wedding, big and grand, an extravaganza. You deserve the best. Doesn't she want that for you? Maybe not. At least that's the way it seems."

Erin visits home, bringing the groom's family list. "Mom we need to go over the list and arrangements."

"It's already May and they are just responding. I don't know about this Erin. What took so long?"

"That's not all, Mother. Chico wants to invite about twenty guests from school and work. We need to include them, as they are wealthy influential people."

"We have twenty, we thought you kids would have twenty, now you have thirty and how many do his parents have?"

"I brought it with me with the addresses. It is one hundred and thirty."

"What! That is insane. We can never fit that many people in the restaurant room. And do you know what the cost would be for that many with full dinner and bar elsewhere?" Catherine's head is spinning.

"We aren't having the reception at Sal's. Marie said they would chip in for half of the cost."

"We don't want that. We want to have a beautiful wedding, the best of everything, with the closest of friends and family who care about you. We are not hosting the 'Event of the Year' here."

"His mother wants us to be happy, so she is willing to pay her share. We need to have a big wedding, nothing small at a restaurant. It must be impressive."

"Who are we impressing? And why? We don't need to impress anyone. We need to have a beautiful day surrounded by those who share love with us."

"You don't want me to be happy," Erin cries. "I want to show his mother that we can do this. She is already making other plans."

"How can you accuse me of that? We discussed this in the beginning. Plans are made by the mother of the bride. Yet his mother is already making plans? When you mentioned that a few months ago, we envisioned the tux and a dinner. What other plans would that be? We, as parents of the bride, will give you the wedding. The three of us will make the decisions. If she wants to be involved that's fine, but it's my daughter's wedding. I will plan it, and it will be prefect."

"Of course, Mother, I didn't mean that she would be making *all* the decisions, but she has booked the church for us."

❧ 26 ❧

Catherine is ready to explode, but manages to control her emotions for the sake of her daughter as she questions, "Marie has picked the church? That's outrageous! What church? And what gives her that right? I'm telling you again, we make the arrangements. You and I will select the church."

Erin is distraught as she responds, "It seems to mean a lot to her to use this church."

Catherine shows her mounting frustration, "Just tell them, we have thirty people coming, counting your ten, and they can have thirty people. We will pick the church along with everything else. That's it."

"I'll relay the instructions, but it's not fair. How can you be like this to me, and her? You are depriving me of the wedding I want. You're making my life miserable."

"Erin, what happened to your excitement of having sixty people comprised of close friends and family? What happened to us planning the wedding? Now tell me who wants this?"

～

Chico relays the information to his mother stating, "These are the demands from Erin's family."

"Oh, really? Well they can't issue a demand to me. We'll have whomever we care to invite. You can tell her we'll pay our share. She has no right to deny us. We concede nothing. Understand me? Nothing. The more tension we create the bigger the wedge we drive between them. If this girl is going to be considered as my successor, Satan, help us all, then we need her to divorce her family."

Hernan overhears the conversation. "Marie, do you realize what you are committing to? Have you thought about the total cost of one hundred people for dinner and open bar?"

"Don't worry, Hernan, I have no intention of actually paying it."

"But you said, I mean, how could you avoid it?"

Marie laughs loudly as she replies, "Well, let them try to collect."

Marie realizes that stronger measures are needed. She gathers two black candles, blessing them. On black construction paper cut into the form of a heart, she writes Chico on the left side and Erin on right. On the back she writes her wishes, girl be gone. "Oya, oh fierce warrior, sister and wife of Chango, I call upon you to remove Erin and her family from our lives. Sever this relationship."

She places the two candles touching opposite sides of the heart. Lighting them she watches them burn. Eventually moving them further from the heart, she says, "Thank you, Oya, for this blessing." Every day over the next week she burns these candles, each time moving them further from the heart.

Tonight, the seventh day, she allows the candles to burn out and tears the heart in half, separating the two names. Marie chants to the gods, "I will keep these two pieces separated until the time my desire comes to pass. Oya, I deliver this disconnected heart to your cemetery gates to be forever buried and forgotten."

Later that evening Chico arrives at Erin's apartment. "Erin, I need to speak to you. If we're going ahead with this wedding, it must be extravagant, stunning to my family and business associates."

"What do you mean, if?" Erin sobs, disturbed by the whole situation.

"Exactly what I said. I can't have my work associates invited to a, beautiful *little* love wedding, I can't exclude my friends, associates and family." Chico says with disgust. "If you are going to be my wife, you must stand by me and support my decisions."

"What about the wedding that I want? Shouldn't that count for something?"

"You're confused. This is not something you want; it's something your mother wants. Are you leaving home to live with me in my life or not?" Erin is trembling and crying. She is confused now and hurt. Chico is tearing her up inside. He refuses to see what she wants, refuses to go against his mother. He is forcing Erin into a situation that should never exist. Forcing her to agree to something she doesn't want.

Two months later, Marie grows impatient as wedding plans have not changed. She needs to step up her spell. She gathers a new black candle, wooden matches, a toothpick, parchment paper and pencil. She writes the two names on the candle and lights it. Staring at the candle, she dissolves into a trance envisioning the future. She draws three triangles on the paper covering them with droplets of black candle wax. Marie repeats the spell until the seventh day when the candle burns out. She walks to the cemetery and digs a small hole at the gate. Marie chants to the gods, "I deliver this offering to Oya. I deliver this completed spell to your cemetery gates to be forever buried and forgotten."

It's September and months have passed with nothing resolved. Speaking with her husband, Marie decides to try a new tactic to drive the gringos away. Her spells are requests that the marriage does not come to pass, but if it does, she needs to have Erin's family removed from their lives. She knows Catherine would prefer not to argue with her daughter. She wants to make Erin happy.

Marie phones Chico. "Hello, dear, you can tell Erin that we're cutting our list from one hundred thirty to seventy and that is the best we can do. Stand up to her and dictate."

Erin relays the message to her mother. Catherine is terribly distraught. She wants to give her daughter the best of everything, but it's becoming impossible. She relents. She'll find another venue.

Chico calls home from his apartment, "Well, Mother, you got your way. Erin's mother has accepted seventy guests, and your agreement to pay for that increase." Marie is smiling as she tells Hernan the outcome.

Catherine calls Erin knowing she is home from work. "I have finally ordered the invitations we had chosen, and placed orders for the flowers, based on your color choices. I have an available banquet room at a nice hotel in Miami and contracts for sit down dinner and an open bar for one hundred. I'm waiting to hear back on the video, photographer, and a lovely musical group."

"It sounds like you have been very busy."

"More than you know. It's not easy to get these arrangements with the date so close. But of course, we had to wait on their list." She can hear Erin sigh. She has been through a lot with her future mother-in-law and has repeatedly tried to make her happy. "The invitations will be here the middle of this month, so set a date for you and the bridesmaids to come here and address them. Let's say October nineteenth. We should mail them the first week of November. I have booked a luncheon for all of us at that lovely little restaurant on the Miami River. You know the one right at the bridge? Be sure to let them know."

With only three months to the wedding date, Marie must increase her spells. Her Santeria spells do not appear strong enough to produce the desired outcome. Although she has spent too little time the past few years working with the Palo Mayombe, she must resort to these stronger means. She departs for her little cabin, which houses her spiritual cauldron.

"I call upon the Palo Mayombe secrets of the ancestral powerful spirits at the house of the dead." She has everything she needs here: skulls, skeletons, potions, candles, spices, and assorted paraphernalia. In her trance, she addresses the Petro family of Lwa. These spirits are jealous, destructive females who take pleasure in curses ordered to destroy love. Marie requests a curse of the worst devastating evil to cross the spiritual threshold into the material world and upon Erin and her family.

A week later, Marie calls Chico. "Could you tell Erin that we are so sorry, but need to add two guests? Your aunt and uncle from Atlanta have decided to make the trip. Hope that isn't too much for her to handle. Just get it done."

"Sure, Mother. That may just send her mother over the edge."

Upon hearing the news Erin phones her mother. "Mother, Marie needs to add an aunt and uncle from Atlanta who changed plans so they could attend."

"Okay, if it's that important, we can add two more."

"Thanks, and I'd like to add ten people from work."

"Well, I don't think ten people who are new in your life are considered close friends. Our list is continuing to grow, and we already have ordered the invitations."

~

Catherine is beside herself. It is October and she is about to explode. She calls her daughter. "Erin, the invitations have not arrived. We are going to need to cancel the nineteenth and reschedule when they get here. Tell the bridesmaids we will keep our appointment to visit the dressmaker Wednesday morning the sixteenth for fittings and then enjoy our luncheon."

Anna, the maid of honor has been Erin's best friend for years. She lived nearby and; they went to high school and college together. She is an honorable person, a great friend and confidant. The other girls are Erin's friends from school and work, except one of the girls, Jane, is a neighbor friend of Chico's family. They have asked for her to be included. With a friendly, vibrant personality, she is a pleasure to have. Everyone enjoys the afternoon on the river sharing their enthusiasm and good wishes. The excitement is electrifying. They agree to get together at Catherine's home to address invitations as soon as they arrive.

Friday, November first Catherine calls Erin, "The invitations are finally here. Thankfully there are no errors; we certainly don't have time for corrections. Make sure everyone can come on Monday to address these. We will only be three days behind the mail deadline."

"Don't forget, Mother, tomorrow we are visiting the church. You'll get to see how the flowers will look and where everything is located, so you're familiar with the layout."

"Yes, I remember the church Marie booked for my daughter."

On Saturday, Frank and Catherine arrive at the church. "It's a bit strange looking, don't you think, Frank? Lots of pillars and doors. How to choose the main entrance? Look at this rotunda, supporting small glass windows, no stained glass visible from the front. Quite stark don't you think?"

"Stark, yes, and unusual," agrees Frank as they enter the church. "The stained glass is inside, actually an uncommon shape inside too. Look at the design over the altar. An extraordinary circle, looks like two hands. Are those hands? Can't tell. Take a picture. Do you have your camera?"

"Of course! Don't I always have a camera?"

"Let's stop on the way home and get them printed."

Upon receiving her photos Catherine immediately thumbs through the prints. "Frank, you must see this print, the last one I took inside."

Frank stares at the three and a half by five-inch photo; a black background with a red streak that begins at the bottom left about two inches high, arches up and over the middle of the page and exits on the upper right side at about one inch wide. "Normally I do not believe in omens, but...."

The following Monday, a few of the girls arrive. Catherine helps them establish a method. They establish an assembly line. Anna has beautiful handwriting, so she addresses envelopes. Erin stuffs them with the invitations, response cards, and small pre-addressed envelopes. Jane places specially chosen fancy love stamps on the envelopes before she seals them. Talk and giggles are abundant as snacks and sodas are served by Catherine during the evening's festivities.

Chico calls to inform Erin to add four more guests from his family. She knows her mother will be outraged. These never-ending requests are a constant source of angst. She will tell her later.

Jane, as the new person in the group, is anxious to contribute. "Has everyone heard about the fuss at Chico's family home last night?" No one has heard anything and is anxious to hear the latest gossip.

"We could hear the argument across the neighborhood. It started early in the evening. I went there and found blood outside on the front porch and feathers strewn all about. Marie was screaming at Chico for marrying a gringo.

"She said, 'I worked many hours spreading the white feathers across the porch and soaking feathers in blood. That should have kept them away. I never thought the wedding would actually happen. Surely the two of you would cancel before the date. No Cuban of our stature should be forced to have a gringo come into their family. It is disgusting and degrading.' "

"Then Marie started comparing the sons. It is worse than having Adriana as a daughter-in-law, that black Jamaican girl married to your brother. Can't you boys find a nice Cuban girl in Miami?" She stops talking as she looks up from the envelopes and notices everyone staring at her with wide eyes and dropped jaws.

Catherine asks, "What's a gringo?"

❧ 27 ❧

"Frank, are you up yet? We have a lot to do today. Our plane leaves at noon and arrives at three. We have dinner reservations at seven. As the hosts, we can't be late. This meeting could mean a great deal to the business, although I'm not thrilled to be traveling eight days before Thanksgiving. If all goes well, we'll be home before holiday flights begin."

Two days later, Catherine and Frank are home celebrating successful meetings. There's little to follow-up before the wedding. Everything is in place. Marie calls Erin to request two more people attending.

Catherine tells Erin, "As you know, final count day is mandated to us by the hotel. Four days from today, November twenty-sixth, is the deadline. Not to mention this constant addition, new guests every week, is leading to huge numbers."

"Don't worry she has offered to pay for it."

~

Two days before Christmas, Catherine's mother, Mary, arrives.

Later that day their eldest daughter, Trish, who is a bridesmaid, arrives with her young son. They have a full house. Erin is there on the Eve to help decorate the tree. Christmas Day is a joyful family occasion of gift sharing; church, turkey, and the beach. It's heartwarming to have them all here for the celebration. Catherine's sister and family arrive three days later. Their large family has reserved a hotel.

∾

On Sunday, December twenty-ninth they have a celebration: Grandma Mary's surprise seventieth birthday party, hosted at the gourmet restaurant where Catherine had envisioned the wedding reception. Grandma is in the center of the long table, looking lovely. Her short blonde hair is backlit by the golden fire roaring behind her. She is surrounded by family. Everyone sings happy birthday to her. The little kids are loving every minute, kissing and hugging Grandma.

Two days before the wedding, all the relatives are at Catherine's. The children sit in the sun building their dream castles of sand. Erin and Chico arrive for dinner. Sporting a sinister grin, he informs Catherine there will be three more people at the reception. Catherine loses all perspective and begins blabbering. "You have done this for months, one, two, three, four people added at a time until it has become an insane situation. You can't have three more. Period."

"But we must have. These are cousins who came to see us get married."

"Then they should have been in your count. Too late now, the deadline was mandated by the hotel, not me. Nothing I can do about it."

"You must call them and explain. This is very important."

"Did you just say I *must* call them? No. I don't think so. I do know how to follow the rules and their rules clearly stated the end date."

"How can you do this to my family? What kind of person are you?" Chico sounds indignant.

"Excuse me, but I'm doing nothing. Your family is the one with constant changes. At this point, I'm not in charge of the situation."

"If you don't call for three more guests, you can just cancel the reception."

Catherine is sure this is an idle threat, but asks, "What are you talking about? Have you lost your mind? You can't be serious."

"I'm dead serious. You can just cancel the whole thing."

"I think you'd better talk to Erin because this is unacceptable. After all the planning and work, not to mention money, this would be insane."

"Erin, I want to talk to you. In the hallway," he commands, as he motions for her to come. There is yelling and crying, mandating and swearing, which can be heard but words are unclear. The door across the hall opens and a young man knocks at Catherine's door asking that they keep the noise level down. It's very disturbing to him and his crew.

Catherine acknowledges the screaming and yelling is unacceptable. She apologizes and wonders about the word *crew*. Her little niece comes over to her and says, "Wow, Aunt Catherine how lucky you are where you live! I wish I lived across from Slash."

"Slash? You know him? What kind of name is Slash? And how would you know a Slash?"

"Because he is famous!"

"Really, Angie? For what?"

"For singing. He heads Guns n' Roses, you know, the band."

Catherine's ears perk up, "No, I don't know. But if you say so, okay. Sounds like a rock group."

"Yes, it is. Do you think I can get his autograph?" Angie begs.

"We'll ask him tomorrow, after he's rested."

Chico enters the apartment. "I spoke with Erin; we've definitely decided to cancel the reception."

"I want to speak with her first." Catherine is furious she needs his permission to speak alone with her own daughter.

Erin appears with Chico. She is obviously upset beyond words. With swollen red eyes, she's barely able to talk as she slobbers through her statement. "Chico will be my husband, my family, so if he says to cancel, then do that, cancel." He won't leave her to speak privately with her mother.

Catherine is distraught. "Erin, you know tomorrow is the last chance we have to cancel, twenty-four hours' notice or we lose the deposit. We have until then, so take tonight to think about it."

Catherine is awake, shaking and nauseated, all night. The next day she phones Erin who informs her mother she has not changed her mind. Catherine speaks to Chico attempting to convince him how devastating this would be. He refuses to change his mind.

At two o'clock Catherine calls again. "Erin, you don't realize what you are doing. After the wedding you need to have the reception. If not, you'll always regret it."

"No, Mother. If my husband isn't happy, then I'm not happy. This is my final word, cancel."

Catherine must now tell her family there will be no reception. Waiting until the last minute, emotionally distraught, she sends a fax to the hotel so they have the cancellation in writing.

Grandma says, "Catherine, I'm sorry for you. I can't even imagine your hurt. Now, how many phone calls do you need to make to inform everyone?"

Catherine looks at her mother through a river of tears, and with the saddest eyes as she says, "Two."

"Two? Really? You had over a hundred-people attending, now you only have two phone calls?"

"Well, those two calls represent four people. The other sixteen people on my guest list are family, standing right here."

Catherine pulls herself up and loudly says, "Angie, come here.

We are going to knock on a neighbor's door." It's midday so she hopes no one is still sleeping. She takes Angie's hand and walks across the hall. She knocks. The door opens.

"Good afternoon, Mr. Slash. Sorry those visitors disturbed you yesterday. They are gone now; we really are quiet people. Could I introduce you to a big fan? A big enthusiastic fan? This is Angie."

"Hello, Angie, you sure are a cutie."

"Oh, could I get your autograph, pleeease?" she asks blinking her dreamy blue eyes.

"Sure thing. Duffy is here too; would you like his?" Now blushing bright pink, she is speechless.

Angie is thrilled, and it made Catherine's day. Something to smile about, saved by a Slash!

The rehearsal dinner was either cancelled or they were not invited, which pleased Catherine in either case. *One less decision for me to make. One less day to spend with these crazy people.*

The next morning Catherine awakens after a restless night, feeling severely depressed. The kids and Grandma are downstairs on the beach. She grabs a coffee and joins them.

"You should have been here earlier to see the sunrise, Catherine," her mother says "Barely piercing the horizon was a bluish white light that magically turned to a golden orange. Gradually, it produced a fire brightness that literally bounced off the little clouds giving the appearance of monstrous flittering fireflies." Catherine feels good to know her mother is appreciating the day.

By afternoon, her sister's family is at the apartment, all dressed for the wedding. Of course, some are partaking in the ceremony. Erin's sister is a bridesmaid and her brother an usher.

Upon arriving at the church Erin's family takes a few photos outside. Catherine still finds the church disturbing: The design, lack of windows, the eerie pictures, and hidden doors.

Inside is total chaos because no one is in charge. No one took over Catherine's organizing position. People are scrambling and asking her where to go. "Where's the dressing room? Where's the bathroom? Where do we line up to enter?" An usher appears to escort Catherine and Frank to their seats. "No," states Catherine. "As the mother of the bride, I'm the last to sit."

The usher returns a bit later. "I'll escort you now; all the guests have been seated."

"Maybe the guests are seated, but Chico's mother is not. I sit after her."

"But she told me to seat you first. I thought that was a nice gesture."

"No, it's not a nice gesture. It's a breach of protocol. The bride's mother sits last. I'll stand here until she sits. If it takes all afternoon, so be it." She turns to Frank and says, "That woman is a witch!" Catherine thinks she hears a small voice, *"Little does she know."*

~

Marie mutters to herself, "Little does she know. I remember the advice of the Palero priest when I discussed my dream. This girl is my yellow dog and will be in my kitchen, meaning in my family. So, I need to deal with her, control her. Then does this mean Juan's wife is the skinny black bird? If so, I can control her as easily as my premonition. Close the window on her neck and chop off her head."

~

Finally, fifteen minutes later, the groom's mother is escorted down the aisle. The usher arrives to walk Catherine and Frank to the front pew on the bride's side of the aisle. As they walk, Catherine directs his arm to a pew midway, leaving the front pew empty.

There is no way she can place her approval on this wedding when they have systematically destroyed her daughter's beautiful family day of love.

Following the ceremony, Catherine and her family head for a restaurant she arranged the day before as they have not been invited to any reception, if there is one. They have a great family time. The kids were excited banging wooden hammers on crab claws. This was the kind of celebration they all needed. It appears Catherine is pounding the table with her hammer harder than anyone else.

Three weeks later, Catherine and Frank move, as planned. They relocate out of the country. The planning, packing, and handling arrangements had been an added stress factor for them both. They look forward to a relaxing Caribbean villa.

It's a year before mother and daughter speak again. Catherine invites all the family for Christmas. Trish and her son are excited about coming. They had been there a couple of months earlier to celebrate the grandson's fifth birthday. Catherine is surprised to learn Erin will be coming for the holiday, suspecting Trish has convinced her. She arrives alone one morning, the week before Christmas. It is a strained reunion, certainly not the usual holiday warm and fuzzy feeling, but a beginning. Catherine thinks Erin realizes how Chico's family manipulated a disaster, but does not bring up the past. Erin leaves the same day.

Four years later, Catherine and her husband move back to Florida. Relations remain extremely tense between parents and daughter. Perhaps because of their close proximity, Erin again visits a few hours over the holiday while her brother and sister are in town. She tells them, "Marie has been driving me crazy to have children. I want to work. That degree was hard to get, and I want to make use of it." Again, she comes alone and leaves by nightfall.

It's almost a year later when a surprised Catherine says. "Hello," in a questioning tone. She hears, "Hello, Mom, it's Erin." Catherine is frozen in surprise, but thrilled to hear her daughter's voice again. "I'm calling because I want to tell you something. I want you to just listen. I do not want to hear you say anything or I will hang up. I'm not asking you for advice nor your opinion, so don't give it. What I'm going to say is already decided and in motion. I'm only calling to let you know because you are my mother. Do you agree?"

✢ 28 ✣

Icy silence hangs in the air. It doesn't seem to Catherine that she has any choice. She could agree and hear what Erin is considering, or refuse to agree to the terms and never know what Erin is talking about. Although she doesn't want any advice from her mother, at least she's willing to share something in her life.

The following day she calls with her decision. "Erin, this seems like an important decision you have made. I hope you sought consultation on the matter and took time to reflect. It sounds life altering."

"Yes, I have received expert advice along with guidance from our church pastor, and Chico's mother has helped me see things clearly. So, I don't need your input on the matter."

Catherine is unnerved. Erin sought to consult Marie but not her own mother. She is on the verge of tears to be so thoughtlessly thrown to the side. She manages a controlled voice level as she replies, "Well, really, you leave me no choice."

"Be sure now. I don't want to hear comments or any excuses as to why you are offering an opinion. So, you promise?"

"Yes, I promise to say nothing."

Catherine hangs up the phone. She is suspended in time, as it ceases to exist. Near collapse, she is so weak she can hardly stand.

Frank sees her distress and helps her to a chair. "What happened, Catherine? Who was that on the phone?" He sees she is trying to speak, but no words are uttered loud enough nor clear enough for him to understand. "Let me bring you some water."

When he returns, she can't even hold the glass. She holds up her index finger as a signal to wait, to give her some time. Frank patiently sits with her, an arm across her shoulders as he continues to pat her hand until she can speak.

Through her tears, Catherine struggles to say, "Frank, I can't believe what has happened to Erin. Our beautiful daughter. Always so strong, self-confident, and completely sure of herself. How could she have fallen prey to these evil people?"

Frank is holding his breath, unsure what has happened to Erin, but certainly fearing the worst as he listens to his wife. "My dear, please tell me exactly what you heard."

Catherine can now breathe and is gaining control of her thoughts. "I always thought Chico's mother was the true wicked witch of the south. Now I know it. Our beautiful child, who was always so loving and understanding, had a strong Catholic education. Her beliefs were unbending, seemingly, until now. I fear stating what she told me, somehow, perhaps, makes it real."

"Please tell me, maybe I can help."

"No, you can't help, I can't help. No one can help. She made me promise that I, which includes you, would not offer any advice on the matter."

Frank is pacing around the living room, "Okay, just tell me. Is she alright?"

"I don't think so. I think she is so confused by the advice she's been getting that she doesn't know what she is doing."

"You said she didn't want advice. Now you are saying she has gotten advice. Which is it?"

Catherine replies in her normal strong voice. "She does not want advice from us! She has been getting advice from Chico's mother and guidance from Marie's church."

"Regarding what? My God woman, tell me."

"Erin is pregnant."

"Marvelous," Frank shouts jubilant at the news. "So, what's all the fuss?"

Catherine proceeds in her whisper voice as if this is a sacred secret. "The baby is not well. Seems it has a genetic defect that can be passed through Irish genes. After she told Chico, she heard his mother say, 'I knew marrying a gringo would bring trouble to our family. She has corrupted our blood line.' Erin is crushed. Still, Marie consults and advises her, telling her she must get rid of the baby. Erin believes that the best thing for the baby is not to be born, as it won't live long anyway, and it may be in pain. Although speaking out of turn, I did tell her that a baby aborted this late can also be born alive and would also experience pain."

Catherine did promise not to speak, but must find a way to convey to Erin, that this is completely wrong. Erin knows her mother's feelings on the matter, which is why Catherine was forced into silence.

Frank is frozen in place as he listens. "How can she not know she is being manipulated? Obviously, they've destroyed her self-esteem. How could she not want to hold that precious life even if only for a moment, if only for one breath? Smell the baby's head, gently massage a tender back, watch those tiny fingers wrap around her finger as they wrap around her heart? The baby is a part of herself to whom she can give life." Catherine is now crying and shaking uncontrollably, rationalizing that maybe Erin will rethink her decision. Maybe she will change her mind. Then again, maybe not, as she continues to listen to Marie and that priest. What kind of priest would give that advice? He should be excommunicated; the church is always against abortion for any reason."

Frank tries to be optimistic. "Maybe as some time passes by, and she connects with the child, she will change her mind."

"No, I don't think so. Marie has her completely brainwashed. It's Erin's problem, and she needs to make it go away."

"Well, no doctor would do it this late. Plus, I believe it's against the law."

Catherine disagrees with him, "I think it's legal if, a doctor deems it medical."

~

The following day Erin phones her mother, unaware that Chico is listening in on the conversation. "Mother, I want you to know that I am scheduled to do this procedure next Monday. I check in to the hospital at seven in the morning, and they will begin administering the drugs then. I'm having some problems with the staff though. I have been through quite a few doctors who have refused to do the procedure. Finally, one has agreed, but so far we cannot find any nurses to assist."

"Why are you giving me this date? Is it because you expect me to be there?"

"Yes, I thought you might want to be involved. And help get nurses involved."

"Erin, having not been a part of any consultations or discussions prior to the decision making, why ask me now? And didn't you think I might, as you say, 'want to be involved' at that point too?" Catherine is so hurt, she can't believe how slighted she was on a decision involving her own daughter and unborn grandchild. That family has brought the worst dread to her daughter and crushed her heart.

Erin interrupts her mother's thoughts. "I knew what your

advice would be and didn't want to hear sentimental arguments over this, it needed to be judged and analyzed on an unemotional level."

"Really, Erin, judged on an unemotional level? This is a life! A new life sent to you as a blessing."

"You promised not to offer advice. So, that is the date if you want to come."

"I will be there to help you, my daughter. I surely will not assist the procedure in anyway like motivating nurses when I myself am against this whole decision."

"Goodbye, Mother."

Catherine relays the conversation to her husband.

"I don't understand the hospital part of this, Catherine. Why isn't she going to an abortion clinic?"

Catherine inhales deeply as she plunges into another desperate conversation. "Frank, sit down. Abortion clinics will handle any procedure up until pregnancy reaches twelve weeks. After that time, the woman needs to be in the hospital and go through all the steps of giving birth. Erin is way past that so she will be at the hospital. Things could go wrong."

"Well, there you go. No doctor would do it this late. It's too dangerous."

Catherine disagrees with him, "I think some might, even though it might also be dangerous to the mother."

Frank slumps so far down he appears to be part of the chair. He is speechless trying to wrap his mind around this evil madness that has engulfed his beautiful daughter. He imagines the type of doctor who would perform an abortion so late. Erin could die.

Chico phones Marie. "Erin has been in contact with her mother. She even invited her to be at the hospital. I don't want to encounter a scene there."

"Don't worry. She won't change her mind for a variety of reasons. Catherine will not argue. First, I won't be there, until the end. For the moment, my job is done. I will take control of the situation after the abortion. Secondly, Catherine no longer has any influence on her daughter. And, of course, Erin is under your total control. You just need to exercise it. She will never mentally recover from this. She will always blame herself, her genes, and her decision. Son, she will look to you for guidance. Be prepared to guide. If you are going to stay married to this girl, you need to exert complete control for her to be one of us."

"Well, I hope I don't have a problem with Catherine."

"You can handle her. She blames you and even me, but she knows Erin made the decision."

On Monday, Erin checks into the hospital early in the morning, accompanied by her husband. All the usual procedures occur slowly, very slowly. It is hours before she has a room. Catherine approaches the nurses' station asking the head nurse, "Could you tell me why it is taking so long just to get a room? Treatment has not even started, and she has been here five hours just waiting."

"Treatment? Treatment you say? Madam, this is not a treatment. It is a killing! No one wants her here. No one wants to check her in. None of us want to be a part of this. We are here to save lives."

Catherine is dumbfounded. "Please believe me when I say, my feelings on the matter are the same. I don't want her here doing this procedure. I don't want my daughter to go through this and live with it the rest of her life. But the hospital accepted her as a patient, and she has a doctor who signed her in. This terrible ordeal needs to be handled with a bit of dignity, if possible."

"I feel sorry for you, Grandma to be. I won't participate, but neither will I stand in your way. I'll try to find you a nurse. No promises."

A nurse never comes to the room. Every time anything is needed, from a drink of water to a towel, Catherine goes to the nurses' station to ask for it.

Chico approaches Catherine. "Thank you for being here. I could never have managed this by myself. I never intended to. I assumed the nurses would handle everything. They are doing nothing to help. It's outrageous."

"Chico, they don't believe in what you are doing and refuse to be a part of it. You must respect their views and values involved here. They see it as facilitating murder. As medical professionals, clearly understanding life and death, murder is what they perceive."

"Do you know when they will start the procedure?"

Catherine wonders why he's asking her. "What is the procedure? That is, as you understand it."

"I have no idea what they are doing or when. Only that they are doing an abortion."

"Do you mean to say that the two of you have not had any medical instructions, regarding timeline and risk, from a doctor?"

"We, rather, Erin does not have a doctor for the procedure. The hospital was to assign one who would agree to do it."

"Are you beginning to see a pattern here that you two are the only ones who want this?" Catherine asks. "Do you see that everyone else considers this a terrible mistake? Can you wake up and cancel this fiasco? Go home. Have the child. And deal with what comes your way. Whatever happens, a new life is always a blessing, filling a need in your life and your soul. It brings a peace and grace to a troubled world. A peace like no other."

Catherine has no idea what an Anencephaly baby is or what it means to life. With all the people who have been consulted by Chico and Erin, Catherine is not among them. She is not allowed to make an informed decision based on facts. She only knows her granddaughter is being taken from her.

Later she studies the procedure, becoming aware of the defect, and the possibilities of life and death for the child. She also learns that her daughter has been misinformed; it's not an Irish trait, though Chico's family has been blaming Erin and Catherine.

❧ 29 ❧

There are hospitals with ground-breaking in utero surgeries and procedures. Catherine wonders if anyone made any inquiries outside of Miami. Her concern leads her to search on her own. She finds that some women have a psychiatric complicated grief reaction, depression or post-traumatic stress disorder. She learns women who terminate for fetal anomalies experience grief as intense as a spontaneous death of a baby.

Arriving at seven-thirty, Erin suffers all day, through the night, and into the next day. Long after discussions end, Catherine is still reluctant to accept that the late stage abortion is going to happen. Obviously, this is something Chico's family has planned and worked for. Erin's caught like a butterfly in a net. No room to escape, any attempt only causes further entanglement and suffering.

Chico's the instrument of delivery of his mother's desires.

Catherine continues to cry and pray for some type of intervention. She asks, "God, why are you allowing this to happen? Why is my grandbaby, whom I already love and want to protect, being put to this torturous test? Where are you? You must intervene to

195

prevent this tragedy. I don't think I can mentally survive this." She is despondent.

A piercing scream breaks Catherine's concentration, ending her prayer. Erin has bolted to sitting position and screams, "I'm bleeding to death."

Catherine's completely unnerved as she grabs Erin and attempts to comfort her and reassure her, while she calls for a nurse. Of course, none comes. As Catherine tries to ascertain what's really happening to Erin, she suddenly realizes the problem. "Erin, calm down honey. You're not bleeding to death. Your water broke, that's all."

"What does that mean?"

"Wait a minute here. Do you mean to tell me that with all the great counseling and advice these people gave you, no one has prepared you for what would happen to you?" Now Catherine knows these people are the devil. They have convinced Erin that they're the experts and know what's best for her and the baby. And they would help and guide her through the decision. Where are they now? Where's that consoling comforting priest? Where's Marie, the all knowledgeable advice-dispensing witch? Where's that loving husband who would stand by her?

Catherine continues to cry and pray for intervention. "God, why are you allowing this to happen? Why is my grandbaby, who I already love, being put to this torturous end? Where are you?"

A thought is forming in her mind, perhaps an answer to her prayer. Yes.

In deepest sleep one night I dreamed
That on the beach I walked.
God was by my side each step
And quietly we talked.
Then on the sky my life was flashed;
The visions all serene.
Two sets of footprints in the sand
Were there in every scene.

But then I noticed in some scenes
Of suffering, pain, and strife...
Just a single set of footprints
At the worst times of my life.
God...you said you'd stay by me
In good times and in bad...
Why then did you leave me
Each time my life was sad?"
"My precious child," God answered,
"When your life had pain, I knew;
The single set of footprints
Were the times I carried you."

"Oh, God. It's just You, me, and Erin."

Catherine is not aware of the evil forces plotting against her. She needs to look back, enabling her to see the future. While Catherine is crying, praying and standing by her daughter as much as she is allowed; Marie is working against her. She and her congregation have been performing their ceremonies on the grounds of the Ft. Lauderdale Airport. "We will meet as dusk leaves us at the southwest end of the airstrip. You will see the Ron Gardner Aircraft Observation Area. Most of the information on line is in Russian. If you are from the early Castro days, you can read the instructions. Chico has assisted her and is learning the basics of control.

Many hours of pain later the baby makes an entrance to this cruel world. Erin has already made donation arrangements to science. The University of Miami medics are here to transport the baby for research, as so little is known about this rare affliction. Erin is emotionally drained. The two of them, mother and baby have been to hell and back—mentally and physically. Catherine is exhausted, the only person by her daughter's side to help her through this ordeal and to see her partially-formed grandbaby girl. She walks slowly out of the blinding-white surgical room.

She enters the waiting room to inform the others, where she encounters Marie and Hernan. They are comfortably relaxing in soft, overstuffed, sea foam-colored chairs. Marie is enlightening everyone on the medical facilities being overtaken by the robots. Catherine is wondering why this woman is free to walk around in society. She needs a padded room with a lock.

Catherine updates everyone. "The little girl was not born alive, an outcome which was expected. She will now be taken to the research facility. Hopefully some good, through the research, will make a difference in future children." She collapses on the lumpy sofa.

Marie goes from comfortably relaxing into emergency screaming mode. She begins waving her arms around and loudly demanding, "You must stop them! They cannot leave here with that baby girl. I need to have her...now!"

Chico runs to Erin's birthing room saying, "Yes, we need that baby, now."

Catherine is shocked and confused, asking herself *We? Why? For What?* She manages to stand on her rubbery legs and follows Chico into the room. He is accosting Erin. "Where is the baby?" Erin just looks at him through her fog. "Where is the baby, Erin? I demand to know! Now!"

Catherine recovers and answers for her daughter. "Why do you want to know, Chico? Why does your mother say that she *needs* to have that baby? What is going on here?"

Still groggy, Erin finally speaks and asks, "Chico, what is this all about?"

"My mother wants the baby for about an hour or two. Her religious beliefs demand a special death ritual be done."

"The baby has already been baptized, Chico."

"This is an additional, special Spanish blessing."

Erin questions him. "Why is this the first I'm hearing about a blessing? Weren't you going to tell me? She can't have it. The baby must be at the facility as soon as possible to be viable for research. Something good must come out of this tragedy. Tell her it's impossible. I'm sorry."

Chico leaves and then returns a few minutes later. "Okay, we discussed it. She will just do a quick blessing so the medics can take the baby shortly. You can manage that right?"

Erin is exhausted and not having the strength to argue, she says, "I guess. It must be quick, very quick. When the medics say they are leaving, you must have her relinquish the baby immediately."

"Yes, it'll be quick. I'll get a wheelchair so you can come with me, Erin."

"I don't want to go. I'm exhausted and mentally drained. I'm not up to a ceremony."

True to his persona, Chico issues his demand. "But you must come. You must. As the mother, you must be there."

Erin turns to Catherine and says, "Do I have to go? Do I really have to go, Mother? I don't want to—and I don't even know what this is."

Catherine is astonished her opinion is being sought on anything at this point. "Erin, you don't need to do anything you don't want to do. You make your own decisions."

"Good, then I'm not going."

Chico again orders Erin. "You must come to see the baby. You need to be comfortable and accepting of this. And reassure the gods."

"I have seen the baby. Remember, I was there when she was born? And I have no idea what you are referring to as 'comfortable and accepting,' and *what gods?*"

Chico storms out, furious at this decision. He has lost a debate, and to Catherine of all people.

Catherine and her husband make sure Erin is never alone. He conveys this to the staff.

Later in the day, Chico approaches Catherine and Frank. "I want you to know something. I promise I will destroy your family. Erin took your advice today over my orders. That's going to cost you. Let me tell you now.

"*First*, I have a business opportunity that I will accept, moving us out of Florida, far from you. I'll separate your daughter from every member of your immediate family; you, her sister, and children. Her brother will hate her and you, but he'll be my sympathetic friend. All extended family members will see me as the nice guy, and they'll side with me against anything you say or do.

"*Secondly*, you'll be ostracized when our other children are born. You won't be invited to baby showers. You won't even know when they arrive. You'll no longer be invited to visit our home. You won't be welcome. Your daughter will not let her children visit you.

"*Lastly*, you have just completely lost your family. Remember I have her ear every day, filling her with reasons to hate you a drop at a time."

Catherine is staring at him in disbelief. She is perplexed. *How insane is he to think he can drive us apart?*

A few months later Chico is listening in as Catherine receives a call from Erin. "Mother, I want to let you know we have some really good news. The company that employs Chico has broken into two different companies. He has chosen to go with the new division, so we are moving to Atlanta. It means a large pay increase and a future vice presidency."

All Catherine hears is the ringing in her ears of Chico's statement; '*First...*

A year after moving, Erin calls. "Mother, we just moved into our new house. I would like for you to join us for our first Christmas here. Chico and I realize our parents are not the best of friends, so we agreed to take turns at the holidays. We would like you to come this year and next year they can come. We can alternate every year."

"How nice and very thoughtful, Erin. We would love to come. It's an honor to be asked first."

"Well, actually Chico's parents couldn't come this year. His mother has to work."

Frank and Catherine arrive on Christmas Eve. Erin's sister Trish and husband Steven have also been invited. The house is a huge three stories in a gated community. Erin confides in her mother that they have been trying to have another child with no luck, and she is very discouraged. Her mother wonders if this is Erin's penance for her abortion decision, but she does not say that. "Erin, there is an old wives' tale; move to a new house and have a new baby. Maybe that'll work for you. We'll see next year, right?"

Catherine is taken aback as she sees Chico and Steven cooking a turkey outside in a tub of boiling oil. The two young men are not getting along, they argue about everything. After carrying the turkey to the kitchen, Chico accuses Steven of splashing oil on his expensive kitchen backsplash tile and wants him to pay to replace it. Trish is furious at Chico's accusations.

Erin is completely stressed, but still attempts to make sure everyone has a pleasant visit. Two days later the visitors are going home. They are ready, even anxious to leave their relatives, their expensive house, and their miserable existence behind.

Catherine muses, *well, next year his parents will come. I'm sure things will be different.*

Summer arrives, and Catherine receives a call from Erin. "Mother I wanted to let you know we are expecting a baby in November. We waited to tell anyone until we knew this baby was going to be healthy."

"So, now I'm just anyone? I am your mother!"

"You know; I didn't want you upset."

"Really? Well you missed. I would like to have known early on. Our friends in the Bahamas are expecting also in November, but we have known that for three months."

"Well, I didn't want to listen to you or your advice."

"Excuse me. Did I say anything last time? Do you recall you asked me to say nothing? And that is exactly what happened."

"Yes, well now I am telling you this time."

~

As November approaches, Catherine asks about hosting a baby shower.

"No thanks, Mother, I've already had three so there's nothing I need."

"Well, I wish I had been there for at least one."

Catherine and Frank anxiously await the call. They are already packed, excited to welcome their grandbaby.

~

"Mother, I'll be going to the hospital any day now. I don't want you to come to the hospital. I'll call you when I'm home."

"Dear, most young mothers would like to have their mother with them for support. I was the one with you every minute the last time." Trying to make light, Catherine adds, "I see that old wives' tale of a new house actually did work."

"Yes. Well, we would appreciate it if you were not here this time."

Catherine knows where this control is coming from. *"Secondly..."*

~

A few days later, on November 8th, finally, Erin calls. "Hello, Mother, we're at the hospital and have a beautiful healthy boy. His name is Ethan."

"Oh, ah, I can't wait to see him and hold him. I'll be there to help when you get home. You can rest and gain your strength."

"No, we have decided we don't want you here now. We'll establish a date when neighbors, friends, and family can come to see the baby."

"What? Now I am classified with the neighbors? How dare you!"

Moments later the phone rings with a call from the Bahamas. They hear an exhausted yet excited voice. "We have a beautiful healthy baby boy! We can't wait for you to see him. Come as soon as you can."

Catherine calls Erin every day to see how she is feeling, and hoping for a change of mind, allowing her to visit. Four days later, during the call, Erin informs her mother she is being released the next day. Catherine cannot tolerate this treatment. She helped Erin through a terrible time, and now she's thrown aside because Chico decides he can separate them? *Not going to happen.* In her mind, she hears him say, *"Lastly..."*

𝔥 30 𝔥

"I'm not about to stay home because Chico does not need me this time. After a nine-hour drive to Atlanta, I want to see our grandbaby boy. I'm determined, Frank." They approach the guard gate at the complex.

"We're here to help the new parents," Catherine explains to the guard. He smiles and lets them through the gate. They park across from the house and await the family's arrival. Hours later the car pulls in the driveway. The excited grandparents drive in right behind them. The young couple is stunned to see them. Chico addresses the couple, "We expected you to obey us."

Upon entering the house, Erin addresses her parents, "Didn't I tell you not to come? You weren't invited and were explicitly told not to come?"

Catherine is outraged. "I felt confident when we got here, and you realized what it meant to welcome our new grandson, you would be glad we came. You'd realize we came to help."

"You can take a few pictures of Ethan and then you will leave. I am going to bed." Chico escorts them to the door. Their long drive home is wracked with heartache.

~

Marie is furious with the gods. Another boy! *Her* two children and now a grand*son*. She asks herself; *how could they do this to me?* Her inner voice tells her what she does not want to hear. *The spirits have been telling you how to get what you want. Placing demands on the gods is not the way. They sent you a girl, a girl that you rejected, Marie, rejected because you were working to destroy the marriage. The loss of a child often does that. You were hoping Chico would then find a nice Cuban girl.*

~

Marie and Hernan arrive the following week. Erin is surprised, Chico hadn't mentioned this to her, so she questions him.

"I did tell you, Erin. I know you've been under a strain lately with the new baby, and I need to go out of town for a few days, so I asked my parents to keep you company and help you out."

"But you assured me you were taking a six week leave of absence to help here at home."

"Yes, but something came up that I need to handle. You like the big money, don't you?"

"I could've had my parents stay if I knew you weren't going to be here."

"Well, I feel better if it's my mother looking after things, rather than yours."

Erin isn't pleased, but she knows when to back off.

~

Marie is there to do her special Spanish blessing as she did for the first baby. She makes herself at home, taking charge, she ushers Erin to bed for a nap. She wastes no time picking up the phone and contacting her Atlanta friends from long ago.

"Be sure to arrive tomorrow at noon. The timing is important. Erin will sleep. We have a two-hour window."

That evening Marie prepares dinner. Unbeknownst to Erin, dinner consists of a specially slaughtered blessed chicken and a special drink to help Erin relax. She retires early, and Marie begins gathering everything she requires for tomorrow's ceremony.

Erin awakens late morning and descends the stairs for breakfast and to prepare Ethan's. She finds Marie busy in the kitchen. "Why don't you feed the baby breakfast, Erin, and then I'll feed him lunch while you take a nap. You look tired."

Erin *is* tired. She doesn't understand this sudden onset of exhaustion. She readily agrees to the timetable. Marie gives her a special vitamin drink which will help her tiredness. By noon Erin's sound asleep and doesn't hear the doorbell.

Marie opens the door to a group of friends who arrive together in one vehicle, a van, so not to draw the neighbors' attention. They enter the home carrying the requested supplies and set them all in the dining room.

"Angela, light the candles in each corner of the large wooden table. Place the fruits in between the candles. Now bring Baby Ethan as we begin chanting. Place him in the center of the table, next to last night's specially slaughtered blessed chicken and the special drink made of the chicken's blood."

The ceremony begins with her calling upon the Egun; the ancestors play an important role. As the Congo drums begin softly, Marie is chanting; "I acknowledge and offer prayers to our elders who've passed on, asking they become spiritual guides to this child. I ask the Egun to possess me and communicate with this gathering." The fruit and special chicken are shared among the group with a taste on the baby's lips.

Within two hours the ceremony has ended. Erin awakens towards evening and admits she feels much better and thanks Marie for her help.

Three weeks later, the Christmas holidays explode on the scene. Frank and Catherine are in Key West with friends. This year is Chico's parents' turn to visit, so they aren't invited. They're upset to miss Ethan's first Christmas, at six weeks old.

"Catherine, it's the New Year holidays. Things are much more pleasant and loving in the Bahamas. Let's go now," Frank suggests. "We will be early and relaxed for the baptism of our friends' baby." Frank is the godfather. He adores this little boy, his namesake, and will watch over him. They spend the time relaxing and enjoying themselves.

Two months later they're invited to Ethan's baptism, along with all the relatives, friends and neighbors. Catherine has booked a hotel room realizing that Marie and Hernan will have the spare room in Chico's house. She'll never consider this Erin's house. Erin will live there as long as she bows to Chico.

They have been traveling extensively on business but arrive back in the states in time for the christening. "Erin, we brought this adorable fluffy stuffed animal holding a basket, a gift for the new baby." It's a long two days. Catherine is sickened every time she meets with Chico, knowing how he belittles and controls Erin.

Marie addresses Catherine in a superior tone, "Catherine, you should be happy we are here and have helped produce this child."

"What could you possibly mean by that?"

"Simply, Chico and Erin have been trying for the last seven years to have a child to no avail. So, you should be thrilled that we were around to make that happen."

Catherine is a bit shaken and unnerved but tries not to let Marie see that, as she asks, "Whatever do you mean, Marie? How could you possibly help them produce a child?"

"Are you familiar with the spirit Abiku, the spirit predestined to death?" I was able to prevent him from accessing Erin's womb so she could have another child, a well child, unlike the first birth."

Catherine feels faint and leaves the room to join Erin as she wraps Ethan's blanket, preparing to leave for church.

As the baptism progresses, the priest unwraps the child's blanket. Catherine attempts to stifle a sound of shock, not successfully. The open blanket exposes a bruise on one leg and a chain on the baby's ankle. Erin becomes hysterical screaming, "What is this! What is this!" she demands.

Marie is indignant and responds, "Don't be such a snob. This is giving them a child to stay here on this earth with them. The chain is applied after a light swat with a wooden broom."

Catherine is confused, "How can you believe such nonsense?"

"It worked, didn't it? He stayed here, though it did require some threats."

Catherine is horrified by this whole business. "What threats?"

"We threatened to cut off a finger or toe. Or maybe burn him. It is a matter of life cycle and rebirth. The old to the new."

Catherine questions Erin's approval of such disregard.

"Mother, I am exhausted at her threats and innuendos. She gets me hysterical and the result is meaningless. If that's what she thinks, it doesn't matter. Just forget it."

Marie is fully aware of Catherine's knowledge regarding Chico's infidelities. Catherine can't understand why Erin didn't leave him before children were involved. Even before the first pregnancy, Erin knew Chico was cheating on her.

Catherine had opened a joint account listing her and Erin as the two signatures. She had put $5,000 in this account for Erin should she need to leave him. She learns Erin has forged her name and given the funds to Chico.

Frank, who does most of the cooking at home, helps with the cooking and cleanup so Erin isn't overwhelmed and has time to enjoy the festivities. As the weekend winds down, the long-distance visitors begin to leave Atlanta. Chico approaches Frank and accuses him of scratching the stove top and demands a check to replace it. He informs Frank, "You owe me nine hundred dollars." Chico smiles pleasantly the whole time he is insulting and racking up the cash. Is there anything this person wouldn't do for money? Frank and Catherine just want to keep the peace.

A few days later Erin calls Catherine. "Thank you very much for your baptismal gift to Ethan. I just, today, found the thousand-dollar check you left in the stuffed animal's basket, saying this was for his new bed. I should have known you wouldn't just give him a stuffed toy!"

"Really? The cute little toy wouldn't have been enough of a gift for you to thank us?" I don't know what has become of my daughter. I think she has been devoured by the big bad wolf."

The following months are so busy Catherine doesn't have a free minute to think about unpleasantries. In September, they make their usual trip to Manhattan to celebrate Frank's brother's seventy-fourth birthday. It's good to get away and enjoy family.

Closing the summer, they plan a trip to the Bahamas to visit their close friends and see the baby again. Departing the plane and heading toward immigration, they find their friend Kendall waving as he approaches them. "I wasn't sure you would get here or even that your plane would take off."

"Why would you think that?"

"Because of all the bombings in New York."

Well they know what a dry comedic humor their friend possesses, so they chuckle. "Sure, bombings, really?"

"Come look at the television in the customs office and you'll see it on the news."

They step into the office belonging to the customs officers and see two planes have flown into buildings, demolishing them and killing many people. Catherine turns to him chuckling and says, "Which Denzel Washington movie is this?"

"I'm not kidding here. This is real."

A customs officer steps in to hear the claim. Looking at Frank and Catherine, as tears fall on his cheeks he says, "Yes, this is a very sad day. So many lives lost."

They find this so hard to believe, impossible to comprehend. How could such a thing happen?

～

The next week at the Princess Resort is difficult. More information brought true reality to the disaster. The hotel is gracious to its guests and keeps them informed of the situation. "There's no travel allowed back to the States. It will be weeks before anyone can fly home. We're granting everyone a fifty percent discount on their room rates, just our small way of helping to ease the pain."

Catherine can't wait weeks. Frank has only one week's supply of medication. Over the next few days, she arranges a boat to the Fort Lauderdale harbor, and contacts the Fort Lauderdale police department. She asks them to escort her and Frank into the airport to retrieve their car.

It's like entering the twilight zone. Two lone people with a police escort entering a huge dark parking garage full of cars empty of people. The patrol car leaves them and an eerie feeling creeps through their bones, as if they are the last two people on earth. They walk through the deserted rows, viewing the circumference aglow in icy blue light. Driving out the garage they feel compelled to give thanks.

The next morning at breakfast Frank sits next to his wife, taking her hand he begins, "Catherine, I have been thinking about what could have happened to us, to our family. A couple of weeks ago, we were in Manhattan. You were taking pictures of the twin towers' neighborhood. With the timing a bit different, we could have been killed. We need to try to make things work with Chico and Erin. No one knows how long they have here on Earth. I want Erin's son and future children to know us, to be in our lives. I want them to know we love them and treasure them."

"You're right, Frank, we need to seize the day, as they say. We have a November first meeting in the Bahamas. Let's fly from there to see our grandson on his first birthday."

When Catherine and Frank arrive at the birthday party, they enter through the side door into the kitchen. Immediately Frank notices the stove top isn't new. "Erin," he says, "I gave Chico a check for a new stove top and this doesn't look new."

"You're right, it's not new. We decided it wasn't bad enough to replace," Erin says.

Marie is in the dining room chuckling, pleased to know her son has caused an upset. He's learning; first create little problems, then let them fester and grow.

"Okay, everyone into the dining room for birthday cake," Erin announces as she lights the candles. Everyone is singing. Ethan is mesmerized. Suddenly the huge clock sitting atop the china cabinet falls right in front of Ethan, hitting his high chair tray with a chest-pounding thud. Five or six inches over and it would have crushed his head.

Erin screams a mother's blood-curdling scream, as she grabs the child. "Marie, you almost killed Ethan!"

"Oh, Erin, you know I didn't mean to knock that off the cabinet. It was an accident."

"Was it just a few days ago that I said, 'No one knows how long they have here on earth?' Frank whispers to Catherine.

Ethan's crying, frightened and confused. Erin's shaking as she holds him. Catherine tries to pet and offer comfort as she stands next to them. Erin turns to Catherine, "That woman almost kills this child every time she comes here."

Catherine looks very confused at this statement and later questions Erin.

"It's just whenever she's here there's an 'accident'. Chico says we need to chalk it up to her age. You know she is a lot older than you are, Mother. Maybe it's her age, but I worry about Ethan being hurt when she's with him." This trip isn't bringing a total solution to our relationship, but maybe we're beginning.

❄ 31 ❄

Four days later, the shortness of life is again brought to the forefront of Frank's mind. To return to Florida, they head to the Atlanta airport. They hear a report on the radio, "There's been a downed plane. At nine fifteen this morning in Belle Harbor, Queens, New York. American airlines flight five eighty-seven went down, killing all two hundred and sixty passengers and some people on the ground. Just two months and one day after the 9/11 attack, the government is unsure if this is the result of terrorism; they are investigating." The Atlanta airport became a navigating nightmare.

The first Christmas in their new home, Catherine and Frank are awaiting the arrival of the family. Erin arrives at two in the morning, awakens early and rushes through the gift exchange. She immediately starts loading the car to leave, hurrying off to Chico's family home in Miami.

Catherine walks to the car and asks, "What's your hurry, dear?

You arrived in the middle of the night. At least you could spend some of Christmas morning with us. We have a lovely breakfast spread planned."

"I'm not sure Chico will want to stay. He's anxious to get to Miami. Most of his family is gathered there."

"And most of your family is gathered here. You have a week in Florida. Would it be too much to spend a few hours here?"

"I'll ask."

"Ask? Ask who? Ask what? You need permission to spend the morning here when you'll be spending six days in Miami?"

As Catherine reenters the house, their little dog is begging to go out. Catherine feels bad that in the confusion and haste she's neglected the little thing. She opens the door and they walk out to the dog's favorite area. Erin's large vehicle is parked between them and the young couple. While she can't see, she hears Chico saying, "Stay here? Stay for what? I'm done. Get your fucking ass moving and finish packing this car."

Catherine looks down at the little dog; an animal so sweet, trusting, and loving. Like a baby, like Erin as a young girl. A girl who, with her parents' guidance, grew to be self-reliant, independent; head strong and determined, and always said what she thought. *Now she is refusing to stand up for herself and refusing my help. What has happened to her?* Through her trickling tears, Catherine mutters to herself; "She is a person I do not know. How did this happen?"

With Frank now retired, Catherine informs him, "The summer is my first chance to leave work and visit Atlanta. Let's plan to stay a week and spend whatever time we can with Ethan. Let's take him swimming, golfing, sliding and especially the zoo. He'll love showing us his zoo." Luckily, they could fit this visit in between a trip to the Bahamas and a heavy schedule of visitors arriving.

They arrive while Chico is away on a business trip, making the visit much more comfortable and thankful they don't need to put up with his attitude. The "dictator" never allows anyone to forget who's in charge, who makes the decisions, and who gives or denies permission. Erin works full time at an extremely demanding job involving some travel. Yet Chico has forbidden her to have house-cleaning help. She writes a grocery check every week with a small amount extra, to be able to pay for help a couple of hours a week. They are both making six figures, yet he denies her help. It's all about control.

Erin pours Catherine a cup of coffee with news, "Mother, we're having a second child."

"That's wonderful, Erin. A boy or a girl?"

"We don't know. We chose not to know in advance."

Catherine teases, "So, when is *she* expected?"

"We aren't exactly sure. We'll keep you posted as time goes on."

They treasure their time with Ethan and enjoy the five-day stay, leaving before the weekend. After arriving home, Catherine crafts a little "Ethan Takes Grandma to the Zoo" book by hand. It contains animal pictures she took at the zoo along with a story. He's the main character telling her all about each animal. He loves it.

Fall in Atlanta emerges dressed in leaves of red, brown, and shiny gold. The vibrant colors spark an excitement in the air. Catherine and Frank arrive just in time to help decorate for Halloween. Skeletons hang by the door, pumpkins on the front step, and eerie music plays at the front walkway. The grandparents are having such fun with Ethan who is giggling at every decoration. All of a sudden, an icy wind blows and the witch rides in on her broom. Marie has arrived.

"Well, after all, it is Halloween." Catherine mutters to Frank. "Perhaps we could place her next to the pumpkin."

"I don't think we want to traumatize the little kids coming to the door", he replies.

Walking into the kitchen, he overhears Marie calling to Ethan. "Come and we can make a witch's brew. I will teach you, just like I taught your father."

Ethan comes bouncing into the kitchen. Excited, as always when he accomplishes something new. "Mother, Abuela, helped me make a magic Halloween drink! Do you want to have some?"

"Sure, sweetie. Goodness this is awful, Marie. What are you teaching him?"

"Just a little magic, Erin. Don't be such a stuffed shirt."

Arriving home, Catherine purchases pink booties and mails them to Erin with a note, "Think Pink." Next week she sends a cute pink dress, followed weekly by pink socks, pink hat and every week something pink with the same note. She has no idea that Marie is wishing the same thing.

More than wishing, Marie is again seeking the Palo Mayombe. She is having difficulty locating Reverend D, the same priest who helped her years ago. Her sister suggests she meet with one of the priests teaching at the college.

"There is a Santeria course at the college?" Marie is shocked.

"Not exactly. There's a course titled 'Comparative Religion.' This being Miami, known as little Havana, it contains a great deal of Santeria in the course."

"Who teaches the course? Is it Dr. D?"

"No, but I do know the instructor and can introduce you. In the early seventies, he was ordained to the priesthood of Sango and has dedicated his life to the study of Santeria."

"Luciana, I'm surprised you are so knowledgeable. You know the African based Chango religion is named after our god representing thunder and lightning? And that it originated in our Yoruba homeland?"

"Yes," she laughs, "You are not the only one who knows their history."

Within the week, Marie schedules a meeting with the Sango priest at the Miami Fontainebleau Hotel. She explains her years of wants and worships, "Yet I have boys, boys, boys. My daughter-in-law is expecting again, although she is not of our persuasion. My son has worked with me and matured in the Santeria religion. He handles and manipulates all aspects of his life very well, including his wife. But I still want a girl."

"I will work on this and put together some spells and prayers that may help you. Can you come by my church next week? How is Wednesday?" he asks, handing her his card.

The following week she visits the priest, trusting that his instructions will bear merit.

"Marie, you must proceed in precise order. Light the red and white candles next to each other, then sit on a pink blanket. On your piece of paper write; I wish to have a girl. Fold it and light it on fire. While it is burning chant; I wish Erin a baby girl, three times then dunk the piece of paper in a bowl of water.

"Now if you can get your son to commit also, give him these instructions. Place nine pink rose petals and a pink baby item in a plastic bag. Next, take a long pink candle and break it in three places. Place the pieces in the plastic bag, with the baby's name written on a piece of paper. Then tell him to chant these words: The bearer of children, I come to thee in hopes of what shall be, bring a baby girl to me.

"He should say this chant three times. Then he needs to place the plastic bag containing the items under her mattress. This is best before conception, but can also be useful at the end of each trimester.

"If you are sure she has already conceived tell him to shake the rattle three times over her head. Put the rattle in a box with a religious token, and sprinkle with this herb mixture. Hide the rattle somewhere in the baby's room and recite: Little girl, your journey has begun, but the best is yet to come. Live long, live well. Let no one break this spell."

Marie drives to her sister's house. "Luciana, thank you for referring me to the Chango priest. He gave me information on certain gods, some worship practices and spells. I'll be in Atlanta mid-December and will follow the priest's instructions. I trust it will work."

~

Three months later, many friends come by to visit Catherine and Frank and bring get well wishes along with a happy birthday.

"Congratulations, Frank! Eighty. Wow! A mile-marker birthday by anyone's standards," is recited repeatedly. He's having some medical problems, but they're manageable. Three days before Frank's party Catherine receives a phone call. "Erin's just checked into the hospital in labor. Please don't tell her who called you."

Catherine's sick to her stomach. She can't believe the call she just received. She hears an echo in her ears; *"Secondly, you'll be ostracized when our other children are born. You won't be invited to baby showers. You won't even know when they arrive. Mission number two completed. You weren't invited to the baby shower. You didn't know about the arrival."*

But I did know. I knew about the baby girl; I knew when they were at the hospital. My sources are reliable. I may not be there, but I can see that beautiful pink baby in my mind.

She picks up the phone and orders a pink flower arrangement to be sent to Erin with a welcome baby girl card and today's date. She attempts to persuade herself that she isn't traumatized by her daughter's rejection, by the fact that she wasn't even told about the baby. Chico has managed to shut her out of her daughter's life.

∾

Frank is having chest pains, though he convinces himself it is psychosomatic or maybe too much coffee. At the same time, he knows Erin's estrangement with them is killing him and Catherine slowly. His wife is not going to quit fighting for her daughter.

∾

Erin phones Catherine a month later, "We'd like you to come and visit and see Baby Anna, named after my best friend. We're having an open house next week for people to come by and see her."

"How nice your mother is invited to come by and see her new granddaughter along with the neighbors. Well, I'm much too busy at work to leave now. Perhaps if I'd known in advance, I could've planned."

"But you did know in advance. I want to ask you who told you when I went to the hospital to have Anna?"

"I won't tell who called me, let's just say I have my ways. Mainly we know it wasn't you who called!"

"It was my sister, right?"

"I will tell you that it was *not* your sister."

"Why are you really not coming next week? You're getting even with me?"

"I'll come for the christening, if I'm invited in time. Do we have a score to settle? I'm not aware of that."

"You're mad that we didn't call you when we went to the hospital. Right?"

Catherine is thinking, *you're damn right and you don't even remember your father turns eighty this week. Every thought is to satisfy Chico.* The conversation ends in a stalemate. Catherine sighs. *What is she afraid of? Why has she abandoned herself? Her desires, her dreams, her family?*

❧ 32 ❧

Christening day, Marie enters the kitchen. "Hello, Catherine and Frank. We arrived three days ago to conduct our special Spanish blessing as I did for the first baby girl."

"That didn't go very well, did it, Marie?" Catherine bites back.

"Things I want always seem to work out in the end. You look tired, Catherine. Why don't you have a seat, and I will make you a special vitamin drink. It will make you feel rested and so much better."

"Are you going to the church with us, Marie?"

"Of course, I would not miss my granddaughter's baptism," she replies to Erin.

"Really, I thought maybe your special Spanish blessing was enough," Catherine injects.

"It is enough. You're right, the baptism is not necessary, but I know you Catholics like to have the ceremony, a mere formality."

~

As they enter the church, Catherine glances up, expecting the ceiling to fall in on them. The priest welcomes everyone and begins the christening.

Chico's mother may be a Santeria priestess and a Palo Mayombe worshipper, but there are practices she has not yet mastered, including the initiation ritual which she performed three days ago.

To bless the child with the sacred candles, the priest opens the child's christening gown. Catherine gasps, and mutters unintelligible words. It sounds like "snake, snake". The open gown reveals a coral and white object encircling her neck, not a snake, a type of necklace, but she is sure it *was* a snake. She wonders, *did it change?* Now she doubts herself. "What is this?" she asks. Everyone looks around the group and stops on Marie. She appears to have no knowledge of the situation.

Back at the house, preparing for dinner, Erin asks Marie if she has any idea how this necklace appeared on her daughter.

Marie confesses, "Yes I do. It is not a necklace; it is a bracelet. Made with specially chosen natural stones. They will protect her from evil and illness. Like your guardian angel, it will protect her from all harm."

Erin thinks nothing of it. *One can't have too many blessings.*

Catherine is hopeful that maybe someday Erin will realize what's going on in her own home.

May arrives two months later. Catherine loves gardening this time of year. The amaryllises are sprouting their blood-red blooms. Still a little Florida cool; birds of paradise are in bloom, with a note of summer on the way.

For Catherine, the best part of May is Mother's Day. The one day when children let their mothers know they are appreciated, even if they forget to say "thank you" throughout the year.

Right on schedule, a beautiful bouquet of roses, with a vase held by a stuffed Teddy Bear, arrives from Trish. Catherine finds an e-mail from Chico in her computer. Maybe Erin used his address to send a message.

Catherine,

We just went through the toughest stage in our marriage to date. Our commitment to this marriage led us to seek counseling. We each started individually and then went together. For me, the problem lay greatly in the way I was viewing her and her actions: all related to you somehow. When I looked at her, I saw you. Her facial features, hair, clothes, posture all resembled you. It was a constant reminder. Then there were actions: she was decisive without discussion, could not discuss her feelings.

I have sought advice from multiple family members (both families by the way) about how to best confront you regarding many issues.

I accept the check for $1,000 you recently left at the house as additional reimbursement.

This means he's keeping the baby's baptismal check gift Catherine just left there. By additional, he means he is also keeping the one she left previously for Ethan's baptismal gift, as payment towards whatever he considers the full reparations. Catherine is shocked by what she is reading and can barely read on.

Chico continues his attack for ten pages telling Catherine how terrible she is. He numbers accusations 1 thru 25. He accuses her of ruining Erin by keeping her chaste. She needs to loosen up. He goes on further to accuse Catherine of not being sympathetic when Erin lost the first baby.

How can he accuse her of that? Catherine was there every minute of Erin's labor, explaining to Erin what was happening to her during childbirth. Chico had thanked Catherine saying he could not have managed alone. Catherine is exhausted, collapsing into her favorite reading chair. She is not sure how much longer she can endure this fight.

Strange he does not attribute any failures or communication problems to his many affairs or his disrespect for Erin's ideas.

~

Catherine sits in solitude recalling Chico's threat shortly after the wedding. *"I will isolate your daughter from her family. It'll take time, but I'll make sure she divorces herself from all of you. She will not see you, or talk to you. Eventually she will not let you communicate with our children. You will never be a part of our lives or our children's lives. Do whatever you want, take any measures you think might work. Nothing will work. I control her. I give her everything she wants and in exchange she does as she is told. You know she still talks to people about how you refused to buy her a pair of Jordache jeans when she was a teen. With me, I allow her to buy anything she wants. I have a house she lives in that is bigger, nicer, and more expensive than yours. There's no way you can overcome that. No matter what I do she will never leave me and her cushy life.*

"I want you to know that includes her sister Trish. Her life and her husband and their children are worthless. They should never be allowed to interact with my family. My children will excel in everything because they are better than any of yours."

~

Catherine is having difficulty comprehending this whole measure. She knows Erin did not leave when Chico was running around with other women. She did get him to go to counseling, only to find out later that he never went to the appointments. He only wrote a check for the hour so she never knew until much later.

The next time he got caught Erin forced him to leave the house. That did not last long; she probably ran short on funds. He moved back in, sleeping quarters redirected to the den. That ended quickly as he was so sorry! Now, she doesn't look, doesn't want to know. If a wife knows, she would need to do something about it, and that is not a consideration. He travels often for work, though sometimes it is not all work.

As long as he keeps throwing mud at Catherine and money at Erin, convincing her to see things his way, he will have no trouble keeping Erin a safe distance from her mother and her sister.

❄ 33 ❄

T he summer of 2005 is extremely hot. Catherine has another conference to attend but not in Miami, it's in New Orleans. "Frank, is everyone crazy to book a conference there in hurricane season? We had three major ones' last year making landfall in the exact same spot."

Business is always enhanced at this annual marketing event, but Frank is not well and cannot travel. Someone would need to stay with him. Two loving nieces volunteer to do just that. They delight in the thought of staying here on summer break listening to his famous storytelling and are excited to celebrate their twentieth birthday with him.

Catherine leaves on Saturday, August sixth after checking the tropics. They are calm. She returns home in four days, late into the night due to difficult flight connections. Her nieces leave the next day. "Thank you for being here, girls. Thank you! I was relaxed knowing you were here." She wishes they had more time with her, but school is starting.

Eleven days later, the foreboding forecast of disaster comes over the weather station. "Large hurricane has formed in the warm

Bahaman waters and is heading to the US coastline. Everyone in Florida should be preparing." She nervously recalls monster Hurricane Andrew entering the Bahamas, where she lived, thirteen years ago.

Two days later she is calling 911, Frank is unconscious on the couch. Paramedics are there quickly. At the hospital, the doctors tell her to call and assemble family members. Catherine prays and waits, unaware of time passing. It's freezing in the hospital or maybe her blood has stopped pumping. Trish arrives first, having hung up the phone to race directly to the airport, jumping on the first departing plane. Two days later, early morning on Monday, August 29th Frank passes, surrounded by caring family members: his wife, daughters and a granddaughter was also here to help with the newspaper notices, phone calls, and arrangements.

Hurricane Katrina made landfall the same morning. Catherine doesn't know of all the other people, approximately two-thousand, some entire families, who suffer greatly and also pass on this day in New Orleans. Her children are keeping all news media, television and radio broadcasts, from her while she grieves.

A week later they tell her of the horrific event. She is disoriented by the news. "Why weren't they evacuated? Where was help? Where were the government agencies and the charities? How could so many people be left helpless?"

The more she hears on the news the more depressed she becomes. "I was just there, standing by myself, on the dock looking over the calm blue waters of the Gulf of Mexico, so peaceful. Boats of every description and size, rocking in mesmerizing cadence. Sailboats waltzing beside the boardwalk. I can't believe all that is gone. I had taken the little bus to view the different neighborhoods. Those quaint old areas—wiped out? All those people displaced? So many perished."

Catherine is still depressed when her sister, the nieces' mother, arrives to help her. She brings her eldest daughter and young grandchildren. They are a welcome distraction, an overall relief.

The sisters are reminiscing happier times leafing through a photo album. They come across the couple's last trip to Manhattan. "I remember when Frank and I visited New York two weeks before 911. He mentioned how lucky we were, saying none of us know how long we have. Now, my near escape from Hurricane Katrina. Yes, you never know."

The following week Erin calls, "I'd like to come and visit with Ethan and Anna. I think they can help you relax, and you'll enjoy them. My friend Anna will also visit with her little son."

Grateful that Chico isn't on the list of visitors she replies, "That would be great, Erin." They all love playing in the pool and riding in the little boats. Catherine is beginning to smile again; little children do that for her.

It's holiday time. Catherine is grateful that Erin and the grandkids come to her home for a few days before Thanksgiving. It has been a mind-disturbing three months of disasters. She takes them for a lovely boat experience on the Loxahatchee River stopping at Trapper John's and a big climb to the lookout point in the park.

Of course, a day later they leave to meet Chico at Marie's house for Thanksgiving Day dinner. Before leaving Erin asks, "Mother why don't you come to our home for Christmas this year? It's your first year alone, and it'll do you good to be with us and the kids."

Christmas! Catherine is surprised by the first invite in five years. Although they agreed to alternate, Marie and Hernan were invited every year, Catherine was not. This year will, at least, be a comforting Christmas, being with the children. They will fill a part of the hole in her heart.

She loves them more than life. Catherine is envisioning the excitement when the children see their gifts. A beautiful full size one of a kind collection doll, ordering a special designed case. The doll is larger than Anna. Ethan will be thrilled to get this professional camera. Catherine had taken him on a photoshoot. Upon returning he spent hours with Catherine at the Photoshop program. He loved it. Now he will have his own real camera.

Arriving at Erin's house she finds Marie is there. Catherine is sick. She addresses Erin, "I thought you invited *me* this year."

"Yes, we did. We also invited Marie and Hernan."

"Why is that, when we agreed to alternate years?"

Chico chimes in, "I'm not going to tell my parents not to come just to satisfy you."

Catherine is irate. "This alternating-years formula was not my idea, so don't try to push it on me. I only agreed to it, you suggested it. I've had a very rough time the last few months, I don't need this aggravation. I was envisioning a lovely holiday. This is torture—an appropriate ending to this year." She stays the night in Anna's room. She has no choice as she cannot drive in the dark. The next day, Christmas, she departs for Trish's home, an hour away.

January is Catherine and Frank's anniversary, a difficult day since he's gone. Trish sends a lovely basket of goodies. Not even a call from Erin.

Mid-summer, she visits New York; it's one year after Frank's death. She has invited all her family with their spouses and children for the memorial service. His brother hosts a lovely luncheon following the services. Chico stands and begins an endearing tribute to Frank — this same person who has caused so much pain in Catherine's family.

Ethan is six, now entering kindergarten. He has been attending preschool not far from home, yet so excited to be in real school now. Erin drops him and her daughter off. Thankfully the school offers day care. She is expecting her in-laws from Miami to visit today. She instructs Marie, "Go to the house. I'll pick up the kids after work. It may be a little late, don't worry."

Late in the day, Erin arrives at the school. "I'm here to pick up Ethan and Anna."

The clerk leaves and shortly returns quite disturbed, "Erin, they aren't here."

Erin's beside herself. "What do you mean? Where are they? Get the woman in charge out here, now," she screams.

The supervisor appears explaining, "They aren't here, Erin. Someone picked them up earlier."

"Who signed them out? Let me look at that sheet."

"I can't see that anyone signed them out."

Erin is nearing hysteria, dialing the police, when a teacher comes to the front office. "Erin, I was here when the children left. The woman said she was their grandmother."

Erin cannot believe what she is hearing. "Do you mean someone proclaims to be a relative and you give the children to her? I thought there was a sign out system here, and only those whose names *I* have placed can pick up the children. *Isn't that right?*"

"Yes, that's right, but she seemed so genuine." The teacher is now close to tears.

Erin dials Marie. "Marie, do you have Anna and Ethan?"

"Yes, Erin. They are at the house with us."

Erin addresses the teacher, "Do you realize what happened here? My near breakdown? And what could've happened if the woman was lying and took my children? You had no idea to whom you were giving my children."

Erin returns to the phone call, verbally attacking Marie. "How dare you pick up my children when I specifically told you not to and that I'd pick them up later."

"Well, I wanted to spend some alone time with Anna, and Hernan could visit with Ethan. We did not want to miss any time with them. You understand."

"No, I don't. We'll discuss it when I get there."

~

Erin rushes home and enters the house, still shaking with anxiety. "You nearly gave me a breakdown. You went against my instructions for my family. How dare you? And how safe were they riding with you? Did you have a baby carrier or a child's safety seat in the car?"

"No, but we were not going very far."

"That doesn't matter. Just one block, and my children must be secure. Last time you came you got lost. I had to come find you. How could you be sure that wouldn't happen again? And with my family in the car with you?"

"In that case, we are leaving. If that's how you feel, we are leaving." As Marie struts toward the door Chico enters.

"What's going on here?" he asks as he views his mother's tears.

"What did you do, Erin, to make my mother cry?"

"What did I do? Let me tell you what your mother did, and how she disobeyed my instructions."

"Since when are you giving orders to my mother?"

As he hears the tale, he convinces Erin it was a misunderstanding and his mother had good intentions to spend time with her grandchildren.

As Marie is leaving, she mutters, "I forgot what you told me, Erin. I just wanted to see the kids."

❧ 34 ❧

M arie awakens to an early morning phone call from Havana. It's her old friend, Manuel. "Marie, I have some very unpleasant news for you. This is very difficult for me. I am so sorry."

"Stop, Manuel. Just tell me what it is. Get it over with."

"Marie, your mother, our priestess, has passed away this early morning." She hears his anguish. There is a long silence.

"I'll phone you back." Marie has not expected this. Although elderly, her mother has always been well. She has to think of what to do now. Thoughts and ideas are whirling in her head. Eventually she calls Manuel. "I'll be there as soon as possible. Please get everything ready at the funeral home. We will need a few days there for everyone to have a visitation with her. Priestess Martina was beloved by all. I'll prepare the Itutu Ceremony. Make sure no one touches her for three hours. Then, have her taken to the funeral parlor and get a few ladies to go into our home and set the altar. We will hold the memorial service there."

"Yes, Marie. Will you conduct the service yourself?"

"Of course, who else could do this? We have no other elder to determine the final disposition of her Orichas."

Marie reserves a private plane, a pilot she has worked with in the past.

"Marie, I have a flight confirmed to depart early afternoon. How many passengers?"

"Just two."

She hurries to Luciana's house to relay the sad news.

Luciana is sobbing, barely able to speak. "Oh no, Marie, Mother cannot be gone. I am not ready for this. What will we do? How will we cope? Are you alright?"

"Luciana, we will be on a plane this afternoon. I have had time to consider this day and to prepare. Manuel is making some preparations, but we must hurry. I will pick you up at noon. Be ready."

Arriving at the Miami airport, Marie is glad they had booked a car service, as the traffic is a nightmare. They enter the check-in area of the building and proceed to their boarding location. The two women pace up and down, unable to be still. Waiting seems endless. Suddenly a familiar voice says, "Mother." Marie turns to see Chico. "I couldn't let you go by yourself. Good morning, Aunt Luciana. Since I'm your successor, I must learn everything about the ceremonies. I'm coming with you."

Marie cringes a bit, but knows it's not the time to mention the new female in the family, baby Anna. She knows her son's self-centeredness prevents him from envisioning a new little baby ever taking his place.

"Alright, Chico, but stay close and do as I instruct."

They stand ready to board when a second familiar voice sends a chill down Marie's spine.

"Good morning, my dear. Venturing home for a visit?"

"No, family business actually. And what possible further business could you have in Cuba, Gino?"

His laugh sets her nerves on edge. "You show me yours; I'll show you mine—like old times, huh?"

"You first, Gino."

"Very well. While you were stuck in Atlanta, and then buried in nonsense in South Florida, I have continued to come back and forth, working with new people."

"What kind of work could you possibly be doing? Certainly, you are not moving money."

"You'd be surprised what dealings are available."

"My mother, the Santeria Priestess of Havana—"

Gino interrupts Marie, "I remember her well, my dear. Go on."

"She passed away this morning. We are on our way to the funeral."

"We? Who are we?"

Marie turns revealing her sister behind her. "You remember Luciana?"

"I certainly do." He grins as he eyes her top to bottom.

"And you never met my son, Chico."

"Very happy to meet you, young man. If you're going to be in Havana a few days, perhaps I could show you some popular man sights, and few of the old-time hangouts your mother and I enjoyed. Take my number; here's my card. Family business comes first, so call when you have free time. I'll teach you all about Cuba!"

As they board the small commuter plane, Marie grabs her son to sit next to her. She intends to keep an eye on this one, making sure he has no free time. Gino sits next to Marie's sister.

"Luciana, surely you remember me from the casino."

"I remember a great deal about you, Gino. I'd rather not talk now. Please leave me to my grief."

The short flight is smooth with a nice landing. The airport hasn't changed much, dingy as ever. Upon their arrival, Gino tells

Marie's family, "Follow me, I have a car that always meets me. Ride with me to the hotel. I assume you are at the Nacional."

"We are not," exclaims Marie with a sound of arrogance. "We are staying at our house and we have arranged our own car."

"Okay, fine. I'll be seeing you, I'm sure. Chico, you give me a call, and we'll see some interesting places. You'll hear some fun in-the-old-days stories too."

The family heads out of the airport with Manuel at the wheel, hoping to find everything intact at the house. Marie needs to begin preparations for the Itutu Ceremony, a private ceremony only for a Santeria priest or priestess, conducted by a higher authority.

First, the funeral parlor. She observes her brother Julio standing in the doorway, head bowed. Instantly she is reminded of the saddest moment that surrounded them, the day her brother Juan was killed, forty-six years ago. It should have been a celebratory day with Marie beginning her Santeria priestess studies. Rather it brought sadness; it became a solemn funeral as her brother was killed.

Julio has remained in Havana all these years to help his mother.

The parlor is dimly lit illuminating the dust, extremely depress-ing. The musty smell mixed with the sweetness of flowers is nause-ating. Marie begins by casting the cowrie shells, calling upon Martina's Orisha. She needs to know her wishes for the disposition of her mother's ritual implements and materials. The gods respond, "Martina wishes you, her daughter, to have her religious items, knowing you will honor them."

This evening will begin viewing and visitation by friends, family, and congregation members. Hordes will be arriving to pay last respects. It is dark and steamy as Marie leaves to go to the family home and prepare. As she steps into the foreboding darkness of the early winter night, she sees a line of mourners already down the street and around the corner.

Julio observes for three days as mourners file past Martina's casket. They still seek her blessing and guidance. What will they do? Who will they go to? Surely Marie will go back to Miami.

Martina is moved to the altar at her home, next to the Tree of Life. The Itutu Ceremony will be conducted here. A private ceremony, normally the godfather or godmother would handle arrangements for the Orichas, but at Martina's age there is no one, only her daughter.

Marie cleanses her mother's body and dresses Martina in the clothing worn at her ordination. She gathers the scissors and comb, along with the hair that had been cut from her mother when Martina became a priestess and used during the ordination ritual. She places these items on the icy cold coffin's frame. Marie is assuring Martina tranquility and rest. Thus, she will not return to torment family or friends. Luciana helps her set up the White Table and prepare for nine nights of prayer with the family in vigilance.

On the fourth day Marie begins preparation of the sacrificial offering. She gathers corn, leaves and herbs. Family members assemble at their chapel as Marie begins her sacrifice. Julio brings her a large chicken and places it on the altar. She begins chanting, calling the Oricha to join in the celebration. They are singing the praises of Martina's long one-hundred-and-one-year life.

Marie gathers the chicken, leading the congregation to the Tree of Life. Laying the fowl on the altar's cutting board. Holding it flat and still, in a fell swoop, she chops off the bird's head. Chanting loudly and madly, she drops it to the floor and crushes it under her foot. Swinging the fowl while chanting, splattering blood throughout the space she pauses to drop the head into a jar. Luciana gathers the body to be cooked and served in celebration the next day to the family members.

The following morning produces a muddy depressing sky with

no sun or clouds, appearing as the grayness of death. The family prepares for the funeral mass. Julio carries the items of the sacrifice while he leads the group, past the Tree of Life, into the cemetery. There is a large hole dug next to Juan's burial site. As the candles flicker a golden glow, Julio places all the items he is carrying at the head of the grave.

Marie chants, "This body is placed in the earth, symbolizing the body's nurturing of the earth, as it has nurtured our bodies. We release her to the gods that they may guide her soul into the world of the spirits. May her spirit be always with us and redirected back to earth in another form, perhaps in a family member who is born after we have departed from this earth." They continue with songs and hymns to the Orichas, praising Oya, god of the cemetery. They culminate with a family meal of the chicken and assorted vegetables.

Chico is assisting at every turn as Marie constantly reminds him. He must. "You wanted to come to learn everything."

It's been six days since they left Miami. Chico collapses on the lounge chair. Hours later Marie is shaking him awake. "Mother, I can't even think right now. Even my brain is exhausted. I need a release, an outlet."

He remembers Gino has given him a phone number with an offer to show him Cuba. He picks up the phone, seeking a diversion.

"Hello, Gino. It's Chico calling to take you up on that offer to see the real Cuba."

"Great, Chico, come by the Hotel Nacional. Join me for lunch."

As Chico approaches the hotel he is in awe, the old building has maintained her beauty and stature as evidenced comparing old photos. Approaching the desk clerk, he asks, "Morning, I'm Chico, here to see Gino. Can you direct me to the pool?"

"Yes sir, Mr. Gino is waiting there for you, poolside at the café."

Chico is astonished that the elderly desk clerk would know who he is and why he was there. He enters the cheerful café. The scents are enticing.

"Good afternoon, Gino. Thank you for the offer to show me the sights, especially the old historic hangouts."

"Happy to do so. You should know your family and its heritage."

"I'm surprised I haven't met you before, you being my mother's friend all these years."

"Your mother and I were close years ago and lost touch until recently."

"The desk clerk seemed to know who I was and why I was here. I find that more than a bit strange."

"You'll encounter a few strange things today. I'll try to help you understand. The clerk is easy to explain. He knows every face that has passed here in the last fifty years; that includes your mother and aunt. Times were different then."

"Why would my mother and aunt be here at the hotel?"

❀ 3 5 ❀

"Sit awhile, have some café. Your mother and aunt were here often conducting business."

"What kind of business?"

"Moving money, sharing or selling secrets, circulating warnings of danger, war secrets, evacuating children, and even personal business."

"I know money was moving out when Castro moved in and secrets were for sale, especially at the time of the Bay of Pigs. I guess personal business is conducted at every hotel. How would those things pertain to my mother and aunt?"

"Well, your mother needed money moved for the family. And she needed help in Cuba moving the children during the Pedro Pan lift. I provided help on those two matters along with Father McCarthy. We coordinated all the efforts and movements in Cuba and the US. Your mother even stayed with my sister. She resents that now. Doesn't like admitting she needs help on anything."

"And Aunt Luciana?"

"Everyone shared secrets, real or not. Your aunt knew a lot of inside information that could have helped save this country from

Communism. She also had an American friend helping her. His name was Tom. Do you know him?"

"No, should I? I find it fascinating that my mother was moving money and my aunt was involved in all that intrigue. It sounds like they were secret spies. How did you and mother get the money out? Were they involved in the Bay of Pigs invasion? Did Aunt Luciana sell secrets? Were they traitors?"

"Why don't we visit some of those old haunts? I'll tell you stories as we go. Let's make our first stop in a nice laid back little jazz club called Guarida de Satanas which means Satan's Lair. Your mother and aunt frequented the place. Sometimes with me and once that I know of with Tom."

"That's the second time you mentioned him. Tell me why."

"It was a secret, but a few of us knew, or suspected, he worked for the CIA. He was also heavily associated with the casino groups. He was often with your aunt, seeking information. Luciana thought Tom perceived her to be the evil sister and your mother the good." Gino continues, chuckling, "Assumptions sometimes made by innovative means."

"What exactly does that mean?"

"Ask your mother. Let's get to the club and see who's playing."

The funeral over, the group rides to the airport in unspoken agreement they will meet here this time next year to finalize the ceremony. They discuss the rituals and changes that have taken place.

A sprinkle of rain begins, seeming to form a musical arrangement on the car. No one notices. As they enter the airport Luciana wonders aloud, "What will become of our church, our ceremonies and our congregation here in Cuba now that Mother is gone?"

"Although Mother has been healthy, I considered this situation over the past few years as she grew older, facing the inevitable. I have been in contact with one of our local priests. He worked diligently with us and Monsignor to get our children safely relocated in Miami. He has already offered to do whatever is necessary."

Chico chimes in boasting, "Well it appears we'll now have a Santeria priest replacing the priestess in our home here in Havana *and* in Miami. Namely, me!"

Marie is choking on her emotions with the stress of her mother death, and now Chico's expectations. An overwhelming flood of anger and sentiment—not normal for the priestess with ice in her veins—washes over her.

"You are an embarrassment and should be ashamed. The last day when you were missing would have been one of the most important in your training.

"Our new priest in Havana had just completed his initiation, enabling him to take over for your grandmother. He now begins his *iyaboraje*. You may recall this means he cannot perform any cleansings or healings for a year. He will wear all white during this time and avoid physical contact with those who have not been initiated. When we return next year for Martina, we will also host his end of year ceremony, giving him total Santeria priest privileges and power. How could you not be available for this?"

She knows this won't be a smooth transition. She also realizes that as she gets older, she may not have the time necessary to train the new little one to replace her as Santeria priestess. She may be forced to recognize Chico as the Santeria priest, another stress.

A smooth flight lands the group in Miami amid glaring star-shaped lights. They exit the airport enveloped in vapors of steam as Marie addresses Chico, "You were not at the house the last day. You wanted to come to learn and then you disappear for two days? Where were you? We could have used your help."

"I went to dinner with Gino."

"Where did you go?"

"A place called Satan's Lair. Do you know it?"

"Don't concern yourself. I will speak to Gino." She cannot explain to him.

Chico's phone is beeping incessantly as he is trying to deplane and collect baggage. It's Erin! He answers, ready with his excuse, although he has returned early from his proposed business trip. He had told her ten days, and he's back in nine.

"Why are you not picking up? I have been calling repeatedly for three days."

"Well, you know I'm working, not a lot of spare time. You enjoy the money it brings in."

"That has nothing to do with not taking a mere minute to phone me."

"Okay, what is so damn important?"

"I'm in South Florida. My mother had an attack and was in the hospital."

"I'll get a plane to Miami right now."

"Don't bother I'm on my way home. They released her today."

Christmas day blows in on an icy wind yet Marie demands they all attend her church in the lovely outdoors the lord created. Erin agrees knowing she'll go to Mass after this ceremony. Strong emotions flood some in the group as they approach the park on Little Kennesaw Mountain. Every member is accompanied by flashes of memory from 1965 on this mountain top where many Santeria ceremonies were performed, including Chico's conception. Peggy Sue and Charlie Johnson, the Caluda family's US sponsor, are here. They also remember that demoralizing night and are still disturbed coming here. Today Marie is wearing the beaded necklace of her guardian angel, Ayao, a fierce warrior who lives in the tornado.

They enter the open area where normally a pleasant breeze whispers through the tall grasses. Today Jack Frost brings icicles up and over the incline, cutting through their skin. Glancing over the west edge, downhill into the valley far below, they have come to feel safe here. The treetops below are barren today, their limbs reaching upward, appearing as ghosts reaching for the heavens.

Marie addresses the congregation, directing their offering today to the ancestors. As the ceremony progresses emotions rise and fall with the drum beat. Chanting mesmerizes the group into a trance. The heighten sensitivity establishes Marie's control. Her dancing and swaying lead her to the grandchildren, Ethan and Anna. Taking their little hands, she leads them to the altar. Reverently she calls upon the dead. "Great-aunt, Carlota, the rebel, who is reincarnated in my son Chico, join his children this day."

The Santeria priestess believes that the dead can intervene in people's lives by providing them with protection or rather pestering them.

She hands a vegetable basket to Ethan and a fruit basket to Anna. Through Marie's ranting and singing Erin is trying to hear and comprehend. It sounds like; "Receive the initiation of the warriors. Saints, descend upon us."

Following the ceremony, Erin questions Marie.

"I assure you, Erin, you must have misunderstood. I simply want them to become as familiar with their father's church as they have with their mother's."

A few months later, Catherine is planning a birthday gift for Erin, who is turning thirty-eight. Being deeply involved in the arts, Catherine is always finding that just right, something special. This time it is a statue of a mother with outstretched arms protecting her two children.

Chico arrives home and sees the statue. He starts criticizing. "Your mother is always against me, always trying to remove me from you and the kids. Here is a statue with only the mother and children, no father involved, right?"

"Chico, it's for my birthday, not an anniversary or Christmas. It's my gift picturing me and my children. What's wrong with that?"

"Like I said your mother wants me out of the picture. This is her way of removing me from the equation." Erin stops responding, she knows not to argue a point with him. The statue is beautiful, a carved stone artistic endeavor. She treasures it.

❧ 36 ❧

I t's October and the heat is barely tolerable. Answering the phone, Chico hears Marie say, "You need to be in Miami Airport at nine on Saturday morning. Our flight to Havana departs at eleven. Don't be late."

He responds, "Mother it's going to be much hotter there than last time. I wish we could wait for cooler weather."

"You know this service must be done exactly one year later. Be there, you will have much to learn if you want to become a priest. You'll be happy to know Juan will be with us on this visit. You two can keep each other company and out of trouble."

The waiting year had passed before anyone realized the time. The family is once again off to Havana to finalize the ritual for Santeria Priestess Martina. The flight is smooth as silk. For Chico, it feels like the magic carpet ride, he's not in control. It's taking him somewhere he does not want to be.

Upon arrival, Marie and Luciana meet with the new high priest. He has been working with the Babalawo for the past year and is ready to fully assume Martina's position with the congregation.

Today Marie will host his end of the year ceremony with music and feasting.

Luciana accompanies the family, but informs her sister, "Marie, I remember your year end. It was not very pleasant for me. If you don't mind, I am not going to participate." Marie understands; it was a torturous ordeal for Luciana to come to terms with.

The following afternoon everyone gathers on the veranda at the family home, discussing their past life here and the future they face without Martina. This evening they fast.

Morning breaks. The sunrise is just peaking over the horizon draping the ile' in gold. They proceed to the shrine. Marie feels the ancestors' presence as she enters. She observes a group of elder members in a circle surrounding the altar awaiting the family's arrival. The final ceremony begins.

The waiting year has passed and now the family prepares. The final ceremony begins, a sacred ritual known as *levantamiento del plato* 'the raising of the dish.'

A goat is brought forth to sacrifice, commemorating the deceased soul and offered to Oya. Chico is chosen to make the offering. He approaches the altar ax in hand, places the dumb animal beside the altar, head resting on the blood-stained stone top. Bembe drums beating and hearts pound as the ax is seen rising above the altar. In one quick decisive motion, the head rolls from the altar staining the green grass red. Quickly, the blood is captured in a bowl and slowly disappears as the deceased devours it. A dish is broken, symbolizing the deceased is now departed.

The Bembe drums continue their pulsating beat and the festival begins. In honor of the deceased, they escort the soul.

A few begin to dance and are mounted by the spirits of the deceased Orisha. Luciana is looking on, remembering when she was mounted at Marie's year end Santeria Ceremony.

Martina can now rest in peace.

~

Chico is confident moving about the Havana night life on his own. Gino had shown him the hot spots last year, and he is ready to party. He remembers the first place they visited was Satan's Lair. It was by far the most interesting. He will start there. "Juan, would you like to come with me this evening to explore the exciting spots in Havana?"

As he leaves, he hears Marie yell to him. "Chico, be back early. Tomorrow we have people to see and must get everything done before we depart the next day."

"I'll be back in plenty of time for tomorrow's commitments."

The next morning Marie awakens and calls for Chico to be up, dressed, and at breakfast in thirty minutes. He does not appear. She is furious assuming he is sleeping off a party hangover. She knocks at his room; no answer. She flings open the door; no one is there. Furious, Marie calls for Juan. No answer.

She is ready to disown the two of them. How could Chico involve his little brother in his schemes? He is supposed to be here learning. But she starts out alone. Her first stop is the new Santero. He invites her into his home steering her to the formal parlor. The scent of roses fills the tiny room. His wife brings coffee and little cakes, setting the silver tray on the antique coffee table. Their discussion is light and friendly as Marie is comfortable in his abilities to lead the religion.

Before taking her leave, Marie addresses the Santeria priest, "I congratulate you on completing the religious studies and training. You are now ready to take charge of the congregation. My mother would be so pleased. Is there anything I can answer for you? Do you feel totally competent in your position at this point?"

"Thank you, Marie, I feel comfortable and ready to take over now that my waiting period is completed. Thank you for hosting my end-of-the-year ceremony, the musical ceremonies, especially the Bata Drums, and the prayers. I am anxious to begin my duties, serving our congregation. I have already been asked to consult a few suffering clients, perform some cleansings, and initiations. The Lucumi religion will flourish, I assure you."

~

Arriving back at the family home, errands accomplished, Marie is greeted by her brother. "Chico is here and asked me to calm you if you are upset with him."

"Now, why would he think that?" She enters and walks through to the veranda to find Chico having an early dinner. "Chico, my mother and I spent countless hours here overlooking the garden, enjoying the scents brought by the breezes. Most of what I learned was done right here. Aside from my education at the house temple, the chapel, with my godfather and elders, my mother spent hours here with me answering my many questions. I can tell you are not interested. You do not take this seriously. You think you can just walk away with a Priest title because of your family. No. You will begin now to study seriously or you will be replaced."

"Really, Mother? Who could replace me?"

"Perhaps your daughter would be a regal Santeria priestess"—Marie pauses for effect— "like her grandmother."

"My wife would never allow that."

"Really, does she know about you? About me? About our religion? Perhaps she needs some in-depth knowledge. Do you have such little control?"

Chico is furious, but he knows his mother is right. He has no way out. "Mother I did not want to do this, but it seems I must tell you why I was not with you today. You went to see the new Santeria priest, right? Obviously, you would be discussing death and the ceremonial rituals that go with it. I don't want to spend my time like that."

"Like what?"

"Discussing mundane procedures and ceremonies. I like things more exciting more celebratory, more fun."

"Perhaps you fear the dead."

Silence follows. Chico does not like the unexpected, and that includes the dead.

"Let me tell you. The dead should be respected not feared."

"I do not like the fact that Great-aunt, Carlota, la rebelde, is reincarnated within me."

"That can only help and protect you and guide you in life's right direction."

"But I still have a dead person connected to my body. That's awful."

"They aren't ghosts; they're invisible companions who help us, and only intercede on our behalf with problems and malicious casualties. Like the spiritual bath, remember?"

"How could I ever forget?"

"I know what I must do now," Marie mutters under her breath.

Morning does not bring sunlight to the island or to the family. Chico is searching his mind for a way out of this dilemma. He wants to run this church. But...

The day is dismal. All four depart the house carrying open dark umbrellas to the taxi, appearing like a slow parade of mushrooms.

The airport is depressing with its repulsive smell. An announcement comes across the sound system. "Boarding is delayed due to storms in the area."

"In the area?" questions Luciana. "The storms are right here."

Finally, they depart. "In just over an hour and we will be landing in Miami. I'm glad to be going back, but I will miss Cuba." Marie turns to her son. "Chico, come and spend a few days with me to talk things through."

Tilting his head back as he heads to the counter he says, "No, I need to get home to my family."

❧ 37 ❧

It's May before Marie visits again. This time it's a religious event. Chico's family arrives early in the week for Ethan's first communion. Marie has insisted that a Santeria service be performed before the Catholic ceremony.

"Erin, dear, you do not need to attend the service if you prefer not to join us. I know you are not a big advocate of the Santeria religion." Marie is smiles pleasantly as she speaks.

"I plan to attend anything involving my children," Erin replies.

The afternoon is heating up, but the breeze billowing over the cliff is comforting. May brings the most tepid temperature. Not even the arrival of Marie could upset such a beautiful day.

Marie addresses a number of children, all appearing to be about Ethan's age. A young boy approaches the altar carrying a small cat.

Marie invites all the children to join her on the altar. She begins the chanting. Erin is surprised to see each child ascending the altar with a small animal. *This must be a ceremony similar to our blessing of the animals that we do in October.*

Marie begins a chant. Soon the congregation joins in. The drums begin and the people begin to sway with the rhythm. Erin is relaxed and enjoying the moment. Chico joins his mother on the altar. The young boy delivers the cat to them. They begin a new chant. Suddenly shock waves pierce Erin, Ethan, and Anna's ears, as the cat screams like a human baby. With no forewarning, its stomach is slashed, head removed and blood smeared all over the altar table.

Erin and the children begin to cry. She attempts to reach the altar to save the other animals, thinking they will meet the same fate. Stumbling, she bruises her knee and cannot get up.

When Chico reaches her, she pushes him aside with a look of shock and disdain. "How could you do such a terrible thing? Kill that little cat, and with our children watching."

"It is no different than animal offerings and killings in other religions, Erin. The young boy is blessed to have his pet chosen for the sacred ceremony. His offering was chosen by the gods."

"His offering was chosen by you and your mother, not any gods." She does not know how to respond to such insanity.

The drums' rhythm and the continual chanting by the congregational members add a desperate madness to the moment. The lunacy of the multitude has created a mob mentality. Erin must get herself and the children off this mountain. She grabs their hands, and they run down the hillside. The crowd still succumbing to the music and the chanting has a delayed reaction, allowing Erin to easily reach her children and escape in the car.

Finally standing up to abuse, she bans Chico from the house and spends the next few days trying to understand this madness and how this will affect her children, her family. She investigates the Santeria religion, gathering as much information as she can. Unfortunately, there is not much available. She has some decisions to make. Chico assures her, given he will be the next Santeria priest his children will not see this again.

Little Ethan is so young and does not understand. How will he deal with this? How will it affect him?

~

Catherine arrives for the Communion, staying at Trish's home. They meet Erin at the church just in time for the sacrament. She immediately feels a tension. Even the children are quiet and withdrawn. "Let's walk over to the church hall and see what they have cooked for breakfast. Follow me."

Catherine perceives a severe strain. Something of mammoth proportions has occurred and everyone is remaining silent. It must be a terrible event not being divulged.

~

After days of this morbid atmosphere, she questions Erin. "It's a problem with Chico's parents' religion, she tells her mother."

"What is their religion? I thought they were Catholic."

"Well, in a manner of speaking. That is what they profess, but not all they practice."

"What do you mean?"

"They are Santeria. Not only are they members and believers, but Marie is a Santeria priestess."

"Oh, my God! Erin, what are you going to do? Do you know all the practices of their faith? They believe in gods but disguise them by calling them saints. They kill animals; they abuse children, all in the name of this religion."

"How do you know so much about this?"

"Well, first, I live in South Florida where the religion is prevalent among the Cubans. Also, I have friends in CSI who teach these horrible faith practices to the police departments. It allows informed officers to go into a situation and determine if it's a crime scene or evidence of a Santeria ceremony."

"Mother, are you saying that the police would not be able to ascertain a crime scene?"

"Some of these Santeria practices are so bloody and violent, it can be difficult to determine."

"Tell me what investigators look for."

Catherine is nervous trying to explain some of their beliefs. "Well, I am not a trained expert, but some things are obvious like small animals with knife wounds. They really like using cats. So, if an animal is found deceased, they are able to determine if it was sick, or tortured, killed, and used in a Santeria ceremony."

"This is mortifying to learn. What other things can give clues?"

"They are trained to go into a family home or a school; they may report a suspected incident with a child."

"Like what? Are children suffering?" Now that Erin knows about the small animals, first hand, she desperately needs to know about children.

"They can be. There are religious ceremonies where children are cut. Sometimes severely. Rarely, but sometimes, causing death."

Death. Oh my God. I must protect my children. Do I leave Chico? Can I force him to give up this religion? And can I trust his word. That has not always been true in the past.

"What can I do?" Erin asks as she paces and wrings her hands.

"I cannot advise you. I know what I would do, but at the very least you need to be aware and diligent in your observations. It is not enough that Chico's parents need to be watched whenever they visit, but if Chico is also involved in this religion it could be disastrous. It could mean your children's lives."

Erin already knows that Chico is involved. Heavily involved. She needs to make some decisions.

❧ 38 ❧

When summer heats up, Catherine decides to escape Florida and visit Trish in Atlanta. It's not too much cooler, but they can sit in the pool and chat. It'll be enjoyable. Trish is glad to hear of her mother's plans and calls Erin to come and join them. Catherine arrives first. Erin saunters in about lunch time.

Trish questions her sister, "Where's Chico? I thought he'd come too."

Catherine jumps in before Erin can answer. "They're separated, Trish. I thought you'd know that."

Erin's in shock that Catherine would have this information. She hadn't told anyone in the family. "How did you know?"

"A little bird."

"Trish told you, right?"

"How could I tell her? I didn't know it myself."

Catherine asks, "Did you find him running around and cheating again? I don't know why you didn't leave when this started. When children were not yet involved."

Anger and resentment are building within Erin. She is

extremely defensive, but everyone knows the truth of his philandering.

They don't know the truth of his religious involvement.

"Only I know," Erin tells herself. Has she forgotten; Ethan knows?

~

After months of his undergoing treatment with a psychologist, Erin allows Chico back in the house. She's assured he has learned to be a family unit, to ignore his mother's requests, and give up these crazy religious practices.

~

It's Halloween time. The time of year when Catherine visits her cousin's home in the mountains, photographing the autumn colors, the deer and the bears. She enjoys coming to visit and relaxing. It's so different than Florida, and her cousin is a great hostess and cook. The next week she leaves for Atlanta to help the grandchildren decorate the house. She's excited they've invited her.

Catherine leaves for Atlanta to help the grandchildren decorate the house. She's excited they've invited her.

"Grandma, look at all this fluffy white web. You can help stretch and wrap the stair railings." Ethan is so excited to be with his grandmother today. He loves Halloween.

"Are we going to carve a pumpkin?" She wonders aloud.

"We don't carve pumpkins, we paint them," Anna declares, so excited to be informing Grandma. "Do you want to go trick or treating or stay home and answer the door?"

"Well, my lovely granddaughter, first choice is to be with you wherever that is."

Anna giggles at that answer, happy and smiling. She instructs Grandma we'll go trick or treating.

Ethan jumps in, "I'll be there with you. Are you afraid, Grandma?"

"Afraid of what?

"Ghosts and goblins?"

"No, they're not real you know."

"I know, but there are bad scary people who are real."

"That's true, but I don't expect we'll encounter any."

Everyone is excited as they start out on their adventure. The two children are giggle and laugh hello to friends they recognize. They start toward home, excited to view their loot. Turning a corner, they happen upon a young boy standing all alone crying.

Catherine calls to him, "Are you okay? Are you lost? Are you hurt? Do you need help?"

When he does not respond, Catherine starts toward him to see if he is injured. He screams, "Don't come near me."

Catherine backs away and tries to soothe him. "Tell me your name." No answer. "Tell me your phone number, and I'll call your mom to come here."

Through his tears and choking he yells the number to her. Catherine dials. "Hello, I am calling this number because I found your son standing on a corner crying."

Before she can continue the woman starts to shriek, "Thank God, thank God. We've been out of our minds with worry. Where are you? We'll come immediately." Catherine walks to the edge of the corner to read the street sign to the mom.

"We've been riding in the golf cart looking for him. We're only two minutes away."

"That's good, because we can't approach him. He's too frightened."

As the golf cart pulls up mom and son are both crying as they leap into each other's arms. Ethan is moved by the ordeal and addresses Catherine. "Grandma, he was really very scared wasn't he?"

"Sure, he was. He was lost and didn't know how to get home.

He had no one he knew to protect him. Not knowing us, he thought we might hurt him. So, yes, he was very scared. That's hard to imagine for someone like you who's never been scared."

"Sometimes I'm scared, you know. Sometimes, like if I think someone is going to cut off my head."

"Ethan, you have quite an imagination!"

"Grandma, would you always help and protect me and make sure I'm safe?"

"Of course, I would, Ethan. I love you very much and would never let someone hurt you. If you are ever scared, you let me know."

Arriving home with their goodies, Ethan sits next to Grandma and wraps his arms around her neck. "Please stay overnight with us. We could make some popcorn. Mom and Dad are going to a party so it would just be us three. We could tell stories." Catherine is grateful for the opportunity and readily agrees.

Grandma, Ethan, and Anna gather in the den, and Ethan chooses Catherine to tell the first story. She tells a story of her childhood, how things were when she grew up. He then chooses Anna to tell a story. At five and a half, her story is similar to the three bears. She's never heard of plagiarism.

"Now, Ethan, it is your turn. Tell us a story."

Ethan tells the story of the boy and the little kitten. Catherine is impressed with his story telling ability. "My Ethan, that is an amazing story, you have a remarkable imagination. How can you think up such a scary event?"

"I didn't make it up, Grandma. It's a true story."

"Now Ethan, making up stories is good, and everyone tries to make them seem real, even the scary ones. But we must be honest about what is true and what is made-up."

"Honest, Grandma, it's true. You can ask Mom. She saw it with me."

Anna's now afraid to go to bed. "That's okay, Grandma, I'll get her to sleep. I'm not afraid. Do you know why? Because when I asked you if you'd always help and protect me and make sure I'm safe, you said, 'Of course I would, Ethan. I love you very much and would never let someone hurt you. If you are ever scared, you just let me know.'"

When Erin and Chico arrive home Catherine addresses the issue, telling them the story Ethan had just related.

Erin knows it's futile to deny it and explains to Catherine. "This occurred six months ago and Chico has undergone treatment for all these months. He is fine now."

"And has Ethan gotten any help? He must be traumatized." Catherine is absorbing this story and doubting every bit of it. She knows Chico better than her daughter does. How can Erin be such a fool to believe this? She must find a way to protect her daughter and grandchildren. She promised Ethan but is perplexed on how to accomplish this. She can't move into their home.

Leaving the next morning she asks, "Ethan, do you have my phone number. Is it programmed into your phone? Make sure to call me if you need anything or just want to talk."

Marie visits on November 2nd, just days after Catherine departs. She's here to celebrate the Day of the Dead. "The day when our ancestors are honored with food offerings," Marie tells her daughter-in-law.

Erin agrees to attend the service as she perceives honoring past ancestors an acceptable tribute to family.

Unknown to all, Marie plans to also make the day's ceremony a blessing for her successor. They face a strong wind blowing up and over the steep incline. Thankfully, the children are dressed in winter coats. It's a beautiful, clear morning. Erin pauses with them to view a dollhouse-sized Atlanta laying at their feet, and a sky overhead, the color of a Morpho butterfly. Enjoying the compelling scenery, Erin is totally relaxed.

The ceremony opens with breathtaking music, causing Erin to smile. She begins to hum and enjoy the moment. Chico has assured her they will delight in a luncheon celebration in honor of the ancestors, similar to the Catholic's All Souls Day. They have brought food types previously savored by their ancestors, along with a special blessed wine. Everyone is thoroughly comfortable.

Marie ascends the altar as the drums begin in rhythmic toque patterns. She instructs everyone to remain seated and opens her spiritual mass with moyuba, speaking the names of the spirits. She offers prayers to the elders while the members pray to their ancestral spirits. "Our invisible companions walk among us today and intercede with the gods on our behalf. We address Great-aunt Carlota, reincarnated in our son! Now he is to stand aside. Our new Santeria leader will be Priestess Anna."

Erin is dazed, somewhat wobbly and dizzy. She quickly regains self-composure trying to bring her mind to reality. She is hearing words that begin to come together in her mind, mortified at what she hears. *Is that real? Does Marie expect my little girl to become a priestess in the Santeria religion? Impossible.* She turns to look at her husband and sees he is also greatly disturbed. She's hopeful he can handle this situation, not realizing he desires the position for himself.

Erin frantically calls to the children, "Hurry, run to the car."

Chico is not far behind. The drive home is filled with his reassurance. "I guarantee Mother will never bestow the title of Santeria priestess on Anna. I'd kill her before I'd ever allow that to happen. I promise, trust me. I'll always protect you, as long as you do as I say." And she does. He's always very convincing.

On Christmas Day, Ethan phones Catherine, "Merry Christmas, Grandma. Thank you for my Christmas present! I really love it, but I wish you were here. I miss you so much."

She can hear him choking up, causing pain in her. "I always wish for us to be together, today on Christmas, and every other day." But this is something his father will make sure never happens.

It's Anna's turn to talk to her Grandmother. "Merry Christmas, Grandma. I love you. Do you miss Grandpa?" Catherine is floored, surprised at the question. It has been three years since Frank died and Erin never mentioned Anna's continual grief.

"Of course, Anna. I miss him every day."

"Me too. I want to sit with him while he tells me some more stories." She's sobbing uncontrollably now.

"I wish that could happen for you. Maybe I could tell you some stories that he told me."

Erin takes the phone from Anna. "Sorry about that, but every once in a while, she gets into memories of Dad and is totally inconsolable."

"Why didn't you tell me?"

"I knew she would get over it in time."

"Are you insane? This has been occurring and hurting her for three years and you didn't tell me? Obviously, your plan didn't work."

"I didn't want to upset you."

"That's not acceptable. First, you continually upset me with your attitude and rejections. But, right now, Anna is the one who needs to be talked to and reassured, which I would have done, had I known. It's evident that your children have wanted to know and visit your parents, and you are the problem, as you have deprived them of the opportunity of knowing us. Now she is suffering because it is too late. But I guess that satisfies the demands of your husband. Right?"

"I try to keep peace, and Marie has been strangely ill off and on for the last six months. They can't determine what the problem is. I have my hands full right now."

⚜ 39 ⚜

Autumn turns the leaves vibrant orange; greens fade from the landscape and Catherine plans her annual trip to the mountains and sends an email invite to Erin to come with the children.

Erin responds, "I don't have time to come to the mountains."

Catherine is persistent, "It's only an hour or so away."

"Yes, I know, but we don't have time. Marie is still very ill. The doctors haven't been able to find anything wrong with her. She's often unaware of her surroundings."

Catherine suspects the funny mixtures they ingest and inhale-have caused Marie's problems. She hears the strain in her daughter's voice and doesn't press the matter. She heads to her cousin's home atop the mountains where the air gives up a soft breeze. A welcome cool wave crosses her body. It's her revitalization time, like waking from a long hibernation. From her window, she views a sloping patchwork quilt of Mother Nature's palette, spread across the earth as far as one can see. A large bear slowly meanders past her window, having just missed a herd of deer.

∾

A week later, Catherine is completely relaxed when she arrives at Erin's, as always, for Halloween. Anna is the Snow Princess and Ethan is Purple Rain. Chico is out of town on business. The visit goes smoothly and Catherine enjoys another year helping to decorate. She cherishes time with her daughter and shares in the children's excitement. She is enjoying life. Catherine leaves a couple of days later, assuming Chico will return home after conducting the Day of the Dead ceremony in the park, as Marie is still ill.

Erin calls Catherine, "Would you like to join me and Anna at her soccer meet in Orlando? On this trip, it's just me and Anna. Chico is taking Ethan to a football game."

Again, it is evident that Erin only has the freedom to see her family when Chico is otherwise engaged.

As they sit together at the soccer meet, Erin tells her mother, "By the end of last month, Marie couldn't remember even the simplest things. Sometimes she doesn't recognize people. Doctors are constantly running tests. Chico has been making regular visits, stopping in Miami for a day here and there as he travels to and from clients."

Catherine replies with a sarcastic snap, "Yes, I'm sure he's always the caring son." She thinks, maybe he is getting further religious instructions from Marie.

Catherine plans a trip through Tennessee with Trish. Before returning to Atlanta, Trish contacts Erin. "Would you like to get together with Mother and me? We'll be there on the twenty-sixth."

"Depends on where. It could be a bit touchy sitting in a restaurant trying to make pleasant conversation."

"I guess Chico is in town? Which means he must come with you, right?"

"Yes, and yes. Try to think of some activity."

"How about we climb the mountain? The kids would like that," Trish suggests in an attempt to keep the peace among family members.

"Great. We'll meet you at ten o'clock. By that time, it should be fairly warm. I'll bring lunch." Erin packs a beautiful lunch; tuna sandwiches for her, Grandma, and Trish. Anna also get a tuna with the lady's lunch. The boys, Chico and Ethan have turkey sandwiches.

As they approach Kennesaw Mountain's midpoint, Ethan turns to Catherine and asks, "Are we going to Abuela's church park?"

"No, we are climbing to the top of the mountain to look at the city."

"Oh good. I don't like her church."

"Why is that, Ethan?"

"I just don't."

At the midway point, Atlanta comes into view. Ethan is excited to share the moment. "Grandma, come here, hurry. Look at this," he says as he points straight out from the mountain to the horizon. "It's yellow, wow! I never saw that before. It must be the atmospheric conditions."

"The what? Atmospheric conditions? Where did you learn that?"

"Oh, Grandma, at school of course. It's noon now so the colors change." He laughs. "Have you ever been in the Civil War Museum here?"

"No, I haven't. Let's go when we get down the mountain."

Catherine is pleased to have seen her daughter and two grandchildren. Chico's occasional glances, his attempt to unnerve her and dampen the day weren't successful. Catherine wouldn't allow it. Ethan has a great time taking Grandma on a tour of the museum.

~

The holidays quickly approach. Catherine is never invited, always Chico's parents. She knows the children will call her. At least that's something.

At Christmas, little Anna calls Catherine. Catherine grabs the phone, "Hello, Merry Christmas." A sweet little voice says, "Merry Christmas, Grandma."

"Merry Christmas, sweetie. Did you get my gifts to you and Ethan?"

"Not yet. We aren't home so it probably came after we left."

Knowing that on December twenty-sixth the boys report to a special football camp, Catherine asks, "Oh, I guess you're with Ethan at training football session again this year?"

"No, we're in Florida. We stopped at Aunt Anna's before going to visit Abuela and Abuelo on Christmas Day. We're on our way to the Florida Keys. We are going sailing."

"Why didn't your mother stop here? She drove right past me to get to the Keys."

"Mom said you weren't home."

"What?"

"Yes, Mom said you were in New York."

"What kind of nonsense is that? I am not, nor did I ever plan to be in New York. So, your mom drove right by me. How awful."

Catherine is completely distressed and cannot continue the conversation, but she does not want to upset Anna.

"I am going to hang up now. Have a nice vacation."

Catherine knew Chico's wishes were law, and that's why they bypassed her. The children, not so small anymore, are asking questions and making their own phone calls. They know when they're being lied to.

Catherine knows she must do something drastic. She begins to analyze and determine where she can go with a plan. *This cannot continue. I must think this through.*

E than is eleven now and making his Confirmation. Everyone's invited to Atlanta for the ceremony. Catherine plans to stay with Trish and just attend the church service. She's sure Chico's parents will be staying in the guest room at Erin's.

Marie informs Erin, "I will be arriving seven days early to celebrate a special religious service for Ethan. My church's version of the sacrament."

That evening Erin questions Chico. "What exactly is this religious service your mother wants to do for Ethan? What does it involve, what does it mean? You said she was gravely ill."

"Did you ask my mother these questions? She can answer and explain better than I can."

"No, I am asking you. You're also trained in the religion, and you're the parent."

"I probably know as much about this ceremony as you know about Confirmation. They're very similar. Both ask the child to now be responsible in their decisions regarding their religion. Satisfied?"

"I'm a bit concerned over the unknown. You know, given past experiences."

"Nothing to be concerned over, I assure you."

≈

Marie arrives one week before Mother's Day. The children are out of school the whole week, for spring break.

Erin asks, "When will you hold the ceremony, Marie?"

"On Friday."

"Okay, we'll be there. Let us know the exact time." She is certainly not letting her children go alone with this Santeria group.

≈

On Thursday, Erin plans to assist with preparations at her church. She tells Marie, "I may be late today, so I've asked Norma, next door, to come later and help you with the children."

With Erin gone for the day, Marie gathers her supplies and prepares to leave for the ceremony. She calls Norma. "Could you come and stay with Anna? I need to take Ethan for some religious preparation today."

"Oh, you mean like classes to learn about Confirmation?"

"Yes, dear, something like that."

"Sure, glad to help. I'll be right over."

≈

Before leaving the house, Norma calls Erin to bring her up to date. "You asked me to call if there were any changes in the plans, and Marie has asked me to come and stay with Anna as she takes Ethan to some religious training."

"I'll call you as I'm arriving at the house, wait to go until then," Erin instructs her.

Marie calls to Ethan, "Please help me load the car with these supplies and jump in. We are taking a ride to the park. When we arrive, you can help me carry these to the clearing."

"I thought we were going tomorrow, Abuela?"

"We need to do this today, because too many people know it's scheduled for tomorrow, and that could interfere with connections to the gods."

"There's more than one god?"

"You will see everything clearly this afternoon."

Erin enters the house, Ethan greets her saying, "I'm glad you're home because we're going to the ceremony today, not tomorrow."

She confronts Marie. "What's this, Marie? You were going to do this without parents present? Definitely not."

Ethan tries to explain, "Abuela said too many people know about tomorrow. It'll be too crowded, so we need to do it today."

"Yes, that is right," Marie chimes in. "We have others in the ceremony to consider also. They do not want a big audience there."

"Too bad, because whether you do it today *or* tomorrow, the family will attend."

Erin phones Chico. Getting his voicemail, she asks him to come home, or at least tell his mother it must wait until tomorrow.

After their discussions, Marie addresses Erin, "I will wait until tomorrow for Ethan's ceremony, but I will go today for Jason, the other child."

Erin hasn't been able to find any information on this ceremony in Marie's religion that correlates with Catholic Confirmation. She decides to take a different route to the ceremonial park and watch today's ceremony from the hill. Ethan begs to go with her. "I want to see it before we go. I got to watch First Communion practice, so why can't I watch this sacrament?"

"Okay, let's hurry."

The afternoon is heating up, but the breeze billowing over the cliff is comforting. Erin sees Marie speaking to a boy as she approaches the altar. She is shocked to see Chico there, leading the boy to the altar. "Stand here to my left, Jason."

Marie begins chanting. She orders a congregation member to bring forth the sacrifice. Erin has no idea what's to come. She sees the member bring a lamb to the altar and watches Marie bless the little animal while chanting prayers. The child appears mesmerized.

Smiling, Ethan is enthralled with the ceremony and the lamb.

Marie pauses and again addresses the boy. "Jason, do you believe in the Santeria religion's teachings?"

"I don't know. I'm not sure what the teachings are."

"Do you want to learn about the religion of your parents and grandparents?"

"Sure, I guess so."

"Good. Today we are going to initiate you into the Santeria religion, and bless your life." Again, the whole congregation begins to chant. The boy is obviously lulled into a relaxed state, as is Ethan.

As twilight approaches, Chico lifts the baby lamb to the altar while everyone is chanting. He lays it down gently on its side. Marie slowly raises her right hand and suddenly slams it down on the lamb's neck. Erin is horrified; she hadn't noticed the ax in Marie's hand. Blood squirts in all directions, seeming to disappear into the air as Chico says, "We feed the gods this blood."

The boy begins to cry. Ethan also is crying. He doesn't want to, he's eleven, but he can't stop. Marie lifts the child onto the altar. He's screaming in fear he'll be chopped like the lamb. Marie lays him on his back, Chico holds him still. The child is now hysterical shaking and crying out. Marie pulls out her large Bowie knife, holding it over his chest. He is begging for his life.

Through his tears, Ethan is pleading, "Please, Mother, stop her." Erin is paralyzed in place and realizes she cannot reach the altar before Marie's arm comes down on the child. They watch the knife meet the boy's chest as Marie begins to draw lines with the sharp point. He passes out, his chest bloody from many shallow cuts.

When Jason awakens, he appears not to remember what happened. Marie's watching him closely. She addresses him and the congregation. "Body modification, such as this boy's scaring of the chest, is an accepted practice worldwide. He doesn't understand this purification, but he will in time."

Seeing his mother approaching, he cries out, "Mama, Papa, my chest is burning. Why did you let her hurt me?"

The mother, like Erin, had no advance warning of what would take place. Body modification is a rarely performed ceremony. She comforts her son as Marie explains the religious significance.

Erin sobs uncontrollably. Her chest is heaving; she can barely breathe as she stumbles to her feet. Erin vomits, confused, outraged, and horrified. *This could have been Ethan!* Ethan is crouched behind a large boulder crying like a baby. Erin tries to pick him up to carry him to the car. The best she can do is support him as they stumble down the path.

Arriving home before the others she paces the floor, half out of her mind, wondering what to do. She draws Ethan a warm bath and gets him to sleep. She decides to say nothing until after church. She must make decisions on how to approach Marie and Chico. Tonight, is not the right time for confrontation. She needs support, and tomorrow she'll ask her mother and sister. Erin is awake through the night watching Ethan's bedroom door, fearing the worst.

~

The following day the household is excited for the Confirmation. Erin calls up the stairway, "Ethan, hurry. Shower and dress and be down here in ten minutes."

Of course, Ethan is not downstairs in ten minutes, so Erin goes up to hurry him along.

"Why aren't you ready yet?" she demands as she stares at the back of his white dress shirt. You know we have brunch reservations before church."

"I'm fixing my tie."

"Turn around and come here. I'll do it for you."

"What happened to this shirt? It's all smudged. You can't wear this. Take it off. I'll get another."

Coming out of the closet with a new shirt, she sees he hasn't removed the first one. She begins to unbutton and remove his shirt.

He pulls away, "I'll do it myself."

"I'm going to help you, like it or not. We're running late." While she's speaking, she's fighting to remove his shirt. He's yelling back that he can do it himself.

"Ethan, what is wrong with you? You know we need to hurry for this."

"Mom," he begins with slight hesitation, "after Confirmation, are we going to the park for my Santeria ceremony? I don't want to go. I don't want to see another baby lamb die, and I don't want them to hurt me. Please don't make me go."

"Of course not, Ethan. I'd never let anyone hurt you."

"But you couldn't stop Abuela or Dad from hurting that boy yesterday, and she tried to sneak me there. She might try to do that again without your knowing it."

"I see. Ethan, *that* will never happen. I promise you. Now, let's get to your Confirmation."

~

Catherine and Trish meet Erin's family at Saint Angela's Catholic Church for the ceremony, not knowing what had occurred the previous day.

After the ceremony Erin asks, "Mom, why don't you and Trish come back to the house for a celebration dinner?"

"You know I cannot be comfortable around that woman, and not with Chico either."

"I could really use your support tonight," Erin pleads.

Catherine tells Trish about the invitation and asks what she thinks. Neither is sure what this means as they almost never go to that house, and they're surely never missed. They decide to go, as something must be wrong. Perhaps Erin has a problem.

Back at the house, as Erin prepares the dinner, she gathers the adult women in the kitchen. The children are outside awaiting barbeque, watching Chico at the grill. "Mom and Trish, I wanted you here for this discussion as I will need your support." Catherine and Trish glance at each other given this unexpected request.

"Marie, I want you to know I was at the ceremony in the park yesterday. How could you possibly hurt a boy like that? And what makes you think *I* wouldn't retaliate if you hurt Ethan in such a way?"

"Did you hear me say body modification, although seldom performed, is an accepted practice worldwide?"

"Yes, I did. I don't care where it is accepted, you aren't doing it to my child. It's savage. Evidently, you also acted against the wishes of the other boy's mother."

"Erin, that is not true. The mother completely consented; this is a religious healing ceremony. Nothing wrong with it. You just do not understand the situation fully. Let me tell you that this boy was suffering severely, mentally and physically. He was possessed. This blessing will relieve his suffering."

"If that's true, why were you also going to perform this ceremony on Ethan?"

"Both children will go through it to become church members.

They must be purified. Ethan must be cleansed of your tainted Irish-Catholic blood. It is even more important for Anna as she will be my successor. Our new Santeria priestess." As she turns to walk away, she sees Chico in the doorway.

He utters in shock, "What is this I hear that Anna will be your successor? We discussed this last month, remember? We agreed I would be the new Santeria priest."

"You know it must be a female, if possible."

"Not necessarily. A Santeria priest has equal power with a Santeria priestess."

"That is true, but in our family, it has always, for many generations, been a priestess."

"Mother, you know you won't be able to complete her education. You couldn't even perform today's little ceremony without my help. And in Cuba you wouldn't have made it through the Itutu ceremony. Admit it; you need me to take over."

Erin is living in a nightmare. Her husband wants to be a priest in charge of his mother's church, and his mother wants her little granddaughter to be a Santeria priestess and perform these terrible rituals.

Not knowing what to address first, Erin jumps on the last surprise first. She glances over to Chico with a puzzled look. "When were you in Cuba?"

Marie answers before Chico can even think. "He was there with me, twice in 2006 and 2007. He does not need to obtain permission from you. He does not need to answer to you."

"Will you both stop! What happened today will never happen to my children. Do you understand me?"

Chico's cell rings. "What is it? Really? Maybe we could do something to take care of that. I'll try to make the arrangements as soon as possible. It is vital that this happens quickly."

Catherine and Trish listen to the one-sided conversation, unaware of the content.

"I always knew she was a witch," Catherine mutters to Trish. Although she doesn't fully understand the problem, Catherine is relieved to finally hear Erin fight back and take some control.

Chico ends his conversation and turns to Erin, saying, "I have to go now." As he leaves the house with his priestess mother, Chico passes Catherine and whispers, "I'll get you for this."

To his wife he states, "I'll be back for my things. Just remember, Erin, *you* are one of my *things*, my major possession."

A cell phone rings. No one answers, as no one hears the ringing. The recording begins. "Hello, Marie it is with a heavy heart that I tell you the newly ordained priest has suffered a heart attack and died. We are of the hopes that your son may be available to come here and lead our religious group. Please call me as soon as possible to make arrangements."

❧ 41 ❧

Catherine is trying to make sense of things in her own mind. *Finally, my daughter is standing up for herself and her children. It has been a long time coming since Chico threatened me and Frank when he said, "I will separate Erin completely from her family. That is, you and her siblings." I never thought that was possible. I never thought Erin could be brainwashed, or so accepting of his dominance. Finally, Erin is taking control.*

Catherine addresses her daughter, "Erin, do you have a plan in mind?"

"Yes, at least an outline of one in my exhausted mind. After what I saw at the last Santeria event, there is only one solution for us to remain safe. I never thought it would come to this."

Erin is not getting any rest tonight; her mind is racing.

The following morning, as the sun rises over the little hilltop, it spreads a new light of day into the kitchen breakfast nook. Over coffee, Catherine attempts to fully understand her daughter's situation and plans.

"Erin, first, please tell me what happened the day before Confirmation that was so upsetting to you, and apparently to Ethan also. It had to be horrendous for you to react so strongly."

Her daughter describes the whole event, including Marie's attempt to take Ethan for a Santeria ceremony involving body modification. She explains that Chico was not only present, he was involved.

"Erin, I need to ask, dear, why you gave up total control of yourself to Chico. Why? In exchange for what? It certainly was not his love for you. You were always such a strong-minded individual, fighting for your rights. At school and work you were always so confident. What changed you so drastically?"

"Mother, I needed to think of my future. I foresaw security for me and the children with Chico. I could never afford what he can provide. I've already sacrificed myself for years to live this lifestyle. For what, to just walk away?"

"So, what are you trying to say? You may take him back? Certainly, you wouldn't even consider that after the threat to Ethan. Not to mention the fact that either your husband or your daughter will head a Santeria congregation. Would you want your daughter to face that?"

"Of course not, Mother."

"You have choices. You may not like any of them, let's analyze the situation. Then you need to fight. Those are the only two choices, stay or fight. I'll help you."

"I'll help too," says Trish.

Erin is so upset she can barely think or reason. "Where do we start?"

They hear a scream from Anna's room, she is screaming and crying. A man is carrying her off to a waiting car. Ethan is screaming, "stop, leave my sister alone." The two women race to Anna's room, they see a man handing her off to her father, who carries her to a car. The child is hysterical. Phoning the police, she reports her daughter missing and in danger.

∼

Two days pass, with no word on Chico's whereabouts nor on the condition of the little girl.

Erin is so upset she can barely think or reason. Where do we start?"

∼

Chico's plan is to go to Miami, where his friends will help him secure a boat and escape to the Bahamas. There, he will be a recognized as a priest in good standing. They know him and his mother, and he will be respected.

The plan works. Marie rents a car and drives Chico from Atlanta to Miami. With his connections he secures a boat and a captain. It's only 90 miles to get from Florida to Freeport, Grand Bahama.

"This should be an easy crossing we almost never have storms this early. Never in May," volunteers the captain. "We have a strong boat, clear skies, and a great mate to help when needed. Be at the pier at 6:30 in the morning, Chico."

It's a beautiful clear day as they set out to sea, waving goodbye to Marie. They are casually cruising along. "We just hit the half-way mark. Say, mate, how about fixing some lunch?"

"This is the life," comments Chico. "I could get used to this!"

Suddenly the sky turns dark. The captain has almost zero visibility.

"What happened here, Captain?" Chico asks, a bit unnerved. This is a situation he cannot control. He is accustomed to being the one in control.

They skim close, too close, to a passing cargo ship. "That was invisible to me," states the mate. "Too close for comfort."

"How do we get out of this mess?" questions Chico. He is completely unnerved as he buckles on his life jacket. No sooner has he spoken than the back end of their large boat clips the passing cargo vessel, overturning them. He is bouncing like an injured fish, up and down, over and under, choking and gurgling. The waters settled. he cannot see the captain, mate nor the boat, assuming all is lost at sea. The night comes and he is panicking, knowing no one knows where he is.

By morning, fighting the weather and the immense heat reflecting from the sun on the water has exhausted him. He can hear a motor approaching, somewhere nearby. He begins screaming. Finally, a sailor on the trawler spots him and maneuvers through the turbulent sea to pick him up. They are headed to New Orleans. He knows the area well, as this is his college town.

Chico is contemplating, now what to do? Get back to Miami, back to Atlanta, head to Bahamas as planned? Maybe stay in New Orleans for a while. He hopes he can find some old friends to put him up for a while, as he has nothing; no money or credit cards. Everything was lost.

He recalls when his mother came to visit him; she walked up Bourbon Street to the Lafitte Guest House. He tries that first; maybe the owner will give him some credit.

"Excuse me madam my mother, Marie, stayed at this hotel a number of years ago when I attended college here. Maybe you remember her. She had asked for room twenty-one."

"I recall, as it was an unusual request. Most people do not want that room."

"I know the history. I came here hoping you could extend me some credit. I was in a boat accident and lost my wallet."

"I heard of the rough waters and a few boats down. You are lucky. I can extend you a few nights' credit."

Chico now must find a place to eat. *Mother and I found an interesting old building during our religious tour. Maybe someone will remember me, though it's very unlikely.* He walks a block and recognizes the crumbling building where they had lunch.

The Lafitte Blacksmith Shop, where the pirate ran his smuggling business, is damp and smelly, lit only with candles, almost the same as his visit years ago. There are few people here. The bar itself appears unchanged; hundreds of years old, with the silver backing on the mirror flaking off. He recalls the smell and reconfirms he would prefer not to be in here. The tavern is still playing a Cole Porter's song, "You do that voodoo...."

The waitress is humming a tune as she approaches the table. "What's your name, honey?"

"No, it's still Betsy. I remember you. Here a few years ago with an older lady, right?"

"I see you're continuing to burn the fireplace in all types of weather. It's never allowed to extinguish, right?"

"Yes, do you remember why? Often, you can see his red eyes staring back at you through the grate. You might see him from here. He is guarding a treasure between the bricks in the fireplace, which is why it is never extinguished."

"Honey, oh sorry, I mean, Betsy, could you possibly extend me some credit? I have lost my wallet."

"Yes, I think we can arrange that. What would you like to eat?"

Chico visits the churches he had seen with his mother. *Perhaps I'll run into an old classmate that could help me out financially, or at least I can pick up a few ideas for my church when I get to the Bahamas.* He returns to a congregation he and his mother had visited. It was composed of five different groups; the Yoruba people, the fiery spirits of the Congo, the Taino, modern-Haitian people, and the spirits of the dead, by way of the French Catholic. He speaks with the caretaker discussing religions and faith. "I am on my way to head a church in the Bahamas." They discuss the events of the world and churches today.

"I'm happy you wondered in here young man, Come again."

Chico makes his way back to the diner and visits the rest room to wash up. The door is difficult to open and he recalls his mother issuing a complaint, it is stuck. He pushes; it won't budge. Finally, it pops open. He stumbles and falls down the stairs. Not badly hurt, he limps back to the Lafitte Guest House. It's only a short distance to 1003 Bourbon Street.

The ghost of room twenty-one, Marie, walks at night. Chico hears the footsteps and the swishing of a gown. He is a bit unnerved as he remembers his mother instructing him on the different religions during their walk through the churches' meeting areas. He is confident this Marie surely would not harm him.

By morning Chico is refreshed and needs to find a way to Bahamas.

He sits beside the fireplace where he sat yesterday, watching the flames dance. He remembers the story of the treasure. Surely there must be some semblance of truth. Maybe there is a treasure. He analyzes the structure for any damage or weakness visible. Mother had told him it was in the chimney section of the fireplace. Chico knows it cannot be Jean Lafitte controlling the flames. Perhaps a worker comes at night to make sure it does not burn out. If the fire never goes out, the treasure will remain in the possession of Jean Lafitte, according to Betsy.

Chico returns that night after closing. The fire is still burning. He waits. There are no walls and no doors, only the liquor is locked up somewhere. He waits for hours, nothing happens. The fire does not diminish. Why? Finally, he locates a mop and bucket. He approaches the fire attempting to squelch the flames, carrying buckets of water, to no avail. He attempts to circumvent the flames and smother the burning embers with the old tablecloths. That does not work either.

Upon visual inspection, Chico decides to walk the wall inside the fireplace and then climb up, as he perceives enough space between the outer wall and the chimney. There is roughly five feet between the outside visual wall and the inside wall surrounding the fire. He surmises, "I can always turn around and go out if it gets too hot." He begins his climb up the masonry bricks. He sees the damper is open, an easy climb. As he nears the top the damper slams shut preventing heat loss. Smoke encompasses him. He can't breathe stuck within the sloping walls of the smoke chamber where combustion products are compressed into a smaller space in order to exit through the chimney. As he compresses, he slowly dies a little at a time.

The next morning Betsy arrives at the diner as usual. "Why is it so hot in here this morning, too early for this much heat."

Everything is in order, just as she left it. She asks the manager, "Has Chico left an envelope for me? He mentioned he would come by today to settle his account."

"No one has come by to see you nor leave an envelope. But I believe I heard Marie Laveau and Madame Lalaurie walking about last night."

Early every morning for nearly a week, as Atlanta awakens well before dawn, Erin visits the Little Kennesaw Mountain; perhaps today they have a ceremony planned. She pulls her SUV out of the garage and heads toward the mountain, approaching again from the back of the park.

Even in the May heat, she can feel the intense temperature of flames emanating from the sacred ground. It feels like Hell. Slowly and cautiously she crawls, military style, to a vantage point. The open altar and the practitioners are barely visible. Sweat streams from her forehead into her eyes. She peers through her binoculars, but is not able to locate her daughter.

Erin waits. Hours later, hungry and dehydrated, barely conscious of the melodic music, she thinks she sees Anna. A woman, elaborately dressed in colorful beaded costume, leads a small girl by the hand to the altar.

The child, also dressed in beautiful beaded attire, is smiling as she approaches the altar. The child is entranced, as she hasn't seen a ceremony before today. The music begins; the members chant and sway. Anna looks joyfully at the little lamb.

Erin is paralyzed by fear but attempts to move into the field. As she crawls forward, a loud thundering blast deafens her ears. It is the Bata drums. The sound is like a thousand soldiers marching forward, out of sync. Tears form as she realizes she may not possess the strength to save her daughter.

While she is laying there immobile, she sees a white cloud floating into the ceremony. It suddenly gathers momentum heading to the altar. Descending rapidly, it encompasses the entire altar and all the worshippers. Erin watches the metamorphosis of the cloud as it becomes a blinding light glowing before her. She hears screams but cannot determine what is happening. She only knows she must somehow save her daughter.

The cloud of light parts and gives Erin a glimpse of the field. Rubbing her eyes, she sees an old ragged woman who begins to scream and rant. Erin realizes she is chanting. There is a rhythm to her piercing cries, and her body movements match the Bata drums.

The earth explodes with a vengeance; fire spurts into the crowds. The throng of people disperses, screaming in madness. The old woman turns her attention to Marie, who is frozen in shock.

"Marie, with this ax and cross I curse you to an eternity of fire. You have created a monster in your own image, built on the dead, those who have no soul, forced to transverse the living and the dead.

The old woman addresses her cries. "Did you hear my son Jason cry out when you frightened him by killing the little lamb? Did you pay attention when he cried and begged you not to hurt him? Did you relent when he beseeched you for mercy as you cut into his chest? What compassion do you have for others? You and your son deserve the ravages of Hell!"

"But you, Marie, with this ax and cross I curse you to an eternity of fire. You haven't even asked of your son. Do you even care about his well-being? Perhaps not. But, if so, you can find him over at the largest tree in the meadow. Similar to your Tree of Life we hear of in Cuba. This is the Tree of Vengeance. Just desserts to you both."

The old woman picks up the little girl and soothes her cries. Placing her on the ground she says, "Little Child, walk towards the cliff there and you will find your way."

As the child departs the old woman turns her sights to the ravaged body on the altar slab. "We leave you, Marie, here to suffer and die. Please, take your time."

Erin's eyes begin to clear. She sees a form moving towards her. She runs towards Anna who is slowly approaching the cliff. Grabbing her daughter, she cries tears of joy.

"Mom, you're squeezing me too hard!"

Erin loosens her grip, picks up the child, and weeps, so grateful that she is unharmed. Offering prayers of thanks, she turns to carry the little one down the sloping cliff and looks right into Catherine's eyes holding tears of gratitude.

In Grandma's hand Erin sees little fingers, Ethan's.

ACKNOWLEDGEMENTS

A special note of thanks to Judy Lucas, successful accomplished author and founder of a group that helps writers become authors.

Abacoa Writers Group, whose support and direction are invaluable.

Creative Writers, headed by Jay Gilbert.

Judy Ratto, friend, author, editor and always there for me.

SeaQuill Writers and Patty Perrin, who are always available to help anyone in the group.

Judy Martin, my daughter, for offering her endless confidence and encouragement.

Thais Brossell, a friend, writer and five-star Beta Reader.

Dawn Watkins & King Brown who encouraged me from the inception of this project through to the end, including a final read through.

ABOUT THE AUTHOR

Patricia is a photographer and the author of the acclaimed **Shadow of His Smile**, the story of her husband John, Tony Bennett's brother and mentor. As a photographer, she captures images with strong dynamic geometric configurations. As an author, she strives to capture life, which often offers undefined lines of demarcation. In both mediums, she takes the viewer or reader on a voyage into unfamiliar territories; historical, personal, religious and more.

Patricia is active in the community. She has been the Director of the Town of Jupiter Art Committee, and is the founder and host of "Meet the Authors" at the Town of Jupiter. She is currently the Co-Chair of the North Palm Beach Cultural Alliance, a member of the Chamber of Commerce, a contributing member of The Lighthouse Art Gallery, and a member of Business 2 Business for Women. She serves on the boards of the Lighthouse Camera Club and SeaQuill Writers Cooperative. As a member of Creative Writers and the Abacoa Writers Group, Patricia organized the first annual Abacoa Writers event. She cares for an acre garden and is a long-time annual member of Disney.

She continues her pursuit of photography and writing.

The Shadow of His Smile: Brothers Together in Life and Song

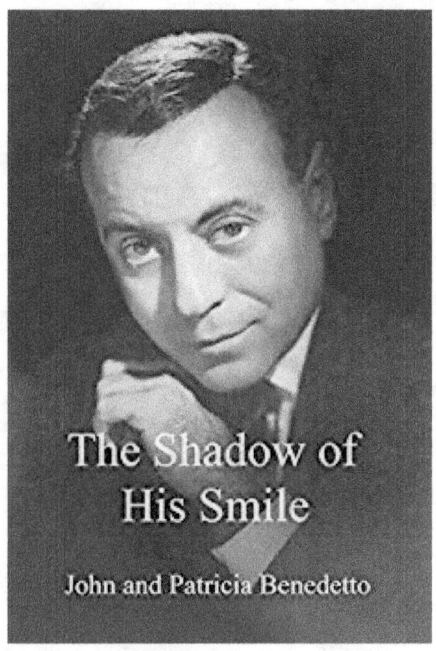